"You think I'm making all this up."

"No. I…"

Craig gave a half laugh that hurt her to hear. "I don't even blame you. It's crap. None of it explains a woman walking out on her kids without even saying goodbye."

Robin felt a thrill of fear. "But…didn't she?"

His expression changed. A mask seemed to close over his face. "Yeah. If you call what she told Brett saying goodbye."

Robin didn't know what Julie was supposed to have said; she'd heard rumors that Craig would have been arrested except for his son's story.

He'd pulled back and now stood waiting, remote. "Will you call for Brett?"

"Oh. Yes, of course." She passed him, but paused in the living-room doorway. Turning back to him, Robin said, "Craig, I…"

"Don't lie. Don't say you're sorry." His voice sounded heavy, slow, wary. "Don't say anything."

Dear Reader,

As a writer and reader, I am fascinated less by the big dramatic scenes than I am by the aftermath. Someone survives a childhood trauma and most bystanders assume that the story is over. But is that really the end? I want to know what comes next.

I'm also fascinated by mystery, although like most of you, I really like to feel secure. The unknown is terrifying. So what happens to a man and his children when they are faced with a dreadful unknown: the disappearance of a wife and mother?

Of course, I don't write about the drama of the disappearance, or the following days. I take up the story a year and a half later, when they have lived with this awful unknown for seemingly endless months.

Think about it. Your husband, your daughter, your mother, disappears. No blood, no clues, no goodbye notes. Did he choose to walk away? Was she abducted? Is she dead or alive? How do you live a normal life as you search for answers that may not be found? And what if finally you get an answer, but it's not one you'll ever fully understand or be able to explain to your children?

Can you fall in love in the midst of this turmoil, this anguish, this guilt and anger?

I hope you'll be fascinated by this story and these characters.

Best,

Janice Kay Johnson

Mommy Said Goodbye
Janice Kay Johnson

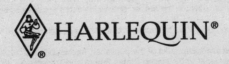

TORONTO • NEW YORK • LONDON
AMSTERDAM • PARIS • SYDNEY • HAMBURG
STOCKHOLM • ATHENS • TOKYO • MILAN • MADRID
PRAGUE • WARSAW • BUDAPEST • AUCKLAND

ISBN 0-373-71197-2

MOMMY SAID GOODBYE

Copyright © 2004 by Janice Kay Johnson.

This edition published by arrangement with Harlequin Books S.A.

® and TM are trademarks of the publisher. Trademarks indicated with
® are registered in the United States Patent and Trademark Office, the
Canadian Trade Marks Office and in other countries.

www.eHarlequin.com

Printed in U.S.A.

Books by Janice Kay Johnson

HARLEQUIN SUPERROMANCE

*Patton's Daughters
**3 Good Cops
ºUnder One Roof

HARLEQUIN SINGLE TITLE

MISSING MOLLY (Part of WRONG TURN with Stella Cameron)

Don't miss any of our special offers. Write to us at the
following address for information on our newest releases.

Harlequin Reader Service
U.S.: 3010 Walden Ave., P.O. Box 1325, Buffalo, NY 14269
Canadian: P.O. Box 609, Fort Erie, Ont. L2A 5X3

CHAPTER ONE

A MAN SUSPECTED of murdering his wife can pretty well count on being left off guest lists.

Laughter, the clink of ice in glasses, the shouts of children and the smell of barbecued beef drifted over the fence from the next-door neighbor's.

Craig Lofgren stood on his back deck, the lid of his Weber kettle grill in his hand. Just like that, he was hit by a fist of anger and loss so powerful, he reeled back a step.

"Daddy?" His daughter tugged at his free hand. "Daddy, what's wrong?"

He swallowed and opened his eyes. His voice sounded hoarse to his ears. "Just taking a whiff. Smells good, doesn't it?"

The anxiety on her face faded and she nodded. "You haven't lit the charcoal yet."

"I'm doing it, I'm doing it." Somehow, he found a grin for her. "Hungry?"

Abby—who just turned nine—nodded, then gave a wistful look toward the fence. "They're all there, aren't they?"

There was no point in pretending. She knew as well as he did why they were excluded. "Sounds that way."

Solemn, she nodded again. "I think I heard Brett putting his bike in the garage."

"Yeah? Go ask him if the teacher lists were posted yet."

The intense emotion had passed, leaving bitter resignation in its wake. He dumped charcoal in the kettle, making no effort to be quiet, poured on lighter fluid and flicked a match. To hell with it if he cast a pall on the block party. Let 'em whisper about him. Feel a tiny twinge of guilt, or at least pity, because they had made his innocent children pariahs with him.

Once he was sure the charcoal was burning, Craig went in the house and sought out his eleven-year-old son. Brett had ridden his bike to the school, where rumor had it the lists had been posted showing which classrooms kids would be in and who their teachers would be when school started next week. Abby was the one who'd worried all summer about whether she'd be in the same class with her friends. But Brett, who professed not to care about school at all, had been the one to leap on his bike the minute Abby said she'd heard the lists were up.

Craig headed upstairs when he heard his daughter's squeal.

"Daddy!" She popped out into the hall from her brother's bedroom. "I got Mrs. Jensen! She's super nice!"

"Great." He gave her a hug and went into Brett's bedroom. As usual, it looked as if a burglar had ransacked it. "Who'd you get?"

Shoulders slumped, Brett sat on the edge of the bed. "Ms. McKinnon."

Damn. Some of his earlier anger and tension gripped Craig again. He'd hoped for any other teacher for Brett.

Carefully, he said, "She's supposed to be good."

Brett nodded without looking up.

Craig hesitated, then stepped over piles of clothes, a soccer ball and God knew what else so that he could reach the bed and sit down, too, right next to Brett. Abby stood in the doorway and watched, her jubilation gone and her face pinched, as it so often was these days.

"What's the deal?" Craig asked.

He hadn't expressed any of his concerns and hadn't realized Brett had his own. The truth was, Robin McKinnon was said to be the best sixth grade teacher in the district. Right now, Brett needed someone who might be able to inspire him, energize him, discipline him.

Craig just wasn't sure Robin would even try. She'd been a friend of Julie's, which meant, in this town, that she would believe heart and soul that Craig had murdered his wife and hidden the body. Or ground it up into bits and fed it to some farmer's pigs. Who the hell knew? Craig understood there were a dozen or more theories. Every one of them involved him as a crazed killer, a man who couldn't stand the thought that his wife wanted to leave him. Nobody had considered the theory that maybe Julie Lofgren had just up and walked out on her family. Or that a stranger had abducted her.

If the police had had one grain of proof… But they

hadn't then, a year and a half ago when Julie disappeared, and they didn't have one now.

Which hadn't changed a single mind. The community had closed ranks against him. His lovely, innocent wife! they cried. A devoted mother and president of the parent-teacher organization two years running, she was well-known in Klickitat. Craig had never been anything but Julie's often-absent husband, Brett's dad who came to games when he could, Abby's father who had missed her second grade parent-teacher conference because he was flying to Juneau.

Now, every single person in Klickitat knew who he was. He couldn't go to the grocery store or get gas without feeling eyes on him, without knowing he was being judged.

He'd hoped that Brett would get the man just hired to teach sixth grade. Someone would have told him Brett's sad story, of course, but at least he might not share the fervor of the people who'd known Julie.

No such luck.

After a long silence, Brett muttered, "Ms. McKinnon used to come to games and stuff."

"She was a friend of your mom's."

Brett didn't say anything.

"Her boy—what was his name?—was a friend of yours, wasn't he?" Craig remembered.

"Malcolm."

"You know, she's not going to treat you any differently because your mom disappeared."

"Yeah?" Fury blazed on Brett's face when he lifted his head. "Everyone does! They either feel sorry for me,'' he spat out, ''or else they're wondering if I saw anything. You can see what they're thinking!''

Yeah. You could.

''Robin knows you.''

''So?''

Craig groped for an answer to the unanswerable. So she'd known Brett, known Julie, even, casually known Craig. She, too, had shunned the entire family after police cars with flashing lights were seen in front of the Lofgren home. She hadn't called to find out why Brett quit the Little League team. Malcolm hadn't called to invite Brett over to hang at his house.

Brett bowed his head again, but tension still ran through him. ''She'll think you killed Mom.''

''I'm not the one in her class,'' Craig said. ''Brett.'' He waited until his son met his eyes. ''I can ask for a change of teacher if you want.'' No response. ''Otherwise, we'll give Ms. McKinnon a try. If you're not happy, then I'll have you changed to a different room.''

''Why can't we move?'' his thin, dark-haired son cried. ''Where no one knows us?''

Because this is purgatory, Craig thought, *and we've been consigned to it.*

''You know why.'' He wrapped an arm around Brett's shoulders and squeezed. ''We're outta here the minute the police find out what happened to your mom.''

''But they think you killed her.'' Brett searched his face. ''Don't they? So, are they even looking for Mom?''

"Sure they are." Craig hated his falsely hearty voice, never mind the fact that he was lying to his kids despite his vows never to do so. No, the cops weren't looking for Julie, because they were sure she was dead. Fish bait. What they were doing was waiting for him to screw up. Head out furtively some Tuesday afternoon for that storage space, rented under another name, where he'd hidden the bloodstained tarps. Or maybe even the body. The cops were probably listening to this conversation. Craig was willing to bet the house was wiretapped. *He* was the suspect, and the cops were dogging his every footstep.

Abby, still in the doorway, let out a sniff. "I miss Mommy."

Craig held out his hand to her and lied yet again. "Me, too, Punkin. Come here."

She plopped onto the bed on his other side and wept a few tears onto his T-shirt. Brett continued to sit stiffly, saying nothing.

"Daddy?" Abby said after a moment. "Did you light the coals?"

"Light the…" He swore and leaped up. "I forgot all about them."

They'd burned down to fiery embers, perfect for barbecuing. Abby brought him the plate of steaks, which he laid on the grill. Juice sizzled as it hit the coals. Soon, the scent of their meat cooking mingled in the air with the smells from across the fence.

And finally, he and his children ate, near to the laughter and conversation in the next yard but not part of it, isolated as they always were now.

Because one day Julie had vanished, leaving behind her car keys and purse. Who would befriend even the children of a man who must have murdered his wife?

ROBIN MCKINNON sat in her classroom and waited for the bell that would bring students rushing in. Hands flat on her desk, she took one last survey of her newly hung decorations, the welcome she'd written on the blackboard, the arrangement of the desks, the names she'd stenciled onto cards and taped below each wooden cubby where her sixth-graders would park their backpacks and lunches.

Her gaze paused halfway, on one name: Brett Lofgren. She both dreaded and anticipated seeing him walk in the door. Notes from Brett's fourth grade and fifth grade teachers made it clear that he had become a troubled boy since Robin had known him. And no wonder! How horrifying for him, to be torn between fear that his mother had abandoned him and his sister and the more frightening possibility that his father had killed his mother.

The Tribune had reported that Brett claimed his mother had said goodbye to him; his story was one of the major reasons Craig Lofgren hadn't been arrested. But what if he'd made up that story to protect his father? Imagine as the weeks and months went by and his mother wasn't found. Would he start wondering if his father *had* murdered her?

She shivered, thinking about it, remembering Julie Lofgren. Robin had met Julie through circumstance, just…oh, two mothers who often sat together at sporting events, rooting for each other's kid, talking in that idle way you did when a Little League game dragged on for hours. After several years, she'd have sworn she knew Julie, the bubbly, pretty woman with dimples and an irresistibly childish delight in the triumphs of her children. Robin had talked about her husband, then their marital troubles and finally the divorce. Just before Julie disappeared, a year after Robin's divorce—when she and Glenn had become embroiled in an ugly custody battle because Glenn was trying to impress his new girlfriend—Julie had listened sympathetically.

In turn, she had confessed to problems in her own marriage, nebulous but enough to make her lower her voice and to cause the light that imbued her to dim. She had never once suggested that Craig was abusive or that she was afraid of him, but she was never quite specific about what was wrong at home, either.

Robin felt guilty that she hadn't stayed in touch with Brett. He and Malcolm were more soccer buddies than close friends, rather like their mothers, but Mal would have been okay with inviting Brett over. She just hadn't thought to suggest it, even though she'd read all the newspapers with her friend's face constantly in her mind, wondering at her fate, first thinking about Craig as a distraught, loving husband, then as a violent man who wouldn't take rejection. She and Malcolm had had their own turmoil about the same time, thanks to Glenn…. But that was just an excuse. Robin prayed that Brett's closer friends had been more faithful.

The bell rang, its shrill clamor making her start. Feet thundered in the hall and two boys jostled to be the first into the classroom. Other children pressed behind them.

"Children" was still the right word, although they wouldn't like to hear it. This was her favorite age, these boys and girls on the brink of so much more: of physical maturity, of making decisions that would direct their lives, of being genuinely cool, of "going together" meaning more than the words. You could mistake a sixth-grader for a sophomore in high school one minute, a fourth-grader the next. Like the boys' voices, cracking and squeaking and booming, these eleven-year-olds wavered between childhood and adolescence. She liked to think she could still have an effect on them that she might not be able to in another year or two.

She smiled as they poured in. "Take a seat. Any desk is fine today."

A few she knew well, because of extracurricular activities or because they were younger siblings of former students. Others were familiar faces, because she'd seen them in the halls every year. A few were new to the district.

As always, she marveled at how much less mature the boys were than the girls—a sad fact that had the girls longing for middle school. A curvy brunette sauntered in, flipping her hair and eyeing the boys sidelong. Pants darn near as low and tight as Christina Aguilera's hugged her hips; her baby tee, snug over a buxom chest, announced that she was a "princess." Slipping quietly into a front seat was another girl, slight as a fourth grader, who would undoubtedly pretend with friends that she was interested in boys, even though she still played with Barbies at home.

Boys punched each other, rocked their desks, guffawed and shouted at friends passing in the hall. Most were shorter than the girls, just beginning a growth spurt that would have them looking like men in only a few years.

Unless he had changed extraordinarily, Brett Lofgren hadn't yet made an appearance. Robin scanned faces yet again. The second bell rang, making a few kids clap hands over their ears. She started toward the door with the intention of shutting it.

A tall, handsome boy with his father's dark hair and gray eyes ambled in. She'd have been fooled by Brett's air of nonchalance, by his sneer, if she hadn't seen how fixed his gaze was. He walked right by her and sat down without meeting anybody's eyes or speaking to a soul.

It might have been her imagination, but there seemed to be a brief hitch in the noise level, a moment when others snatched a surreptitious look, then ostentatiously turned back to their friends and began chattering again. Brett slumped in his chair and began tapping his fingers on the desk.

Robin closed the door and cleared her throat. Quiet spread slowly.

"Good morning. Welcome to sixth grade, and your last year at Roosevelt Elementary School." She smiled in acknowledgment of the cheers. "I'm Robin McKinnon, and I look forward to getting to know all of you."

She called roll. Most said, "Hey!" or "That's

me.'' Brett flicked a hand in the air and didn't look up. They talked about seating and agreed to start the year wherever they liked.

''After the first few weeks, once I get to know you, I'm going to start assigning seats.''

Groans.

She smiled. ''It's important for you to learn to work with people who aren't your best friends. There are rewards, too, in getting to know kids who aren't in your circle, who maybe have different interests. And finally, I know you'll concentrate better when you *can't* whisper with your best friend.''

Brett, it appeared as the day went on, *had* no best friend, at least not in this classroom. He spoke to no one. Some of the girls made tentative efforts to flirt with him, not at all to Robin's surprise; Brett was not only good-looking, but his sulky expression gave him a James Dean air. The other boys were downright wholesome in comparison.

She handed out paperwork for them to go over with their parents concerning her expectations, both for behavior and quality of work. They reviewed math, so she got a sense of where they were, she distributed texts and talked about her requirement for reading: a report a month, each written after reading a book from a different category on a list she gave them. She wanted them to read widely; one sports book was okay, for example, but not nine. The kids always grumbled early on, but her experience was that they found their interests broadening when they dipped into a biography or a play or science fiction or a classic.

At morning recess and lunch, Brett waited until last to slouch out of the classroom door. Robin peeked to see what he did on the playground and saw him shooting baskets by himself. He moved as if he did this often. He'd feint, dribble, shoot and rebound like a pro. As good as he was, no other boy went to join him.

Oh, dear, she thought. Usually she arranged desks in clusters of four once she started assigning seats. Brett was going to be a dark cloud over every group stuck with him if his attitude didn't improve.

It didn't.

Although there were no incidents, he stayed sullen through that first three-day week.

On the following Monday, Robin saw another boy poke him as they waited in line to go to P.E., and heard Brett snarl a startling—and forbidden—obscenity.

"Brett!" she snapped. "You will not use that word at school again. Is that clear?"

Eyes filled with dark, churning emotion, he stared at her for a long moment. Then he gave a curt nod.

"Please apologize to Trevor."

This pause was even longer. Finally he mumbled something that she suspected was as unintelligible to Trevor as it was to her, but she decided not to make an issue of it.

Oh, dear, she thought again.

Tuesday, Amanda Whitney, she of the baby tees and tight jeans, sat down beside him and began tossing her hair and giggling as she tried to coax him to talk.

Brett leveled a cold stare at her and said, "Will you just leave me alone?"

From the other side of the classroom came a boy's voice. "Jeez, Mandy! Stay away from him. He's probably a killer like his dad."

Brett erupted from his desk, sending the chair flying. Shoving aside other desks and kids, he lunged toward a cluster of boys. He crashed into Ryan Durney and the two went down.

Robin yelled, "Stop, *now!*" and grabbed Brett's arm before he could punch Ryan.

Ryan scrambled away, his eyes wild. The rest of the kids had gathered in a semicircle, looking scared.

"Back to your seats!"

They went.

Gentling her voice, Robin asked, "Ryan, are you all right?"

He gave a jerky nod.

"Please take your seat, too. I'll talk to you in a minute."

She marched an unresisting Brett out onto the small, railed porch of the portable building. Mercifully, the porch of the next portable and the covered breezeway into the main building were deserted. When she released him, he put his back to the railing and waited, head bowed and lank hair hanging over his eyes.

"What were you thinking?" Robin asked.

After a minute, he shrugged.

Her heartbeat was slowing at last, but she still felt shaken by the violence of his reaction. Sixth-grade fights were usually...clumsier. She had never seen an attack so purposeful. Given another ten seconds, he would have hurt Ryan.

"I should send you to the principal's office," she said. "I won't hesitate to do so if you ever, *ever,* start a fight again. Is that clear?"

He nodded.

"What Ryan said was unkind. It was also spoken out of ignorance."

Brett's head shot up. He said hotly, "My dad would *never*—"

Robin held up a hand. "But that isn't the point. You cannot go through life attacking every single person who thinks something you don't like."

"I should just let people call my dad a murderer."

"I didn't say you couldn't correct them, or even argue. When," she added sternly, "the setting is appropriate to do so."

His face set in stubborn lines.

"Have you ever said to Ryan, 'My mom left my dad. Just because the cops can't find her doesn't mean she's dead'?"

"Nobody will believe me. The cops don't."

He had a point. She gave up on reason and said, "If another kid taunts you, I want you to come to me. I'll talk to him or her, just as I'm going to talk to Ryan. But violence will only convince them that they're right."

Anger simmered in his eyes. "Dad didn't—"

Interrupting, Robin said, "Right now, I neither know nor care. He's not in my classroom. You are. He isn't the issue here, any more than are the parents that I know don't encourage their children to do their homework or who don't care enough to come to parent conferences. *You* are responsible for your own behavior, for how you handle your problems. Parents might be part of the problem, but your response is yours alone." She waited a moment. "Do you understand?"

Jaw still clenched, he jerked his head once.

"Fine." She touched his rigid arm. "You may return to your desk."

Stepping into the classroom, she gestured to Ryan, who took a circuitous route to avoid going anywhere near Brett. Robin steered the other boy outside the classroom door.

"I'm glad you weren't hurt."

"Jeez! He was like an animal!"

"You said something deeply hurtful."

His face became wary.

"Tell me, Ryan, do you know anything about Brett's parents for a fact?" She waited, then continued, "Or have you been listening to gossip that is no more informed than you were a few minutes ago?"

"Everybody says…"

"Has Brett's father been arrested? Tried?"

He hesitated, then shook his head.

"Don't you think the police would have arrested Mr. Lofgren if they had any evidence whatsoever to suggest that he killed his wife?"

"But…"

She overrode him. "In this country, we believe people are innocent until proven guilty. Mr. Lofgren is nowhere near being proven guilty. Perhaps more to the point, in this school, and especially in my classroom, nobody deliberately attempts to hurt another person's feelings. Am I making myself clear?''

Looking both mulish and sheepish—speaking of animals, she thought with a certain wryness—Ryan nodded again.

''Then this incident is forgotten. You may go back to your desk.''

Of course, she was lying. The incident was not forgotten by either boy, or even by her.

Wednesday, she had her students begin journals, which they would leave in their desks every night.

''I'll read them from time to time.'' She wandered among desks, touching a shoulder here, smiling there. ''Not to correct them. I want you to write freely about your experiences, your thoughts, your feelings. I'm checking only to be sure that you are in fact using your time to write. Still, be aware that I may read any particular passage, so in a sense you are writing for my eyes.''

She gave them twenty minutes to open their spiral notebooks and—for the most part—stare into space. Each day it would come easier, until the majority of students actually enjoyed this time, took up where they left off, explored contradictory emotions, forgot that they were writing for anyone but themselves.

On Thursday she interrupted a shouting match between Brett and a pair of boys from April Nyholt's class. They said, ''I'm sorry, Ms. McKinnon,'' and retired from the battlefield looking smug. Brett smoldered.

Robin wished he could see that his attitude was most of the problem. Other kids in this school had

had notorious parents. Students had buzzed a couple of years ago when a sixth-grader's mother left her father for another woman. But the girl had had the sense to say, "She's my mom and I love her, but…it is so-o freaky!" Everybody had sympathized and quickly forgotten. Brett didn't let anybody forget.

Robin didn't look at her students' journals until Friday. She asked that they be left out on the desks. When the room was empty, she walked from desk to desk, flipping open the journals.

Some had only a few lines.

I'm going to my dad's tonight. I hate going! It is so boring!

Robin smiled at the multiple underlines beneath "so," even though she felt sad at how many children were shuttled between divorced parents' houses with no regard for where they preferred to be.

One boy wrote in some detail about a Seahawks game to which his uncle had taken him. The excitement shone through, and that provoked another smile. Several kids couldn't spell, and she made a mental note of their names. Ryan wrote about "that Lofgren kid" trying to beat the crap out of him. "All I said was…" Robin sighed. Her little lecture had apparently not had much impact.

Perhaps deliberately, her route brought her to Brett's desk last. She opened his journal, started reading and made a small sound of shock.

Oh, dear, was no longer an adequate response.

CHAPTER TWO

CRAIG DID NOT expect to hear from his son's teacher on a Friday evening. In fact, he didn't expect to hear from her at all. Last year's teacher had never once called him in for a conference, even though Brett's grades sank throughout the year and the principal did summon Craig several times. When Craig showed up for the traditional November parent conferences, Ms. Hayes had appeared uncomfortable and kept their talk as short as she could manage without outright rudeness.

Last week, when he'd asked how the first day of school went, Abby's face had brightened. "I really like Mrs. Jensen. She's letting Summer and me sit together."

Brett shrugged.

Craig had tried a couple of times in the intervening week and a half to talk to his son, but Brett always mumbled, "It's okay."

Don't borrow trouble, Craig warned himself. He didn't want to assume Brett would do poorly this year. Time was supposed to heal, wasn't it?

Craig had been gone the past couple of days. He'd flown the polar route to Frankfurt and back. As usual, his father stayed with the kids.

Dad had already fed them when Craig got home at seven-thirty that evening. Waving off Craig's thanks, he said, "See you Tuesday," and left.

As he did every single time, Craig wondered what he'd do without his father, who'd retired nearby a few years back. Who else would stay in this house? Something told him that motherly types would not line up outside his door if he ran an ad in the weekly paper asking for live-in help for half the week.

Weary, Craig said hi to Abby, engrossed in a favorite TV show, and to Brett who was hunched over the computer playing Snood. In one way, he was stung by their lack of interest in his arrival home. In another, he was pleased. Abby had clung to him after her mother disappeared. Every time Craig had to leave, she'd sobbed and begged him not to go. Brett had hidden his feelings better, but Craig could feel his anxiety, too. He'd considered quitting his job, maybe seeing if he could fly for a local carrier like Horizon, so that he could be home every night. But just recently, he'd seen an improvement. The kids were beginning to have faith that their Dad would always come home.

On his way to the kitchen, he gave something approaching a laugh. Faith? Hell, maybe they just liked Grandad better. Craig knew damn well that his father wasn't as demanding as he was. Abby and Brett had manipulating Grandad down to a fine art.

Without interest, Craig gazed into the refrigerator. His father had left a covered plate. Craig lifted the tin foil, saw leftover spaghetti, and stuck it in the microwave to warm even though he wasn't very hungry. He had to eat.

The microwave was still humming when the phone rang. Craig started. The telephone in this house didn't ring often.

He lifted the receiver and said cautiously, "Hello?"

A woman's voice, sounding tentative, said, "May I speak to Mr. Lofgren?"

"This is Craig Lofgren."

The microwave beeped. He ignored it.

"Oh. This is Robin McKinnon. Brett's teacher."

His heart sank. So much for his foolish hope that Brett's notoriety would wear off and that he might start joining the pack again, so to speak. It seemed Abby was, even if none of her friends were ever able to come home with her to play.

"Yes?"

"I'd like to set up a conference with you, Mr. Lofgren. To discuss Brett."

"What's he done?"

There was a moment of silence. "It's not so much what he's done as how…unhappy he seems. He's very isolated, you know." In this pause, Craig sensed she was searching for words. "He's angry."

Angry. That meant Brett was still starting fights. Rubbing the back of his neck, Craig said, "Is Monday too soon? I'm an airline pilot and I fly out again Tuesday."

"Can you come right after school on Monday? At two-thirty?"

He agreed. "Should I be speaking to Brett about something specific in the meantime?"

"No-o." She seemed to draw the word out. "I'd rather talk to you first."

"Is he doing his work?"

"In a perfunctory way."

Damn it, Brett was a smart kid. He'd been a top-notch student until… Craig grunted. Until his world fell apart.

"Did you say something?" the teacher asked.

"No. I'll see you Monday."

He replaced the receiver, then stood frowning into space for a long minute before remembering the spaghetti. He ate without tasting it, dumping half into the garbage. What was Brett doing? Beating the crap out of every kid who said, "Hey, did your dad bury your mom in the backyard?"

Yeah. Probably. Craig could even understand the temptation. There were days he was angry, too. When he sure as hell wanted to punch somebody. He was angry that he couldn't grocery shop locally without mothers shooing their kids out of his path or all conversation dying around him. He was angry at "friends" who hadn't known him at all. And some-times, on really bad days, he hated the cops, and es-pecially Sergeant Michael Caldwell, the investigating officer who had made up his mind from the get-go that Craig had killed his wife and had hounded Craig for the next year.

A week ago, he'd felt sick to realize that he was happy to see in the newspaper that Michael Caldwell

had died in a car accident. An easygoing man, Craig
had never truly hated before.

And he was lucky enough to be able to escape the
miasma of suspicion and judgment when he went to
work. Co-pilots and crew came from all over the
country. Some didn't even know about Julie. Others
had never met her and had forgotten the notoriety. In
the air, he was just Captain Lofgren.

Besides, he had a lifetime of lessons in self-
restraint to draw on. Brett was at a tough age anyway.
What scared Craig was the long-term effect of all this
anger on Brett. Hormones were putting him through
the wringer already. He was *supposed* to be slamming
doors and sulking. He wasn't supposed to have discovered that theoretically decent people seemed to
need to have a leper in their midst whom they could
despise and fear. He wasn't supposed to have discovered already what it was like to *be* that leper.

Craig tucked Abby in and heard about her week.
Summer's mother, thank God, had allowed her
daughter's friendship with Abby to continue. Summer
didn't come over here, but Craig could live with that.
Abby had asked a few times, Summer—or her
mother—had made excuses, and Abby had quit asking. But they had her over often and kids her age had
been oblivious to the police investigation. Some of
them had probably heard now—mothers must give
some explanation why little Bridget or Annie couldn't
play at Abby's house—but even in fourth grade they
were too young to care, apparently, about grown-up
stuff they didn't really understand.

"Can I go tomorrow?" she asked, as he pulled the covers up and smoothed them.

He realized he'd missed something. "Go where?"

She rolled her eyes in a good imitation of her brother. "To Mt. Rainier."

"Just for the day?"

"We're taking a picnic and stuff. Summer's brother is bringing his yucky friend, so she *needs* me."

"Of course you can go. Maybe I'll take Brett fishing."

Her nose scrunched. "If you catch something, I don't have to eat it, do I?"

Craig laughed. "No, you don't. Your loss."

"Uh-huh."

Still laughing, he kissed her good-night and turned out the light.

He didn't suggest bedtime for Brett for another couple of hours. Then he wandered in to say good-night and stopped in his tracks.

"Hey! Your bedroom's clean."

"Grandad made me."

Hmm. Maybe his father wasn't quite the pushover Craig had feared.

"Good. Did he also make you wash a few loads, or is it all piled up in the laundry room waiting for me?"

"Uh... I started a load. Tuesday night." Then Brett grinned, for a second looking like the cheerful kid he'd once been. "Just kidding. I washed three loads. *And* folded them."

Which meant Craig's dress shirts were probably

wadded in a stack on his bureau rather than hanging in the closet, but Craig wasn't about to quibble.

"Thank you," he said, and meant it.

"Did you know that Grandad doesn't throw his socks away when they get holes in them? He says he doesn't mind a little ventilation."

"He grew up without much money. Even though he's got enough now, he thinks before he buys anything."

Brett puzzled over that. "Oh. But…socks?"

"Maybe we should buy him some for his birthday."

The boy's expression made plain what he thought of socks as a birthday present.

Casually, Craig said, "Your teacher called tonight."

A flare of something very like fear was dampened in a heartbeat. Brett's face went blank. "Ms. McKinnon?"

"Uh-huh."

His son tried to hold out, but couldn't. "What did she want?"

"A conference." Craig waited for a deliberate moment. "Do you know what it's about?"

Brett shrugged. Craig's least favorite response.

"We'll see," he said.

Brett turned his face away on the pillow.

"Do you want to go fishing tomorrow?" Craig asked.

He looked back at his father. "Really?"

"Yeah, why not?"

"Does Abby have to come?"

"Nope. She's going somewhere with Summer."

"Cool! Yeah!"

THEY HAD A GOOD DAY, taking their poles to a small lake where they rented a rowboat and trolled. With Labor Day weekend past, the lake was uncrowded, a few powerboats crisscrossing, one water skier making half a dozen laps before taking a spectacular fall.

The sun was warm, the blue surface of the lake dazzling, the occasional excitement of hauling in a trout of legal length all they needed to save them from boredom. Trees grew down to the shores of the lake, interrupted by summer cabins and docks.

Craig made no effort to direct the desultory conversation, just let it drift along with the boat.

Only once did the subject of Brett's mom come up.

After one of the many long, contented pauses, the eleven-year-old said, "That policeman is dead, right?"

Craig nodded. "His funeral was last week."

"What will they do now?"

"I don't know." Craig flexed his pole and cranked the reel a few times. "It may not make any difference that he's gone."

His son gave him a look older than his years. "He thought you killed Mom."

Craig considered denying it, but dismissed the notion. He wasn't a believer in telling his kids lies.

"Yeah, that's the impression he gave."

"Maybe the other cops don't." Hope was scrabbling here. "Maybe they'll find Mom."

"You know, even if they did, I don't think she'll be coming home."

Brett nodded. "Unless she's, like, being held captive somewhere. I read about this guy who kidnapped women and kept them for, like, six months at a time. Or she could have amnesia or something."

"Almost anything's possible." Craig made his voice gentle. "But the chances are she's either dead or she left because she wanted to."

"Yeah," his son said despondently. "I know. But...hey!" His pole bowed. "Wow, this feels like a big one!"

That was it. Excited about his catch, Brett didn't seem interested in talking about his mother anymore.

Sunday was catch-up day: clean the house, mow the lawn, buy groceries for the week. Brett was even quieter than usual but helpful, Abby as chatty as always.

Monday Craig did errands: the bank, the dry cleaners, the post office. He usually drove to Tacoma to do them, just so he didn't have to endure the stares.

Coward, he accused himself. Or maybe he was paranoid; maybe some of the stares were imagined. Could be that he and Brett both were being egotistical in believing the whole world gave a flying leap about their personal drama.

He still went to Tacoma.

Abby and Brett both took the bus home from school. They'd be okay without him for an hour. Craig parked in front of the elementary school administration building and waited until the buses pulled out and the majority of the parents picking up children had left the parking lot.

While he waited, he tried to remember a woman he'd met a few times but probably hadn't exchanged ten words with. She was pretty, he seemed to recall, but not in Julie's class. He remembered her as too thin, tense. Always nice, but looking wired, as if she didn't sleep. Brett had hung out with her kid and seemed to like her. For some reason, Julie and Robin McKinnon had clicked, which was the part that worried Craig.

Finally he made himself get out of the car and walk in. This was the kind of place he hated most to go, where he was especially unwelcome. A sign on the door read Visitors MUST Check In At Office. The secretary looked up with a smile that froze when she saw him.

"May I help you?"

"Just checking in to see my son's teacher. Ms. McKinnon is expecting me."

He signed in and she handed him a pass that he was supposed to clip to his shirt pocket.

"I'll let her know you're on your way." The secretary turned away.

Striding down the hall, careful not to turn his head to look into classrooms or to make eye contact with passing adults or kids, Craig imagined that she was summoning reinforcements to be sure that Robin McKinnon didn't risk life and limb by being alone with him.

More paranoia.

Turned out that Brett's classroom was in a portable

just outside the double doors at the far end of the wing. If he'd known, he would have parked in the back and gone straight to her classroom without walking the gauntlet. The hell with their rules.

Not a good attitude for the parent of two young kids.

He went up a ramp, knocked and went in.

As Robin McKinnon turned from the blackboard, an eraser in her hand, his first thought was that she was prettier than he'd remembered.

She'd put on weight, but in a good way. It made him realize that what he'd seen back then was worry. Something wrong in her life. He remembered something about a divorce, but that had been a while back, hadn't it? But divorce did bring consequences: money problems, or her boy had reacted badly to his dad moving out.

Now she had a round, gentle face, big brown eyes and light brown hair pulled loosely into a ponytail on the crown of her head. It was beautiful hair: thick, straight, shiny. Heavy silk.

She wore a batik-print skirt in brown and cream and a cream-colored T-shirt. Quite a bit taller than his petite wife, Robin McKinnon was five-seven or -eight, slim but curvy in the right places.

"Mr. Lofgren. Thank you for coming."

She didn't smile. Blocking his awareness of her as a woman, he nodded curtly.

"Please. Come and sit down." She led the way to her desk. When she sat behind it, he followed suit in a creaky old armchair of that yellowed oak being retired from all public institutions.

She looked nervous, but her eyes met his. "We've met before."

"I remember."

"I was very sorry to hear about Julie's disappearance." She said it carefully. Had rehearsed it, he guessed. "I liked her."

He nodded again, keeping his face expressionless.

"This must have been a very difficult year and a half for you."

Craig had lost patience with pretence. "Is there a point to this?"

Her expression told him he'd been rude. "I *was* going to add that it must have been a difficult time for Brett as well."

He sighed. "I'm sorry. Yes. Of course it has been. As you said, he's angry."

"And sad," she prompted, as if he'd forgotten something important.

Craig grimaced. "That goes without saying. Does he miss his mom? Of course he does. But that's not at the root of his problems. It's the whispers, the friends who turned their backs, the cops coming over and over again to interview his father." He heard how harsh his voice had become. "It's the fact that we might as well live in a zoo, with people peering into our cage with morbid interest and fear." He made himself stop. "Does that give you some insight into Brett, Ms. McKinnon?"

She gaped, and Craig realized that he had been leaning toward her, trying with body language to strengthen his description of a life he hoped would horrify her. Would truly let her understand his son.

Letting out a long breath, he leaned back. The chair groaned. Silence swelled.

Her tongue touched her lips. "I'm sorry," she whispered, voice cracking. "I didn't realize…"

"Why should you? Unless you hurried your son to the other side of the street because you saw Brett coming."

There was a fearlessness in her eyes that he hadn't noticed before. And something else—shame.

"No," she said, still in that low, husky voice. "I wouldn't have done that. But I should have encouraged Malcolm to stay in touch with Brett. I let Brett slip from my radar. For that…I really am sorry."

To his astonishment, he believed her. All he could do was nod. His throat seemed to have closed. He met kindness so damn rarely.

Clearing his throat, he nodded at the folder and spiral binder she had squared on the desk blotter in front of her. "Maybe you'd better tell me what's going on."

Blinking, she looked down, then gave her head a small shake. "Yes. Of course." She bit her lip, then lifted her head to meet his eyes again. "From the first day, Brett's been…sullen. He stays to himself. He has no friends that I can see."

"He never did make friends as easily as my younger, Abby. But he had a couple of good friends. One moved away right before…" His jaws tightened. "The other kid pretty much turned his back on Brett. I don't know if it was by choice, or on his parents' orders. Or if Brett's turmoil drove him away."

"Oh, no," she murmured. When he said nothing

more, Ms. McKinnon seemed to gather herself. "He…attacked another boy one day this week."

"He was in fights a few times last year."

"Yes. But this seemed different from the usual elementary school fights. Mrs. Hayes didn't say anything in her notes about Brett to make me think she'd been alarmed by the incidents last year, beyond the fact that they're a symptom. But this time…" Her eyes were unfocused as she frowned, apparently searching for words. "He…erupted. I could see such rage on his face. I think, if I hadn't been here, he'd have really hurt the other boy."

"But you broke it up."

"Well, of course!" She glanced down at the spiral binder that lay between her hands, planted palm-down on the desk. "I've had concerns from the first day, but I wouldn't have called you yet, I would have let Brett settle in and seen how it went, except for this."

Her touch ginger, as if the garden-variety spiral notebook held directions for building a nuclear bomb, she lifted it, turned it around and held it out to him.

Uncomprehending, he took the notebook.

"In my class, everyone has to write a journal. They make entries every day. I do warn them that I'll be glancing through their journals, mostly just to be sure they're writing. Sometimes I read more than other times, particularly if I'm concerned about a student. Sometimes they write quite a bit about their home lives."

What in hell?

Craig looked down at it, strangely reluctant to open the cover. Something had shaken a woman who'd been teaching sixth grade for a number of years. He'd have thought she would have seen—and read—it all by now.

With an abrupt movement, he flipped open the notebook and saw his son's nearly illegible scrawl filling the page.

Lots of people deserve to die. Not my mom—she's not dead anyway—but lots of other people. That cop. I want to go, like, burn a cross on his grave. Or something. So people know he's a son of a bitch.

Actually, "son of a bitch" was preceded by some horrific obscenities. Words Craig hadn't realized his son knew, far less used.

Heart drumming, he continued to decipher the scrawl.

Like Ryan Durney. I wanted to kill him! I still want to kill him!!! Maybe I will. He says I'm like my dad. He thinks I'm a murderer, so maybe I'll be one. I'll just punch him and keep punching…

Feeling sick, Craig read to the bitter end. The appalling stream of consciousness broke off midsentence. Apparently journal-writing time had ended. Hands shaking, he closed the notebook and sat with his head down.

Oh God, oh God. How could this rage, this rot have been filling his son's head without him knowing?

Craig had read about the stunning tragedies at schools like Columbine without understanding how it could have happened without the parents *seeing* that their children had turned into monsters.

Now…now he knew.

Eyes burning, he looked up. "I had no idea."

Voice soft, Robin McKinnon said, "I assumed you didn't."

"He says I'm 'like my dad,'" Craig quoted. He scrubbed a hand over his face. "Does Brett think…" His throat closed.

With clear compassion, his son's teacher said, "I don't know. He did defend you to me, but…what a child says isn't always what he believes, deep in his heart."

Pushing the spiral notebook away with revulsion, Craig asked, "Have you ever seen anything like this?"

"Not…quite. Hints of it." She nibbled on her lip. "These kids have all seen slasher movies, you know. Really grisly stuff. So imagining themselves in that world, if you will, isn't the stretch for them it might have been for us when we were kids."

He nodded numbly, wanting to believe that Brett didn't mean any of this, but unable to.

"This, though…" She, too, gazed at Brett's journal. "It shocked me."

Craig shook his head. "He must have known you'd read it."

"Yes, and that's what gives me hope. I think he must *want* an adult to know what he's thinking and feeling."

"He could have told me."

"Maybe," she said, "he wants to be strong for you."

Maybe he did. Craig remembered the clean bedroom, the folded laundry, the help raking the lawn and vacuuming the living room. Brett didn't even ask about his mother often, he went on as if, on the surface, nothing had changed.

"I suggested counseling. Six or eight months ago. After he started picking fights." He had to breathe deeply a couple of times. "He said no. He was okay." His mouth worked. "He's not okay."

"No. He's not."

"Thank you, Ms. McKinnon." Craig blundered to his feet. "You undoubtedly want him out of your classroom and this school. I don't blame you."

She shook her head and said firmly, "Please sit down. I don't want Brett to go anywhere."

Craig stared at her now determined face.

"This," she nodded again at the notebook, "suggests he is quite troubled. But he's only eleven years old. He has plenty of reason to *be* angry. What he's feeling isn't irrational. The other children *do* stare and whisper, in part because his attitude invites it. But, in fairness to Brett, that's not the whole story. Ryan Durney did suggest that—" Here she faltered.

"I'm a murderer."

"Um…" Her gaze shied. "Something like that. Ryan warned a girl away from Brett, suggesting that…"

"He's just like me." Craig swore under his breath.

"The sad thing is that Ryan isn't an unusually cruel boy. They taunt each other at this age, the boys in particular. They…hunt for weaknesses, in themselves as much as in the others. I really believe if Brett had fought back in a different way, if from the beginning he'd said, 'Jeez, I know my mom took off. I don't

know what that cop's problem is,' the other boys
would have dropped it.''

"But they smelled blood.''

"Exactly.''

He sat in silence, feeling defeated.

"I strongly recommend counseling,'' Ms. McKinnon said.

Craig nodded. "Do I tell him you showed me
this?''

"Why not? I warned the students that what they
wrote wouldn't be private. If he doesn't know how
inappropriate his thoughts and fantasies are, it's time
he finds out.''

"Damn straight,'' Craig muttered.

Voice tentative, she said, "I assume there's a reason you haven't moved to a community where you
can make a fresh start.''

"We've been strongly encouraged to stay put.'' He
made sure she heard the irony.

"I see.''

Weirdly, in the midst of his turmoil, Craig was distracted by the swing of her ponytail when she nodded,
the way light from the overhead fluorescent fixture
shimmered from it. He realized he was staring and
made himself look away, at the blackboard.

"I talked to the administration in Salmon Creek
about moving Brett, but they turned me down.''

"They're desperate to pass a bond issue, and classrooms are bulging. I'm not surprised.''

His impression had been that they hadn't wanted
Brett and his problems. But he kept that to himself.
"I even looked into the Christian school here in town,

but they let me know that they thought Brett's presence would be disruptive." If he'd been a member of their church, it might have been different, they'd implied. He didn't buy that.

His son's teacher asked, "How is your relationship with Brett?"

"Actually…" He cleared his throat. "Actually, it's pretty good. We went fishing Saturday. He helped me around the house yesterday."

"Is he involved in any activities with kids his age outside school? At church? Does he still play sports?"

Craig shook his head. "Everything just went by the wayside…."

She nibbled on her lip in a way that distracted him as much as her glorious, shining hair. "Can you encourage him to take up an activity again? Or is that impossible because of your job?"

"My father would chauffeur Brett." His voice scraped. "But who would have him?"

Her startled expression told him she still didn't get it.

"Try to imagine." Baring himself like this was humiliating, but he didn't see any choice. "I call a Boy Scout leader and say, 'Hi, I'm under investigation for murdering my wife, but I'm hoping you'll welcome my son into your troop. By the way, he's having fantasies about murdering everyone he doesn't like, but I know he'll have a great time learning to tie knots.'"

Robin McKinnon stared at him for a long time, not saying a word. He shifted uncomfortably.

Then, briskly, she said, "I don't see why he

wouldn't be welcome on his old soccer team. Will you bring him?''

Craig blinked. ''The season's already started.''

''I remember him being quite talented. We could use another goalie.''

''But…''

''I'll speak to the coach and call you.''

He still seemed to be stuttering.

''The team practices five days a week. Games every Saturday and we'll probably enter tournaments into November. I really do believe it would be good for Brett.''

''If Brett's forced on the other boys…''

''Remember, most of the boys are from Salmon Creek, not Klickitat. Since Brett and Abby don't go to school there, I suspect most people will have forgotten all the talk.'' Because the Lofgrens actually lived on the outskirts of the school district, the playfields for the Salmon Creek team had been closer. ''I know Malcolm will be pleased to see Brett again.'' Her tone said he'd darn well better. ''The others will follow his example.''

''Just like that.''

''Just like that,'' she agreed.

Shaking his head at her astounding blend of naiveté and kindness, Craig stood. ''If he's welcome, I'll bring him.'' His voice hardened. ''If he's not, please don't set him up for another fall.''

She rose to her feet, too. ''I understand.''

''Thank you, Ms. McKinnon. I'm grateful that you got in touch. And—'' the words seemed to snag in his throat "—that you are willing to give him a chance."

She smiled at him for the first time, momentarily becoming beautiful. "I never give up on my students, Mr. Lofgren. As you will find."

Was that a promise? he wondered, walking back through the school halls. Or a warning?

CHAPTER THREE

"DAD, I GOT PROMOTED to Homicide today."

Ann Caldwell stood beside her father's grave. She hadn't brought flowers, which were allowed only on specific holidays. Instead, she stood straight, as if awaiting inspection, feet braced and hands clasped behind her back. The hot September sun baked her.

Today had been the last day she needed to wear her uniform to work, a thought that brought both pride and a fluttery sense of anxiety. Her uniform defined her in ways she knew to be unhealthy. But she had badly wanted this promotion, so that she could finish her father's work.

Make him proud.

"I'm opening the Lofgren file tomorrow. He won't get away with murdering his wife. I promise."

Hearing footsteps and the low murmur of voices, she bowed her head and stayed silent until a middle-aged couple passed, holding hands. She felt their curious glances, and knew it was the uniform that drew them. The uniform that she wore because she had followed in her father's footsteps.

When she heard car doors open and slam shut, she focused again on the velvet green sod, laid like a carpet since this earth had been opened only ten days ago to receive her father's body. If she searched, she could find the seam where roots had not yet entangled with other roots. But as she'd approached the grave earlier, she had felt a massive sense of disorientation. The ground should be raw. Dad was barely gone! Instead, he might have lain here for a year, or ten years. He might never have seen her receive her badge, or the commendations that she had believed—oh, with her whole heart!—would make him smile and say, "You're a chip off the old block." Or, "You made me proud today, girl."

"I asked to take over your cases, Dad," she told the green swale interrupted only by the brass plaque. "I can finish what you started. I won't be working with Reggie. He's going to be taking a desk job. Can you believe it? Big Reggie Roarke pushing paper? But he says he has high blood pressure and he figures this is the time. I've been assigned to Diaz."

A man eight or ten years older than her, Juan Diaz had looked her up and down with critical dark eyes and then shrugged. "Here's hoping you've got half your old man's goods."

She had felt a tremor inside, a moment of doubt she rarely allowed herself. Then she'd given him a steady gaze. "We'll see, won't we?"

She'd show him. He couldn't be half as hard to please as her father had been.

"Well." Ann took a deep breath. "That's all I came to say. Someday I'll be back to tell you I've arrested Craig Lofgren. I'll put him away."

This one had mattered a whole lot to her father.

More than she'd ever quite understood, except that he'd boiled at what he'd called "rich boy crime."

"They think they're above the law," he'd ranted. "They dress good and they hire fancy lawyers and somehow they walk. They don't *look* like criminals. I could see in this bastard's eyes that he didn't even think I'd suspect him. After all, he'd called us, hadn't he? Full of concern. Where could she be? But he *knew*. By God I could feel it. He knew the whole time."

Dad knew, too. Julie Lofgren was dead, slain by her husband's hand. But proving what he knew was another matter. He had to find her body. Even some blood. A witness. *Something*.

It ate at him, that good-looking airline pilot who must make $200,000 a year but wouldn't let his wife go. Didn't want to pay alimony, or maybe his pride was just stung. Could be he was one of those men who refused to lose anything that had once been his. Didn't much matter why he'd killed her rather than grant her request for a divorce.

What did matter was his cocky attitude. In every way but words he let the cops know they couldn't touch him.

Ann had seen pictures of him; handsome and smug. Tomorrow she was going to open the fat manila folder that held photos, reports and her dad's notes. As soon as possible, she'd visit Pilot Craig Lofgren and let him know that someone was still watching, still waiting. Maybe she could shake him up a little.

Aloud she said, "Julie Lofgren deserves a grave, too. When she has one, I'll put flowers on it for you."

Then, having finished what she came to say, Ann walked back across the grass to her car. She felt stronger for having put into words what she meant to do.

Solving the mystery of Julie Lofgren's disappearance would end any doubts—other people's and her own—about whether she was anywhere near the cop her father had been. Even Dad would have had to concede that if she could accomplish what he couldn't, she'd have earned her badge and more.

After unlocking her car door, Ann took one last look at the curving slope of old trees and new graves.

Even Dad, she thought one more time, would see that a woman could do this job, and do it well.

THAT VERY SAME EVENING after she'd talked with him at school, Robin called Craig Lofgren. She dialed the minute she hung up the phone from talking to Ralph.

The soccer coach had been doubtful but willing. "Yeah, yeah, the kid was good," he'd said. "But if he makes trouble, he's off the team."

"Deal," she had agreed.

In the middle of the second ring, someone picked up the phone. "Hello?" said a high girl's voice.

"May I speak to your father?"

"Who is calling, please?"

Robin smiled at the child's by-rote manners. "Robin McKinnon. Brett's teacher."

"Ohh! Is Brett in trouble? I'll get Daddy."

He came on a minute later, sounding guarded. "Ms. McKinnon?"

"Please, call me Robin." Alarm flared in her chest. What? She was trying to get friendly with a man who might have killed his wife? She cleared her throat. "Um, I spoke to the coach. He says it's fine if Brett wants to rejoin the team."

"Really?" Craig Lofgren sounded stunned.

"You didn't think he'd agree," she realized. Or did he not think she'd even bother to ask?

After a moment, he said, "No. I didn't."

Something in his voice gave her pause: a kind of grief, perhaps, that she had never heard before. The truth was, he didn't expect anyone to give his kids a fair shake. The understanding made her sad and even more determined.

"Will you talk to Brett? The sooner he starts practice, the better. He's already missed two games." She hesitated. "The coach doesn't promise a lot of playing time. Since he's so late starting."

"Brett will understand. The others have earned their positions." He was quiet for a minute. "I talked to Brett about his journal. He claims to have been venting."

"I showed it to the principal," Robin told him. "I had to, you know."

"Is he going to expel Brett?"

"No. I persuaded him to let me handle the situation, for now. He does insist on a psychological evaluation."

Craig swore.

Robin clutched the phone. "I'm sorry."

"No." His voice was deep, raw. "You're going

out of your way to help. I shouldn't have said that."
He paused. "He may even be right."

She hated to concede that Brett could be so troubled. Robin feared her own guilt was manipulating
her in uncomfortable ways. She had failed him, so
now she had to make him better. But if he wasn't
really disturbed, that meant what she had or hadn't
done wasn't very important. For entirely selfish reasons, she needed this one sullen boy to be okay.

And she hated to admit even to herself that her
motives were at least partly self-centered.

She told the boy's father which field practice would
be held on and what time they started. "Will you be
able to bring him tomorrow?"

"I fly out in the morning. My father stays with the
kids. I'll ask him."

"Good. I'll look for Brett."

"Thank you," Craig said, with a depth of emotion
impossible not to hear.

"It wasn't any huge effort. I'm just…nudging."
That was how she often thought of her job: tiny prods,
scarcely noticed, that gradually steered kids in a different direction, or made their parents react differently. She couldn't demand, couldn't order, couldn't
produce revelations that would change people's lives.
What she could do was nudge. "But you're welcome," she added.

"Will you let me know how the week goes?"

"Of course I will." She had a thought. "In fact,
I'll e-mail you, if you like. Brett supplied your address for school records. I don't know if you check it
when you're out of town…"

"I do, when I can."

"Then I'll give you an objective view of how the first practice goes."

"Great. Thank you," he said again.

At school the next day, Brett was quiet and withdrawn, but he did get a 90% on a pop spelling quiz. She smiled at him when she handed the graded quizzes out after lunch. Robin thought she saw a quick flush of pleasure on his face.

She'd already talked to her son about Brett, but she repeated herself on the way to practice that afternoon.

"Brett may not want to come back if he feels ignored."

"Mom…"

She frowned at a red light. They couldn't be late today. Not today! They just *had* to be at the field ahead of Brett and his grandfather. "You'll kind of stick with him, right? Make sure he's not sitting off by himself?"

"Mom…"

The light finally—finally!—turned green and she rocketed forward, ignoring her son's exaggerated grip on the armrest. "His soccer skills may be rusty. Maybe you could give him tips. Not obviously. Make it casual, so he's not embarrassed, but…"

"Mom!"

"What?" Startled, she shot a glance at her lanky, almost-twelve-year-old son, who was tugging wildly at his brown hair.

"I heard you the first time! Brett's cool. Okay? Nobody's going to ignore him. Jeez, Mom. It's not like we stand around. We'll be doing drills or running laps. Okay?''

She took a deep breath. "Okay. I'm sorry. I'm just kind of nervous about this. Since I set it up.''

"I can tell,'' he said with heavy irony.

Robin grinned at him. "Have I mentioned lately that I love you?''

He rolled his eyes. "Yeah, like, ten times a day.''

"I love you.''

"Don't say that in front of anybody.''

"I'm not a complete idiot.''

They both laughed. He trusted her; she trusted him.

They turned into the gravel parking lot and crunched their way to the far end, closest to today's field. Malcolm leaped out, freed his soccer ball from its net bag and tossed it to the grass. Turning back, he grabbed his water bottle.

Robin popped the trunk and pulled out her lawn chair and the tote bag in which she carried a book and a can of soda. Just as she slammed the trunk, a red Honda van pulled into the next slot.

A dizzying sense of déjà vu swept over her. Julie would leap out, calling out, "We made it! Hold up, and we can walk over together.''

Julie had loved her van for everything she could pack into it and for its shiny strawberry-red color. She'd always been willing to drive to any activity, to run anybody's kid home, to whisk across town for someone's forgotten shin guards or jersey. She was every team mother, every room mother.

Robin felt a painful squeeze in her chest, as if only

at this moment did she understand that her cheerful, generous friend was truly gone.

How? Why? she begged incoherently, knowing there would be no answers. And then, *I'm trying to take care of him.* She tried to tell Julie, hoping she could somehow hear, know.

Out of the driver's side climbed an older man who looked a great deal like his son. Robin remembered seeing him at games, although he'd tended to be down on the sideline rather than sitting in the bleachers with her and Julie. With dark hair cut short and an erect carriage, he had the air of retired military. Wearing a polo shirt and shorts, he glanced around, his expression wary when he met Robin's gaze.

"Mr. Lofgren?"

"Yes?"

She smiled. "I know we've met before. I'm Robin McKinnon. Brett's teacher this year. This…" she turned in search of him, "is my son, Malcolm, who has grown about a foot since you last saw him."

Brett's grandfather, too, smiled, his face relaxing. "Robin. Malcolm. I remember you." He nodded at the lawn chair. "Do you watch practice?"

"Yes, usually, unless I have quick errands to run."

"Ah. I wondered if I should stay."

Brett and a pretty, younger girl had gotten out, the girl looking around curiously, Brett pretending he hadn't noticed anybody else's presence.

"Hey!" Malcolm said. "It's great you're joining the team. We missed you."

Bless him, Robin thought. The speech was unusually loquacious for an eleven-year-old boy. They seemed to communicate mainly in grunts and raucous laughs. Malcolm *had* been listening to her.

Brett pretended to look surprised to see her son. "Hey," he said in response.

"Come on." Mal jerked his head. "You know how Coach feels about us being late."

Brett grimaced. "Yeah, I remember."

Kicking their soccer balls before them, the two boys struck off across the field. They were a handsome pair, both tall and athletic in their shorts, shin guards and loose-fitting T's.

Beside her, Brett's grandfather said, "This was nice of you."

"I hope it works out," she worried.

"Your boy looks like a nice kid."

Now she smiled. "He is." She surveyed the little girl, who waited gravely to one side. "Wow, you've grown, Abby."

The girl grinned. "I'm in fourth grade this year."

As they started walking after the boys, Robin said, "I hear you have Mrs. Jensen."

"She's really nice."

"You're lucky. Just between you and me, I think she's the best fourth grade teacher in the building."

"My best friend's in her class, too."

They continued chatting, Abby telling her artlessly about Summer, whose mom said maybe they could go to the water slides at Wild Waves next weekend and if they did Abby could come for sure. Abby got a little shy when she saw other younger siblings playing under the trees at one end of the giant soccer field.

A couple of the ones close to her age were hanging from a low, well-worn limb on the sycamore.

Her grandfather said, ''Why don't you go see what they're up to. Unless you want to watch Brett.''

She wrinkled her nose, hesitated, then sidled over to the trees. Robin saw that she was quickly absorbed by the small crowd of kids ranging from four- or five-year-olds up to a ten-year-old sister who bossed the rest around.

On seeing the new arrivals, Coach Pearce slapped Brett on the back and said, ''Hope you've been staying active,'' and ordered the whole team to take two laps of the field.

Brett loped beside Malcolm, the two finishing near the head of the string of boys.

Robin set up her lawn chair near the picnic table and several other mothers. Brett's grandfather shook hands all around. The others seemed momentarily startled, turned to look at Brett, but smiled and included the boy's grandfather in their idle conversation.

Robin paid more attention to Brett's play than she did to her son's. Brett wasn't as rusty as she would have expected. He must at least have been kicking the ball around. He couldn't have tossed it in a closet and left it there, or he wouldn't have been dribbling the ball deftly between cones, heading it to other players, passing with fair accuracy when he and another player raced down the field exchanging the ball.

He acquitted himself well when they scrimmaged, too. By the end of practice, he was as sweaty as the rest of the boys and was in the midst of them when they grabbed water bottles and drained them, listening while Coach mentioned a few weaknesses and said, "We're playing Puyallup Saturday and they went undefeated last year. Let's make sure they don't repeat that feat this year, shall we?"

"Yeah!" The boys high fived.

"Good practice," the coach finished briskly. "I'll see you tomorrow."

The cluster broke up into twos and threes that started toward the parents on the sideline and the parking lot where others would be pulling in to pick up offspring.

"Brett," Coach added, "I want to talk to you before you go."

In the act of folding her chair, Robin froze. Oh, no! Had Brett not done as well as she'd thought? She saw the boy's face go expressionless in a way she'd seen every day in school and come to dread.

"Sure," he said, shrugging as if he didn't care.

Malcolm hung back, too.

Stacking cones, the Coach said, "I'd like to try you out at goalie tomorrow. You still interested in playing the position?"

"Yeah! Sure. That's cool!" His back was to Robin, but she heard the animation in his voice, saw the way his shoulders relaxed.

She relaxed, too, and smiled at his grandfather who had also been listening. "He did great today."

She repeated the compliment to Brett as the two families walked back to the parking lot together.

Mal scoffed, "Nah, he was so slow I could have

stolen the ball from him any time I wanted.'' His foot shot out.

Brett turned his body, blocking the steal and then going for Malcolm's ball. After roughhousing the entire way, the two boys were grinning when they reached the cars.

''See you tomorrow!'' her son called as they separated.

''Yeah.'' Brett picked up his ball. ''Tomorrow.''

There was hope in the way he said the word, and a little bit of surprise. As if he hadn't anticipated tomorrow in a long while.

Robin had to blink some moisture from her eyes before she could unlock the car.

That night, after Malcolm had gone to bed, she sat at her computer and typed an e-mail, deleting and correcting half a dozen times, as if she were writing the cover letter for a grant application.

Dear Craig.

She frowned at the salutation, changed ''Craig'' to ''Mr. Lofgren,'' then questioned the ''Dear.'' Finally she deleted the whole dang thing. It was too formal anyway.

In the end, she was left with a few bare sentences.

Just wanted you to know that soccer practice went really well today. Brett hasn't lost any skill, and he seemed to have fun. He's to try playing goalie tomorrow. Oh, and he got a 90% on a spelling quiz today!

She added and deleted comments on how nice Craig's father was, how much Abby had grown, how she hoped his flight was turbulence free.

Honestly! They weren't pen pals.

The next night, she had a return e-mail from him.

Thanks for the report. I was hoping Brett would e-mail, too—he has his own Hotmail account—but no. He's probably not wanting to make too much of this. Thank you, Robin.

Nothing chatty. Although he had used her first name. She was glad she hadn't said, ''Dear Mr. Lofgren.''

She hit Reply and typed,

No more thanks, please. Another good day. Brett was dynamite as goalie! I suppose he felt he had to prove something, but he made some spectacular stops. Josh, who is the team's regular goalie, seemed especially determined to crack him. But after Brett skidded ten feet across the turf, stopping a hard drive to the far corner, Josh ran over and congratulated him. Well, he whacked him on the back and then they exchanged high fives. Preteen male congrats.

After a moment, she signed ''Robin'' and hit Send.

The next night, he had replied again.

I wish I'd been there! I did get an e-mail from Brett today, who said, ''Soccer is okay. I need new shoes.

Mine are too tight." I should have thought of that. We can stop somewhere on the way to practice Friday, or Saturday morning before the game. If not for your e-mails, I'd be trying to decide how okay "okay" is. It's just okay? He's not having fun but is determined to give it a chance? He's having the time of his life? So, once again…no. You said no more gratitude. Can I at least thank you for helping me stay connected? Tokyo feels like a world away, not just a few time zones. Craig

Robin didn't hit Reply this time, although she felt a pang of regret. She'd been rather enjoying their exchanges. Tomorrow, he'd be home to see his son play.

She hoped he wouldn't be disappointed if Brett didn't see much action Saturday. Although as well as Brett was playing, the coach might put him in. Without a good backup goalie, Josh had been playing both halves in a mask and pads, but he was a heck of a forward, too.

Robin had no trouble picturing Craig on the sidelines at the game. She'd always noticed when he showed up for the occasional practice and every game when he wasn't working. She'd tried to reconcile the husband Julie talked about so casually, and increasingly grumbled about that last year, with the handsome man who paced the sidelines yelling encouragement, who ruffled his son's hair and said, "Don't worry about it. That was a heck of a shot on goal you took earlier," when Brett had made a mistake and was slumped despondently on the ice chest after being pulled from the game.

The two people—the tall, athletic man with unruly dark hair and the demanding but indifferent husband—never quite lined up and clicked into place in Robin's mind, and she knew why. *Face it,* she'd thought. *You think he's sexy and can't imagine what she'd been grumbling about.*

But even then she had known that the exterior was often deceptive. Then, she'd reminded herself that beauty was only skin deep, etc., etc.

Now she reminded herself that some of the most famous serial killers were both handsome and charming, à la Ted Bundy. Some wife-killers looked like every woman's dream husband.

Craig Lofgren could have murdered his wife and still be a caring father. In fact, he might have killed her for that very reason: he didn't want to lose his children.

So don't be an idiot, Robin told herself when her heart gave a faint flutter at the idea of seeing him. *Concentrate on helping Brett.*

THE NEXT DAY, the team had already begun running laps when Robin glanced idly over her shoulder—not that she was looking for anyone!—and saw Brett tearing across the grass from the parking lot, kicking his soccer ball before him.

When he reached the sideline, panting, he dropped his water bottle, spoke briefly to Coach and took off after the other boys.

Robin was careful not to look over her shoulder again. As a result, her start was genuine when a slow, deep voice said from just beside her, "Did you see the totally cool new soccer shoes?"

She pressed a hand to her chest. "You scared me!" Then she laughed. "Yes, I did. You had to buy top of the line to make all the other boys jealous?"

It was the first time she'd seen him smile since before…well, *before*. This one was slightly abashed. "He begged. I succumbed."

"You were glad he was excited about something."

His gray eyes met hers. "Read minds, do you?"

"My stock in trade. How else do you think I maintain control of a classroom full of eleven- and twelve-year-olds? I have to scare 'em somehow."

He laughed, showing a flash of teeth, his dark face heart-stoppingly handsome. A lock of hair flopped over his forehead, and his throat was tanned and bare with his sports shirt unbuttoned at the top. When her heart gave an uncomfortable squeeze, Robin lowered her gaze.

Which didn't help, as he had his shirtsleeves rolled up and she'd always been susceptible to strong brown forearms and big, capable-looking hands.

Sounding only a little breathless, she asked, "How was Tokyo?"

"It was my third visit this month." His gaze following his son, Craig said, "Prices there make Seattle look cheap. I mostly read in my hotel room. Went out for dinner and drinks with my crew." He yawned. "But they're a hard-drinking bunch. I'm not."

"I thought pilots couldn't drink the night before a flight."

"Our layover lasted two nights."

Out of the corner of her eye, she could see that other mothers were watching them. Two whispered to each other. Most of them had known Julie, too, and had seen Craig at games. This team had been together for several years. Once they'd seen Brett, they had begun buzzing about whether his father would show up, but conversations had tended to die when Robin drew near. Everyone knew she was instrumental in bringing Brett back, and that he was in her class this year.

Craig ignored the others. Robin tried to think what to do, but couldn't decide. Introduce him as though none of them had ever met him? Say cheerily, ''Remember Brett's dad?'' *The one who is under suspicion for murdering Brett's mom?*

She didn't think the other women would snub him, but she couldn't be sure. In the end, she let him handle meeting other parents—or not—as he chose. She not only wasn't his pen pal, she wasn't the team social director.

After drills, Brett suited up to play goalie. He flubbed a couple of attempts to stop balls and looked dark as a thundercloud. Robin saw him steal a glance at his father on the sideline. Craig gave him a thumbs-up.

Jaw setting, Brett turned his attention back to the action heading his way. Josh passed to Malcolm, who thundered a kick at goal. Brett threw himself horizontally through the air and came down clutching the ball.

Applause erupted from parents on the sideline and

his teammates. Robin heard a quiet, *"Yes!"* from the boy's father.

When the practice ended, Brett and Malcolm, dirty, sweating, dark hair plastered to their heads, walked together toward their parents as if their friendship had never been interrupted.

Robin said, "Craig, you probably don't remember Malcolm."

Craig held out his hand. "Well, you've changed."

Mal shook the hand of Brett's father with no more self-consciousness than he would have shown with any adult.

"Great save!" one of the other mothers said as she passed.

"Thanks." Brett blushed as several others echoed her.

The two boys headed for the cars, leaving Craig, Robin and Abby, who parted from her new friends and ran to her father, to follow.

"Good practice," Robin said, to fill the silence.

"Yeah." Gazing at his son, Craig said in a low voice, "I can't believe I didn't think of this. Didn't see how much he missed it."

"It hasn't been that long…"

"A year and a half? That's forever to a kid this age." He made a sound in the back of his throat. "I've been trying to protect them. Believe it or not."

"I believe you." But when he turned his head, she evaded his gaze, because she wasn't sure exactly how far he had gone to "protect" his kids and she didn't want him to see that doubt in her eyes.

"Thank you for that." He waited until she did look at him. "And for everything else."

"I said no more…"

He grinned. "Tough. Right, Punkin?" He swung his daughter in an arc above the ground.

She giggled in delight.

Robin laughed, said, "See you tomorrow," and dug in her purse for her car keys.

"Mom?" Malcolm stopped with his door open, looking over the roof of the car at her. "Can Brett come home with us tomorrow? Spend the night?"

She didn't hesitate. She'd hoped—hadn't she?—that Malcolm and Brett would become friends again.

"Sure, I don't have any problem with it."

"Hey, Brett!" Mal hollered. "You want to come home with me after the game tomorrow? Mom says you can spend the night."

The stunned expression on Brett's face quashed Robin's doubts. He turned to his father, who nodded. Brett sounded hoarse when he said, "Yeah. Sure. Uh…see you." He hopped quickly into the van.

Robin didn't let herself look at Craig. Brett was the one who mattered. She could not let herself feel even sympathy for the boy's father. The police must have good reason for believing he was responsible for his wife's disappearance. Mustn't they?

She backed out, raising the usual cloud of dust, and drove away without a glance in the rearview mirror.

CHAPTER FOUR

THE FIRST HALF of Saturday's game, Brett got in for maybe five minutes. Craig hoped Brett meant it when he said he was cool with not playing much.

"I mean, I missed a season." He'd shrugged.

Julie had disappeared in April. The kids had needed to go to school. But sports hadn't seemed important. And, with every damn thing he did, Craig'd had to consider how it would look. Would an innocent man hurry to put his kids back in regular activities? Supposing he'd killed Julie, what choices would he make? Craig had to try to make the opposite ones. He'd second-guessed himself so often, he'd been like a dog chasing its tail. What was right for his kids or himself got lost in worries about what everyone else would think.

From the sidelines, Brett called a few words of encouragement, groaning when the other team scored and did a high five with another benchwarmer when Robin's son kicked a bullet into the goal. When the coach did send him in, Brett played defense just long enough to give the starter a rest. He did fine, but didn't have a chance to shine. When he was tagged to come out, he trotted back to the sideline without apparent disappointment.

At halftime Brett drank from his water bottle and sucked on orange halves like the other boys, part of the crowd. Craig, standing apart from the clot of parents, felt an uncomfortable squeezing in his chest. Brett had lost so much.

Robin McKinnon had been the one handing out oranges. Craig had done his damndest not to look toward her after the friendly nod they'd exchanged earlier. He couldn't help himself now. She had her head cocked as she listened to another mother talk, but as if she felt his gaze, her eyes met his in a silent moment of communication. She was reading his mind again. Pain gripped his chest tighter.

He couldn't afford to become aware of her as a woman. God help him, he was a murder suspect.

He was also married.

Craig suspected he and Julie would have been divorced by now if she hadn't disappeared. But she had. As Brett had said, what if she'd been abducted and held for a year and a half? What if she escaped to find he'd divorced her? What if her body was found, and he'd divorced his murdered wife for desertion?

He couldn't go on with his life in any meaningful way until the mystery of Julie's disappearance was solved.

Swallowing, Craig looked again at his son. What he would and could do was be sure his kids moved on.

It was time.

Brett was to start seeing a counselor Tuesday evening. That should have happened a year ago. The school psychologist's evaluation hadn't been as dire as Craig had feared, but Brett obviously needed help working through his anger.

Water bottles set aside, the team huddled with the coach, separating after a cheer. With mixed feelings, Craig saw Brett putting on goalie equipment. Was he ready when he'd only started practice this week?

But Brett was grinning and joking with teammates as he ran onto the field, enveloped in an oversize neon green shirt, his hands in gloves.

"He'll do fine."

Craig started.

Robin smiled at him. "Sorry. Did I scare you?"

Yeah. She scared him. But not for the reason she was asking.

"I was worrying," he admitted. "What if he doesn't play well? Will he want to quit?"

She watched his son take up position in front of the goal. "I bet his self-esteem is higher than you think. He knows he's rusty. So do the other boys. But he really has a knack for playing goalie, you know."

"I remember." Brett was fearless. Skinned elbows, scraped knees, bruises mottling his cheek...none of that worried him. He had a good eye for the line the ball would take and instincts that helped him intercept it. Craig let out a ragged breath. "It's just that..."

"He looks happy, and you want him to stay that way."

Craig shook his head. "How do you do it?"

She turned a surprised face to him. "Do what?"

"Know what I'm thinking."

She was the one to sigh this time. "Because I'm worried, too. I got him into this."

Craig didn't say anything. *He's not your responsibility* didn't seem appropriate. Sure, she'd gone above and beyond to help Brett. But in doing so, she'd accepted a level of responsibility. She must realize that.

The two teams lined up. One of the Puyallup boys made a powerful kick and the action was on. When it came close to Brett's goal, Craig watched intensely. The rest of the time, he watched Robin.

She wore a loose-fitting royal blue T-shirt tucked into the waist of jean shorts that showed off long, tanned legs. Her glossy hair was trying to slip out of her usual ponytail. Craig had to shove his hands into the pockets of his khaki shorts to resist the urge to tuck a strand behind her ear.

Her face was so animated, he could tell how the game was going without looking at the field. It brightened, fell dramatically or became taut with suspense. Her mouth formed an *O* as she gasped in disappointment. A moment later, she would laugh in relief or delight at a great steal or stop. Craig wondered if her students appreciated how easy she was to read.

When her head swung toward the Salmon Creek goal, he focused on the game again. The Puyallup boys had a fast break going. Running with them, the ref was watching for an offside violation, his whistle in his mouth. Defenders scrambled to get into position, but they weren't going to make it. Brett advanced out of the goal.

"Too far," Craig muttered.

"Maybe not."

The coach was yelling, "Get back!"

Brett never turned his head, never wavered. Light on his feet, he crouched waiting for the shot.

Parents on the other sideline screamed encouragement. Craig's heart drummed. This wasn't just a game. For Brett, more rode on it. Way more.

The player pulled back his foot as if he were going to boot the ball, then deftly tapped it to a teammate who had come up at a run. A huge, booming kick rocketed toward the corner of the goal.

Brett flung himself sideways. The ball deflected off his fingertips and fell to the ground in front of the goal. Players from both sides scrambled for it. Brett, in another headlong dive, came up with it.

Groans from the other side mingled with exultant cheers from the Salmon Creek rooting section.

"*Yes!*" Craig said, under his breath.

Robin laughed up at him, her face alight. "He was brilliant!"

Bemused, Craig saw his son nonchalantly kick the ball, which soared over the heads of the other boys and rolled nearly to the other goal. "He was, wasn't he?"

Salmon Creek won, 2–1. The boys lined up to slap hands with the opposing players, then ran off, grimy and triumphant. Brett paused by his dad to exchange high fives, then joined the others to grab juice and brownies.

Robin had melted away, Craig realized. He saw her helping distribute brownies, congratulating boys and talking to other parents.

Nobody spoke to Craig as small family groups broke away and headed for the parking lot, but almost every parent called, "Great stop!" or "You did a heck of a job," to Brett. Craig was satisfied.

Brett joined him, water bottle in his hand and soccer ball at his feet. "Wow, I didn't think I was going to be able to stop that one!"

"I never had a doubt," Craig lied, then grinned when Brett made a rude face. "Yeah, okay. Maybe one or two."

"I mean, they *had* me. It was just luck."

Craig stopped walking. "Not luck," he said seriously. "You were good. I saw your focus."

"I really like playing goal." Brett's expression and voice were both eager in a way Craig hadn't seen in a long while. "I mean, it's cool to score goals, but I like the pressure of it all coming down to you. The ball's coming at you, and you've got, like, this tunnel vision. What a trip!"

Craig had felt that way about flying when he discovered it. He remembered his early flights, that sense of being in a bubble, in which nothing existed but him, the controls, the clouds streaming past, the checkerboard landscape below. It all came down to him. There was an adrenaline rush you didn't get in everyday life.

He slapped his son on the back. "I know what you mean."

When they reached the car, Craig asked, "Are you still planning to go home with Malcolm?"

"Yeah." Brett tried to sound as if it was no big deal, but he failed to hide his pleasure. "I'm just going to grab my stuff."

"Do I need to pick you up tomorrow?"

"I don't know." Brett tossed his soccer ball and the bottle on the floor and reached for his duffel bag. "I guess I'll call you. Okay?"

"Sure."

A horn beeped, and Craig turned to see Robin's car stopped behind his. Malcolm jumped out and jogged over to thrust a scrap of paper at Craig. "Mom says to give you our phone number."

"Thanks." Craig smiled at the boy, then waved toward Robin.

A hand waved back from inside the car.

"See ya, Dad." Brett loped off next to his new buddy.

Craig got in his car, but didn't reach immediately to put the key in the ignition. He was alone. It was the strangest feeling. Both kids were off with friends, both spending the night. He hadn't spent a night alone at home since the early days after Julie's disappearance, when the cops were putting intense heat on him and his father had taken the kids a few times to spare them.

Here was the chance single parents rarely had, and he was going to let it go to waste. Well, not entirely—maybe he'd rent a DVD on the way home, something he wouldn't let the kids watch. After all, the TV would be all his for a change.

He grunted in wry amusement. That was sad.

Craig stopped at the grocery store in Salmon Creek and picked up the makings for a meal neither Brett nor Abby liked. Another small pleasure, which was the best life had to offer these days. The bigger pleas-

ures—here, he tried hard not to picture Robin Mc-
Kinnon—were not for him.

His decent mood suffered a jolt when he was half
a block from home. A blue sedan sat at the curb in
front of his house. No rack of lights or insignia on
the door, but he knew a police car when he saw one.
Two people sat in this one.

Waiting.

Craig drove past them without turning his head. He
went straight into the garage and closed the door behind him, popped the trunk and unloaded his groceri-
ies. He was grimly putting them away when the doorbell rang.

He knew better than to ignore it. An innocent man
cooperated. Welcomed an investigation.

On the doorstep were a man and a woman he didn't
know. The man looked Hispanic, with dark hair and
the age-old eyes cops sometimes had. Craig's fleeting
impression of the woman was that she had to be a
good deal younger. Short and big-breasted, she wore
dark hair in a bun so severe she'd never need Botox.
Not flattering. Neither was a mannish outfit of blazer,
slacks and white button-down shirt that made her look
stocky.

He imagined how pleased she'd be to know that
he'd made even that quick assessment.

"Yes?"

To his surprise, it was the woman who answered,
her voice quick and aggressive. "Mr. Lofgren, I'm
Officer Caldwell."

"Detective Diaz," the man said.

She continued, "We'd appreciate a few minutes of your time."

Caldwell? Craig took a second look. God help him, she was nothing but a feminine version of her old man. He should have recognized the eyes right away. Even if he'd missed that distinctive deep blue, the contempt in them should have tipped him off.

Silently, he stood back. They walked past him single file, Caldwell's gaze sweeping over him, Diaz's assessing him more thoughtfully.

He led them into the living room, saying with reluctant civility, "Have a seat." He'd hoped, prayed things might be different now, but he could see on Caldwell's face that nothing had changed.

She sat, back stiff, gaze hostile. "Detective Diaz and I will be handling your wife's case now. We've read the reports. Now we want to hear exactly what happened from you."

"Do you know how many times I've told this story?"

"To us?" Her eyes challenged him. "Never."

God. She wanted him to recite the facts yet again. She thought she could trip him up. And he had to oblige.

"I had a fight with my wife." To himself, he sounded flat, unemotional. "We yelled, something we didn't usually do."

"Who started it?" Diaz asked.

"Julie did. She claimed to have had a bad day. Just little things. You know." He shrugged.

"No." Brows raised, Caldwell looked around his living room, as if it represented an alien world. "Your 'little thing' might not be mine. What made her day bad?''

He unclenched his teeth. ''The dry cleaners didn't have my uniform ready. Abby had been home with a cold, driving her crazy, she said. Julie'd started dinner and then discovered she didn't have a can of tomato paste.'' He wanted to stare her in the face and say, *Are those "little things" in your world, too?* But a man under investigation didn't try to get a rise out of the cop questioning him.

Expressionless now, she nodded.

Because he had to, Craig continued. ''She was angry that I was flying out the next day. Julie'd become increasingly unhappy with my schedule, although I was an airline pilot when we met. It did leave her alone for days on end with the kids.''

''It's my understanding that Julie was president of the parent-teacher group.'' Officer Caldwell pretended to flip through her notes. ''Room mother for both children's elementary classes. She had them involved in a number of activities and seemed willing to drive even when it wasn't her turn.'' She looked up. ''The last is a quote, by the way. From another mother.''

Craig said nothing.

''I'm a little confused. This doesn't sound like a woman who minds being left alone for days on end with her kids.''

He hadn't understood her himself. He didn't know how to explain a chameleon to someone who'd never seen one.

''That was the part people saw. Julie had once told

me she didn't want children.'' She'd actually announced the fact a couple of months after their wedding, when she'd somehow transformed into a career woman instead of the relaxed artist he'd first known. She seemed to have forgotten their talks about starting a family. But he had loved her, or so he believed, and he chose to hope she would change her mind, that she was just going through a phase.

A phase. The gap between that mild description of changing life stages and the reality of Julie's new selves was so vast, it was almost funny.

He pulled himself back to the present. ''A couple of years later, she got pregnant by accident. After that, she…changed. She became supermom. Only, recently the role had started eroding. She still put on the public face, but she got moody, told me she felt stifled. That night,'' he frowned into space, remembering her desperation, ''she told me she didn't know if she could stand being a single parent for even another day.'' His mouth twisted. ''I yelled back that it was time she grew up. She threw something at me.''

''Something?'' the Hispanic officer asked.

''A figurine. A stoneware cat she'd bought at a crafts show. It shattered.''

''And what did you do then?'' Caldwell asked, aggressively seizing back the reins of command.

''I walked out. Literally. Took a few laps of the block, cooled off, then went back in the house. I checked on the kids, talked to both of them, made light of their mom and me yelling like two-year-olds. My bedroom door was shut. I slept in the guest room.''

"In the morning?"

"I had to leave early. At four a.m. I sneaked into the bedroom, showered and dressed. Julie never stirred, although I suspected she was awake. Usually I kissed her before I left. That morning…" His jaw muscles spasmed. "I didn't."

They waited, pencils poised above notebooks.

Craig continued, "I drove to the airport, getting into heavy fog. Checked in, but the place had been shut down. Eventually I got word my flight had been canceled. I thought, good, maybe Julie would feel better if she went shopping, had dinner with a friend. I got home about eleven. Julie wasn't there."

The van, her pride and joy, had been in the garage, so he'd been surprised by the deathly silence in the house. The air had seemed heavy, thick. He'd called her name and gotten no answer. Her purse was on the kitchen counter, car keys lying beside it. Okay, she was upstairs, sulking.

Knowing they needed to talk, he'd climbed the stairs. The bedroom was empty, the bed made. The bathroom door stood ajar. With increasing puzzlement, he stuck his head in, thinking she'd be in front of the mirror putting on makeup, or taking a hot sudsy bath, although he didn't smell the bath oils she liked to use. The bathroom, too, was quiet, deserted.

He heard himself calling again, "Julie? Julie, where are you?" Abby's room—maybe she'd stayed home again today, even if she'd seemed better last night. But no. Her bed, too, was made. Julie had insisted the kids keep their rooms neat. Brett's bedroom was a little sloppier, the comforter askew as though he'd just yanked it in place, obeying the letter of the law.

Craig checked the guest room, the kids' bathroom. Downstairs again, he headed for the kitchen and the back door. Julie wasn't much of a gardener, but she did tend baskets and pots of annuals. She wasn't there, either, and when he checked the soil beneath a geranium, it was dry and crumbly.

He still felt nothing but puzzlement and irritation. She didn't have the car or her purse, so she had to be around somewhere. Having coffee with a neighbor. Maybe, he remembered thinking with a twinge of hope that shamed him, she was having an affair and would leave him. The woman who was his wife had become a stranger to him, and an unhappy one. If not for the kids, he would have wanted out, but he hated the idea of being a weekend father, of disrupting Abby's and Brett's lives.

He changed and went for a jog, then made himself a sandwich and read the morning *Times*. Still no Julie.

"I waited until the kids got home," he told the cops. "I figured she would have told them her plans for the day. When they didn't know, I started knocking on neighbors' doors, then calling Julie's friends. A couple of hours later, I called 911, even though I still thought she'd walk in the door any minute. I was…annoyed, considering I was supposed to be on my way to Paris, that she'd let the kids come home to an empty house."

Sergeant Caldwell's look-alike daughter said, "The investigating officer wrote that you didn't seem as distraught as he would have expected."

"That's because I thought this was a continuation of our fight. There was no sign of a break-in. Nothing like that. She'd told me she couldn't take another day. I wondered if she was having an affair. She knew Brett had my father's phone number and would call him. I thought she was making a point. Saying to me, 'You didn't listen.'"

"You claimed to have no idea where she would have gone."

He didn't back down. "I *have* no idea."

"There was no money missing from bank accounts."

It wasn't a question, but he answered anyway. "She'd made no unusual withdrawals. She might have been socking away a hundred bucks here and there, but she couldn't have left with more than a thousand."

Caldwell's daughter was looking at him with open dislike. "You mean, when she *disappeared*."

His eyes felt grainy, but he didn't blink. Didn't flinch.

She flipped closed her notebook. "I take it that's your theory. Your thirty-eight-year-old wife just…left you. And her children. Without taking a change of underwear, her toothbrush or her purse."

He knew she'd stuck in Julie's age to emphasize how unlikely it was that she had truly changed. Julie hadn't been young enough to be flighty, was the implication.

His voice became ragged, despite his best attempt. "She told Brett she'd be leaving soon. It doesn't seem likely she'd say that, then just happen to get abducted by a stranger two days later.''

Officer Caldwell said, ''On the other hand, if Julie was afraid of her husband, she might have felt a need to say goodbye. In case.''

Craig surged to his feet, rage and despair near blinding him. ''You've made up your mind. Just like your father. You're not going to try to find her, are you?''

Diaz rose, too. ''Mr. Lofgren…''

Craig didn't look away from the woman's eyes, the color of the North Sea from the air. ''Don't waste my time. Use your goddamn wiretaps and anything you want, but if you're not going to listen to me, stay out of my house.''

''Mr. Lofgren.'' Diaz stepped forward, blocking Craig's view of Caldwell. ''You have to understand how this looks to us.''

Craig returned his stare. ''Oh. I understand. It looks like I killed her. Without bloodshed, without witnesses, without reason.''

''She wanted a divorce. That's a reason for too many men.''

''*I* wanted a divorce!'' With shock, Craig heard himself say something he'd never admitted to anyone else. His knees sagged, and he sat back down. Dully, he said, ''I didn't ask her for one because of the kids. But I wouldn't have been angry if she'd wanted out.''

From beyond Diaz, his partner said, ''Unless she intended to take your children. The children *you* wanted and that you insist she didn't.''

Craig braced his elbows on his knees and didn't

look up. "Half the kids' friends have divorced parents. We'd have coped, like everyone else does."

"But," Officer Caldwell said, "as things turned out, you didn't have to."

That's when he knew there'd be no end to his torment.

"No." He shoved himself to his feet again and looked at them without emotion. "I didn't have to."

They left after informing him that they would be interviewing neighbors and friends again.

"And your children, of course."

Caldwell made the addendum offhandedly. Craig's fury ignited again, deep in his belly. She didn't give a damn what she did to Abby or Brett. She was like a Pentagon general, far from the battlefield, dismissing "necessary" casualties. She didn't have to see the blood.

At the door, Craig said, "You may interview each of them once. If you ask anything out of line, if you upset them, you're not coming near us again without walking a gauntlet of lawyers."

She turned back, this absurdly young cop, her expression smug. "Are you threatening us, Mr. Lofgren?"

"I have been cooperative for a year and a half. Neither your father—he *was* your father, wasn't he, and not an uncle?"

Her smugness died. "He was my father."

"Neither he nor you have made any sincere attempt to find out what happened to my wife. Was that a threat? No." He looked at her with all the disappointment and anger that had festered for the year and a half. ''It was a suggestion that you do your job.''

With that, he closed the door in their faces and locked it.

Craig pictured his son's face as he'd said goodbye, relaxed and happy. Damn it, *happy,* for the first time in so long. With despair, Craig rubbed his face. He couldn't even protect his children. What kind of man was he, who had to drive two towns over to buy toilet paper so he didn't meet anyone he knew? Who couldn't even give his kids a basic sense of security?

He'd gone into the kitchen and flipped open the phone book yellow pages to ''Private Investigators'' when one of the last things Officer Caldwell had said hit him.

They'd be interviewing neighbors and friends.

Caldwell and Diaz would be talking to Robin McKinnon. Who had seen Brett's pain-filled writing.

Ryan says I'm like my dad. He thinks I'm a murderer, so maybe I'll be one.

Under pressure, would she interpret Brett's words as an admission that he thought his father might really have killed his mother?

Craig guessed her attempts to help Brett might slam to a stop. Interviewed afresh, reminded of police suspicions, Julie's friend wouldn't want her son having anything to do with Julie's husband even if she did feel sorry for Brett.

Robin wouldn't be breezily friendly on the sidelines anymore. She wouldn't touch his arm, read his mind, ally herself with him.

He felt pathetic to discover how much he minded, how much simple human kindness had meant to him.

Maybe the time had come to put the house on the market and move. To hell with the police. Short of arresting him, could they stop him? Maybe he'd been cooperative too long. There had to be a way for the kids and him to start over.

He couldn't see that happening here, in Klickitat. Once again, in his grief, he felt anger. This time at Robin McKinnon, who had given him hope, but would soon snatch it away.

CHAPTER FIVE

"THAT SON OF A BITCH." Ann glowered at the passing scenery. "Did you hear him? He was threatening us!"

"Was he?" Diaz said mildly. "Calling your lawyer is a constitutional right."

She turned her impatient stare on her new partner, behind the wheel of the unmarked car. "Are you on his side?"

"Side?" He glanced at her. "Do you always make up your mind before you start an investigation?"

He was right. Of course he was right. Shamed, she held her silence for ten seconds or so. Then she burst out, "This isn't just any investigation! You know how much it meant to Dad."

"Yeah, I do. I thought he let it get too personal."

She gaped. "You don't think he was a good cop?" The very idea was heresy.

"I didn't say that." Diaz frowned and drummed his fingers on the wheel. "I admire the way he stuck to this case. He wanted to see justice for Julie Lofgren. But I sometimes wondered…"

"What?"

Sounding reluctant, the other cop finished, "Why he was so sure the husband killed her."

"Don't you ever have a gut feeling?"

"Yeah. Sure I do. But on this one, Michael got personal. Real personal. He didn't like Lofgren. He went on about the ridiculous salaries pilots make, how they're driving the airlines into the ground. 'Spoiled brats,' he said. Spoiled…well, that doesn't mean murderer.''

"Lofgren's cocky," Ann argued.

"Did you think so? He looked pretty beaten down to me."

"We're getting to him." She wanted to believe that. He'd crack. Sooner or later, he would give himself away.

"You're not your dad."

She bristled. "Meaning?"

"Let's…just start fresh. Okay?"

"I'm not going to railroad him, if that's what you're saying."

He spared her another glance from his dark, unreadable eyes. "I didn't say that. I'm suggesting you keep an open mind, that's all."

Tempted to keep arguing, she knew deep down that he was right. She wanted this one for a lot of reasons. To prove herself, mostly. To lay on her father's grave like a dozen red roses. But she had started with an assumption—her father's assumption, not hers.

She hadn't liked Craig Lofgren, either, but she'd been so sure she wouldn't, he could have had a smile like Russell Crowe's, and it wouldn't have melted her. Even if she believed Lofgren had killed his wife, she needed to take a step back. Her father had hit a brick wall on this case. Maybe, if she tried to start as though this were some case handed to them, not one she'd heard about for a year and a half, she would find some way around that wall, or a chink in it. If she put on her father's glasses, she'd see only what he saw.

And fail where he failed.

"Yeah. Okay," she conceded. "I wanted…"

His voice gentler, Diaz nodded. "To finish something that meant a lot to your dad. I get that."

"Where are we going?" She looked around.

The town of Klickitat was just waking up from the 1950s. Golden arches and a chain hardware store had risen on the outskirts, but the main street hadn't changed in half a century. Well, that wasn't quite true. Antique stores and a quilt shop had replaced the small furniture and department stores of an earlier era. Nonetheless, the couple of cafés seemed busy, a one-screen second-run movie theater defied the multiplex that had sprung up on the outskirts, and parking was hard to find.

"A couple of the neighbors work downtown. Figured we could start by talking to them."

She nodded. Somehow, in her mind, she hadn't gotten beyond interviewing Lofgren. But they'd go at this methodically. Someone, somewhere, knew something. They always did.

"Who first?"

First was the only neighbor who had actually been home the day of Julie Lofgren's disappearance. She supposedly hadn't seen or heard anything. "But, hey," as Diaz put it, the woman hadn't been interviewed since the early days.

Lynn Adams lived across the street and a couple of houses down from the Lofgrens. She owned one of the half dozen antique stores that made Klickitat a popular destination.

Ann guessed antiques were okay, but the stuff in this store looked like it had taken a beating. The furniture was all painted white and banged up, metal shelving had rusty dings and faded silk flowers leaned drunkenly from chipped pitchers. It all looked garage sale, but the prices were magnified twenty times.

Summoned by the skinny kid behind the jewelry counter, Lynn Adams emerged from a back room. Ash blond hair coifed and sprayed, she was an attractive woman in her fifties, at a guess, although she was fighting to hold on to her forties. Her forehead was a little too smooth. Ann wasn't experienced enough to guess whether she'd had a face lift or a Botox injection.

"May I help you?" When Ms. Adams heard their purpose, she nodded slowly. "Come on back. I have a small office."

Following her, Ann paused at a glass case that held some tiny, finely detailed porcelain boxes, but flushed when she caught her partner's eye and hurried to catch up. *Stupid,* she told herself. Women cops did not admit to girly tastes.

She secretly resented it when Diaz nodded her to the only chair facing the beat-up oak desk that darn near filled the roughed-in cubicle. He leaned one shoulder against the door molding and slouched there.

Lynn Adams sat behind the desk and faced them. "What do you want to know?"

Ann pulled out her notebook and flipped it open. "Are you aware the investigating officer died?"

"The papers were full of it." Her voice had an edge of fear. "We thought maybe without Sergeant Caldwell, Craig Lofgren would get away with killing his wife."

"Over Ann's head," Diaz said in his calm, deep voice. "We'll continue to investigate, ma'am, but at this point we're still in the dark as to what happened to Mrs. Lofgren. Perhaps you'd help by telling us what you remember about that day. You weren't working?"

"I just opened this shop a few months ago." She smiled with a hint of smugness. "My husband is an attorney. I don't need to work. But I've always had a good eye, and John finally suggested I go into business."

"I see," Diaz said. "That particular day? Do you recall your plans or what you actually did?"

"Of course I recall it!" She looked offended at the idea that she'd forget a red-letter day. "With all the fuss later, naturally I've thought back a million times."

With some impatience, Ann prodded, "And?"

"I went into town first thing. That's the last time I saw Julie. She was just pulling into her driveway in that red van of hers. I assumed she'd run the kids to school and maybe done some errands of her own on the way home. We waved."

"And you were gone…how long?"

"Maybe two hours. I picked up some dry cleaning,

bought groceries and prowled an antique store. Just for fun, you know.''

Diaz asked, ''And did you pass her house on your way home?''

''I always look at people's yards as I go by. It was spring, remember. The Lofgrens weren't gardeners, but I did notice how pretty the flowering cherry between their house and the Lyles' next door was.''

''But you didn't see Julie or any sign of activity?'' Ann asked.

''I didn't see a soul. I went home, unloaded my groceries and the clothes I'd picked up at the dry cleaners, and then decided to putter in my own garden. I put in several hundred bulbs every fall. I take pride in my garden.''

Ms. Adam's tone of self-satisfaction suggested that she gardened competitively. If someone else on the block put in a hundred daffodils, she'd be sure she planted a hundred and twenty.

''So you were actually outside for some of the day? In the backyard, or the front?''

''Mostly the back.'' She sounded regretful; she would have liked to have witnessed the crime.

''I presume the neighborhood is pretty quiet at that time of day.''

''Well, I do remember the Quinns behind us had left their terrier outside again, and he barked all day long. We've asked them again and again...'' Her mouth crimped.

''Does the dog bark nonstop, or because he heard you?''

''Oh...'' She gave a huff of displeasure. ''I suppose he's noisier when I'm outside. He carries on when the school bus comes.''

''And when other cars pass?''

Her expression changed. ''Well…yes. I suppose so.''

''Do you remember hearing vehicles pass?''

For the first time, she looked as if she were genuinely trying to see the day anew. Eyes unfocused, she said, ''Yes. Yes, I think several cars went by. And a UPS truck. I caught a glimpse between the fence slats.''

Ann hid her excitement. Nowhere in her father's extensive notes was any mention of a UPS truck. ''Did it stop on your block, to your knowledge?''

She frowned. ''Why, I think it might have. Is that important?''

''Probably not, but it gives us another potential witness.''

''I don't know how I forgot back then.''

Juan Diaz asked, ''Do you have any idea which house it stopped at?''

Ms. Adams made a humming sound as she thought. ''Not right next door. I'd have heard the doorbell. But somewhere on the Lofgrens' end of the block. The truck came back a few minutes later.''

They learned nothing else from her. She hadn't noticed the few cars that passed. She hadn't heard gunshots, screams or sounds of an altercation. She'd gone in and taken just a short nap, she admitted, before the shouts of kids getting off the school bus woke her.

She also admitted to not knowing the Lofgrens well. No, she wouldn't exactly call herself a friend;

she'd met them at block parties. They waved in passing. She didn't know anything about the state of their marriage, although their nearer neighbors had told her about the loud fight the night before Julie's disappearance.

Rather than hear about it secondhand, Ann and Juan excused themselves and walked the block and a half to the real estate office owned by one of the Lofgrens' next-door neighbors.

Gil Beckman was just ushering clients out when they arrived. "Good timing," he said heartily. "I can give you five minutes."

No more than forty-five, he was soft around the middle with twinkling eyes. His engaging smile didn't altogether convince Ann that he was genuinely delighted to have them in his office.

Sure, he remembered the altercation he'd overheard. "It was the first and only time I ever heard Craig and Julie raise their voices. They weren't that kind. Never yelled at the kids, even."

He'd believed he knew them pretty well, until Julie vanished and her husband came under suspicion. "The usual." He shrugged. "We watched each other's houses when we went on vacation, borrowed the mower when the other fellow's wouldn't start. Craig and I played a round of golf together a couple of times."

They'd socialized a few times when he and his wife first bought their house, but that relationship just petered out. "Wife and I don't have children, so I guess we just didn't have much in common. Craig's schedule had him away on weekends often, too."

"Did you ever give any thought to their marriage?" Ann asked. "In the sense that you noticed they were loving, or that things were strained?"

He laughed. "You should probably talk to Carol about that one. Women notice stuff like that. Anyway, I didn't see the two of them together much the last couple years. I thought everything was fine. That night, when we heard them fighting, Carol said she wasn't surprised, that Julie had confided some frustrations to her."

He gave them Carol's card. She was a mortgage officer at the Washington Mutual Bank here in town.

Diaz leaned forward. "Please tell us about the quarrel you overheard. Could you hear what they were saying?"

"Just a word here and there. Mostly her. She screamed something about smothering, which got me sitting up, but the wife pointed out that Julie couldn't carry on like that if he actually *was* squeezing her throat. Caught a few profanities, mention of the kids…" He shrugged.

Ann frowned. "We've gone through the notes left by the original investigating officer. I seem to remember you told him you heard Craig Lofgren threaten to kill his wife."

"Me?" He looked surprised. "Heck, no! Just that thing about smothering. And that was her, not him." He chuckled. "Can't imagine a man bellowing, 'I'm going to smother you!'"

"No." Ann gritted her teeth. Was he lying now? Or had he lied then, in the excitement of being involved in high drama?

She and her partner thanked the Realtor and left.

"Let's drive," Diaz said. "Washington Mutual's down at the other end of town."

Ann nodded. She waited until they were in the car before she asked, "Do you think he was lying?"

"Lying?"

The raised brows were starting to irritate her.

"Yes, lying. About whether he heard an actual threat or not."

Diaz shrugged. "I had the impression he was being straight."

Damn it, she had to agree. Which left a gaping discrepancy.

A sleek, attractive businesswoman in a red suit with a skirt short enough to bare long elegant legs, Carol Beckman was able to commandeer a break room so that they could talk privately. When she sat, crossing her legs with slow deliberation and no attempt to tug at her hem, Diaz watched with interest. If Ann had been closer, she'd have jammed her elbow in his rib-cage.

Maybe her glance had the same effect, because he cleared his throat and she thought a flush tinged his high cheekbones.

"Ms. Beckman, we just spoke to your husband about his recollections concerning the altercation you heard between Craig and Julie Lofgren the night before her disappearance. He felt that you knew the couple better than he did and were more observant of subtleties because you're a woman."

Carol Beckman flashed a flirtatious smile at him. Ann might as well not have been in the room. Heck, she was invisible next to a woman like this, with her dark hair drawn into a sleek roll on the back of her head, her vivid makeup, the diamond earrings winking on her earlobes. Most of the time, Ann was comfortable with herself and with the necessity of suppressing her femininity to fit into a man's world. Moments like this, she suspected she didn't have to; she just didn't know *how* to make men flutter like moths. Yeah, she'd catch hell if she were caught being girly. Being womanly might be another story.

If only she knew how.

"Julie and I weren't close friends, but we chatted when we were out getting our mail at the same time or just coming or going. I had coffee with her the week before…" She swallowed. "She grumbled about her husband. She said she felt like a single parent, that he wasn't interested in shouldering a fair share of responsibility."

Even given her prejudice against him, Ann thought that didn't sound fair. The man *was* earning the household income, after all. Unless he wasn't helpful when he was home, she reminded herself.

"I had the impression they had other problems," Carol Beckman continued. "She looked unhappy. Fidgety. On the verge of tears. But she didn't want to say more. Her little girl was in and out, and I assumed that was why."

"The quarrel took place…" Diaz glanced down at his notes. "In the late evening?"

"That's right. Gil and I were going to bed. It was a nice night, so we had our window open. I remember he was sitting on the edge of the bed taking his socks off when Julie yelled something about being smothered.'' She smiled. ''He leaped to his feet with nothing on but Jockey shorts and one sock, ready to rush to the rescue. I patted his arm and persuaded him to let them argue in peace.''

''How much could you hear?''

She made a moue. ''Honestly, not much. Craig's voice was loud, but a deep rumble. You know. Hers was more piercing, so I could hear words here and there. Then slamming doors.''

''From the tenor of what you heard, were you alarmed?''

She hesitated. ''Well…no. I mean, our neighborhood isn't the kind where you hear couples fighting every night, so we were shocked, but… Oh, what married couple doesn't occasionally raise their voices?''

Ann wouldn't know. She'd never been married, and her mother had died when Ann was ten. She stole a speculative look at her partner, whom she knew was divorced. Somehow she couldn't picture him…well, fiery enough to bellow at any woman. He was too…controlled.

Face expressionless, he nodded. ''Did you see either of the Lofgrens the next day?''

She shook her head in apparent regret. ''No sign of them. Of course I was at work all day. I didn't know there was anything wrong until Craig rang the doorbell wondering if we'd seen Julie.''

''Did he appear worried?''

She wrinkled her nose. ''More annoyed, I would

have said. He gave a rather curt nod when we said no, thanked us and left.''

Ann spoke up for the first time. ''Ms. Beckman, the investigating officer indicated in his notes that either you or your husband said you'd heard Mr. Lofgren threaten his wife that night.''

She was exasperated to see that Carol Beckman wasn't the only one to appear startled by the reminder that she was present. Diaz actually started.

''Threatened? Oh, no. We couldn't make out enough of what was said to suggest that.'' She paused. ''Although in retrospect...''

''In retrospect?''

''Well, it's rather suggestive, isn't it? That they should have a screaming match, and then she should vanish the next day. Don't you think? So, of course, we've wondered ever since what we *would* have heard, if we'd...well, gone out in the yard.''

''Would have heard'' was not something you took in front of a jury. Ann let her partner thank Ms. Beckman and step politely aside so that she could go through the door ahead of him. Or so that he could watch the sway of her hips. Ann couldn't tell, because he did *not* wait politely for *her* to go ahead.

She'd had a lifetime of feeling this unhappy suspicion that she was some sort of genderless creature. She'd always been a tomboy, mostly to please her father. But suddenly, about the time she turned sixteen, he decided she should become a real woman, only she didn't have the skills. So she kept forging on, trying to please him the only way she knew, only that was never good enough.

He'd give her a dismissive glance. "Chunky thing like you, what good would you be when a perp goes ballistic? For God's sake, why don't you find a husband?"

Because I don't know how! she'd wanted to cry. But also because she didn't *want* a husband; she wanted to prove herself, not wave pom-poms for some man.

She'd made her choices, but it did rankle sometimes to be so lacking in something so basic as sexual appeal.

On the other hand, she decided at a slow simmer, if Diaz had a grain of common courtesy, he wouldn't make his opinion of her lack of womanly appeal so obvious.

He thanked Carol Beckman, held her hand a moment longer than necessary, then walked out without glancing back to see if Ann followed. If she hadn't scuttled at his heels and leaped into the car, he probably would have driven off without remembering he *had* a partner.

She opened her mouth to…what? Bitch that he hadn't held open a door for her?

But he took her by surprise. "Okay. What happened to them hearing Craig Lofgren yell, 'I'm going to kill you if you don't…?'"

Those had been the exact words her father had written in his notes. Don't what? he had asked, but they hadn't heard the tail end of the sentence. She was impressed that Diaz remembered the exact phrasing.

"I don't know," she said, frowning ahead. "They've revised their story, but why?"

He bounced his fist on the steering wheel as he thought. "Maybe it's not intentional. Maybe they've just talked it over endlessly, until they remember it differently. Or maybe they never did hear a threat. Could be they got excited and blew up what they had heard, just to be important or because suddenly all that yelling did seem threatening."

Ann nodded. "Or else they did hear it, but now they're trying to protect Lofgren."

He gave her a sharp look. "Why would they?"

She lifted her chin and met his stare. "I don't know. How about this? Because Ms. Beckman is having an affair with Craig."

"What about the Mr.?"

Ann shrugged. "She's convinced him he didn't really hear what he thought he heard. She seemed to me like a woman who could convince a man of anything."

Diaz's expression changed, and she realized she'd sounded resentful.

In a hurry, she continued, "Maybe they've decided in the meantime that he's a great guy and he couldn't have hurt his wife. But you have to concede that they might be lying."

His fist bounced a couple more times. "What," he said thoughtfully, "if they know damn well where Julie is?"

Ann stared. "You mean...*they* murdered her?"

"Unlikely. I was thinking more that they knew she'd taken off and are covering her tracks."

"By throwing suspicion on her husband?"

"Why not? But now they figure she's made her getaway, so they're trying to get him off the hook."

"That's convoluted," she argued. "The woman walked out on her kids if she left voluntarily! How could they support her doing that? Anyway, they weren't even close friends with her."

"We don't know that Julie and Carol Beckman weren't good friends," Diaz pointed out. "And remember, the Beckmans don't have children. Maybe they chose not to because they don't like kids. Could be they figure she was showing some sense ditching the brats."

Ann hadn't much liked either Beckman, but that was really coldhearted. She shook her head in automatic denial.

"You know, I think the first explanation makes the most sense. They blew up what they heard at the time because they were in the middle of a police investigation."

After a moment, Diaz nodded, then reached for the ignition. He started the car, put it in Drive, then gave her a long, considering look. "There's one other possibility."

"What's that?" she asked, puzzled.

"That they never did say they'd heard a threat."

"What?"

"That your father made it up. To bolster his belief that Lofgren had killed his wife."

She gaped at the preposterous suggestion. "He was a good cop!"

"Haven't we all exaggerated here or there, to support what we know to be true?"

"But...to lie..." Shaking her head hard, Ann said, "No. No, he wouldn't have done that."

Diaz studied her face for another long moment, then shrugged. "Just thought I'd throw out the idea."

"Well, stuff it back wherever it came from!" she snapped.

He didn't say anything, simply drove.

Michael Caldwell might not have been perfect; he'd had a temper and...well, a streak of intolerance. A big, commanding man, he never accepted excuses, not even from his daughter. Ann wished he had loved her more unconditionally.

But he was hard to please partly because his standards were so high! Anger burned in her chest. How could a fellow cop who'd known her father well think for a minute that Sergeant Michael Caldwell would *lie* to make a man look guilty?

As if he'd read her mind, Diaz said abruptly, "I thought it had to be said."

"No. It didn't."

"Forget it, then."

How could she? Ann knew she'd never see the dark-eyed cop the same again. He didn't know what loyalty or friendship meant.

But she did. She believed in her father, and she *would* finish what he had started.

CHAPTER SIX

THE MAN WHO RANG Robin's doorbell wasn't the
same one who'd watched his son play soccer the afternoon before. Robin would have sworn he wasn't,
except that the outside package was the same: dark
hair, gray eyes, broad shoulders, great cheekbones.

But the eyes were expressionless, the mouth tight,
his voice clipped. "Is Brett ready?"

Robin blinked. "I don't know." One hand on the
door, she turned and called up the stairs, "Brett, your
dad's here!"

She turned back. He hadn't relaxed one iota. No
Hey, hope he had a good time. Or *Gee, hope Brett
wasn't too much trouble.*

No conversational gambits at all. He simply waited
on her front porch, as if she wasn't there at all.

No, that wasn't right; maybe he was looking
through her, but he knew she was there.

"Is something wrong?" Robin asked. She hated
how timid she sounded.

His mouth thinned. "Wrong?"

Sixth graders liked to play this game. She didn't.

"You look angry," she said bluntly.

"I have a lot on my mind." *None of your business,*
he might as well have said.

Why had she let herself sympathize with him? And where were the boys?

"You're going to scare your son if you don't hide whatever it is you have on your mind a little better."

A nerve jumped beneath of his eyes. "Damn," he muttered.

"Excuse me?"

"I'm sorry." He bowed his head and pinched the bridge of his nose. "I didn't mean to take out my mood on you."

Idiot that she was, her annoyance melted away. "Um...do you want to come in? I don't know what the boys are doing, but I can offer you a cup of coffee."

That's good, she told herself; *invite a murderer into your house.* A *Buffy* fan, she wondered if this was something like inviting a vampire in once and losing the right to refuse him forever after.

Craig looked at her as if she were crazy. "A cup of coffee?"

"I have some brewed. I was just having a cup myself."

He turned his head each way as if checking to see who was watching. "Uh, sure."

"Do you have Abby in the car?" Robin peered past him.

"No, she's my next stop. She spent the night at a friend's, too."

Robin stepped back. "I could lie and say I haven't cleaned house, but the truth is, I'm a slob."

A reluctant grin tugged his mouth. "Then Brett's right at home here."

"Really?" Letting him shut the front door, she led the way to the kitchen. "That's funny. Mal's so organized, it scares me. He never drops anything on the floor, puts his dirty dishes straight in the dishwasher and lines up his shoes in his closet."

Her house wasn't *that* bad, just…comfortably untidy, in her opinion. She excused herself on the basis that it wasn't big enough. After the divorce, this two bedroom fixer-upper was the best she could afford. With no home office, she tended to spread papers she was grading across the kitchen table—there was no dining room—then have to shove them aside to eat. Their computer stood on a cheap desk wedged in a corner of what the Realtor had optimistically called the "eating nook." Along with occasional embroidery, Robin was writing—trying to write—a young adult novel, with several versions of the first chapters along with notes and some research books stacked helter-skelter on the measly desktop. Poor Malcolm had to work to find room to lay out his binder when he used the computer.

Craig glanced around while she took a mug from the cupboard and poured coffee. "I can see why an organized son scares you."

He was teasing her. That had to be a good sign.

"It's easier to be neat when you're a kid and you don't have that much going on," she protested. "I'm a busy woman, that's all. Lots of projects in the works."

"Uh-huh." There was definitely a smile in his eyes now.

"Sugar? Creamer?"

"Black."

She handed him his mug and picked up her own. "I wonder where the boys are?"

"Lose 'em?"

"I didn't hear the back door, but maybe…" The single window in the kitchen wasn't positioned above the sink. No, it was squeezed between a wall cupboard and the refrigerator. If she ever came into a little bit of money, the kitchen was first on her list of remodeling projects.

She saw them immediately, bouncing a soccer ball between them, off a knee here, a head there. Brett was laughing, his face lit with good humor. The sulky James Dean effect was gone.

"No wonder they didn't hear me. They're practicing headers, or something, out in the backyard." She turned. "Let's go in the living room and have our coffee in peace before I call them again. You can tell me why you looked so grim." When his face tightened again, she said more tentatively, "If you want to, that is."

Bookcases lined two walls of the living room, leaving room only for a couch under the large window, a television in one corner and two easy chairs facing it. The carpet, a faded rust and twenty-five years old if it was a day, was second on her remodeling list. It looked worst next to the cream and taupe striped furniture and gleaming side tables left from her more prosperous married days.

"Please. Sit down."

He nodded and chose the couch. Robin curled one

foot under her and took the big overstuffed rocker. Letting silence settle, she sipped her lukewarm coffee.

"The police came around yesterday."

She didn't know how to react. Did she feel dismay, for his sake, or relief, because her police force was determined?

"So they're still, um, pursuing the case? Even though that officer died?"

"One of the two that visited me was his daughter." Despair carved lines in Craig Lofgren's face, making him less handsome and more...human. "Can you believe it? A daughter, prepared to take up her daddy's quest. Which, unfortunately, was to see me put away for twenty years."

"Are you sure?"

"That she's his daughter? She admitted as much. That she wants to put me away? Oh, yeah." His voice seemed to scrape his throat. "She sat there in my living room looking at me as if I were the scum of the earth. She'd made up her mind."

"Surely they have other suspects." She swallowed at the expression on his face. "Why do they think…"

What an awful thing to ask someone! It really wasn't any of her business. She opened her mouth to say, *No, forget I asked,* but too late.

"Because neighbors heard us quarreling the night before Julie disappeared."

Quarreling. That word could cover quite a lot of territory, from his wife snapping, "Damn it, why didn't you take out the garbage?" to a violent domestic disturbance that had brought the police to his door.

"Did any of them call 911?"

He looked at her as if she were crazy. "Why would they? We raised our voices." Then understanding flickered and his face went expressionless. "Are you asking if I hit her? The answer is no." He set down his nearly full coffee cup and started to rise.

"Sit!" Robin ordered, as if he were a sulky eleven-year-old.

Craig froze, then obeyed.

Frowning at him, she said, "You're the one who raised the subject. Since you did, I'm trying to understand. You and Julie had a fight. Lots of married couples fight. My husband and I did, thus the divorce. Usually the police don't assume a shouting match means you're a murderer."

"Usually," he pointed out, "one spouse doesn't vanish the next day."

"Well, sure, but...hadn't you quarreled before?"

His eyes smoldered with suppressed emotion, but his face remained impassive. "Apparently not loudly enough for the neighbors to hear."

"What was the result of your fight?"

"Result?"

She waved her hand impatiently. "I mean, did she demand a divorce? Did you make up?"

"Oh." Lines in his forehead deepened. "Neither. I stalked out, went for a walk and slept in the guest room. I left for the airport without seeing her again. I assumed her claim of 'smothering' was histrionics."

"Smothering?" Robin stared at him. "What did she mean?"

Strain showed on his face, and he looked away.

"Julie hated being left for days at a time with the kids, even though my schedule actually has me home more than most fathers. I sometimes thought…" He stopped and clamped his mouth shut.

"You thought?"

"Never mind."

She gave him her most severe schoolteacher look. "You can't start that kind of sentence and not finish it."

His expression didn't lighten. "You wouldn't believe me."

"Try me." Why on earth was she challenging him? she wondered in a kind of panic. She'd *liked* Julie. She probably *wouldn't* believe whatever he told her. But…she was coming to like him, too, which might be incredibly dumb of her.

"All right." He looked at her with that blank face she now realized hid a powerful well of emotions. "I was going to say that I sometimes thought Julie didn't want to be a mother anymore."

Robin echoed, "Didn't want to be…"

He squeezed his eyes shut. "Yeah, she was mother-of-the-year. I know. I said you wouldn't buy it."

"Darn it, give me a chance!"

Startled, he met her eyes again.

"She was room mother for both kids, right? She had them in all kinds of activities. Why did she spend so much time with Brett and Abby if she wanted to escape them?"

"Because…" He swore and shook his head. "This sounds ridiculous. Even I know that. It's just that… room mother was who Julie had decided to be."

He hesitated, then said abruptly, "She didn't want kids. She didn't give me a vote. But she got pregnant by accident, and next thing I knew Julie was Suzy Homemaker. She bought pretty pink maternity clothes. She started pureeing and freezing baby food because the commercial stuff wasn't good enough, she read endless 'how to parent' books and decorated the nursery. I couldn't open a single damn drawer in the house because they all had child-proof catches on them. Brett was barely born and she had them signed up for Mom 'n Me yoga and swim classes. I told myself I was glad. She'd discovered she was wrong. Motherhood was turning out to be great for her."

"But you weren't glad," Robin said, trying to understand.

He shoved his fingers through his hair, making it stand up. "It wasn't that. I *was* glad. But the change was so sudden, so complete, I'd find myself listening to her chatter at the dinner table and think, where's Julie? Who is this?"

"People do change."

"Slowly. Painfully. This was more like…" He shook his head, as if unscrambling his thoughts. "More like she'd been possessed. Same body, same face, but even her expressions had changed. The way she thought. She pretty much threw out her wardrobe and bought new clothes—suburban mom. Traded in her Camaro for a Volvo station wagon. This while she was still pregnant. She looked dreamy while she ran the blender turning peas into baby mush instead of irritated because she was stuck in the kitchen." He shook his head again, but this time looking baffled.

"I'd say, 'What happened to not wanting children?' and she'd give this tinkly laugh and tell me she hadn't meant it. She used to pick up speeding tickets so often our insurance was sky-high, but all of a sudden she had a Baby On Board decal in the back window and was horrified at anyone who went a mile over the speed limit."

Robin had known only the Julie he was describing now. The devoted mother, sweet-natured, giving PTA president, classroom volunteer. The woman who'd bandaged knees, handed out treats, cheered on everyone's children.

Julie, driving a Camaro?

"Speeding?"

Craig's mouth twisted into a semblance of a smile. "That probably seems as weird to you as 'Baby On Board' did to me."

She didn't know if she believed him or not. "Um... Have you told the police all of this? They could confirm the speeding tickets, and that she owned a Camaro..."

He laughed, the sound ugly. "And then she got pregnant and reformed her ways. Women do. I can't describe to people who didn't know her how strange this transformation was."

"But...you must have had friends..."

"We'd just moved here from Chicago. We didn't see much of old friends, not as a couple. She didn't— doesn't—have any family, and all I have is my father."

"So you don't have anybody to back you up." How terribly lonely that sounded.

She saw in his eyes that it was—or that he was a superb con artist. How could she be sure what he was?

Wasn't it amazingly convenient that he and Julie had moved here right at the moment she supposedly made her sea change? That she had no family, no lifelong friends, who could disprove his claim that she was...what? Somebody with a split personality? Or just a woman without a sure sense of self?

His face twisted and he blundered to his feet. "You think I'm making all this up."

"No. I..."

He gave a half laugh that hurt to hear. "I don't even blame you. It's crap. None of it explains a woman walking out on her kids without even saying goodbye."

Robin felt a thrill of fear. "But...didn't she?"

His expression changed. A mask seemed to close over his face. "Yeah. If you can call what she told Brett saying goodbye."

Robin didn't know what Julie was supposed to have said. She'd heard rumors that Craig would have been arrested except for his son's story.

He'd pulled back and now stood waiting, remote. "Will you call for Brett?"

"Oh. Yes, of course." She passed him, but paused in the living room doorway. Her back to him, Robin said, "Craig, I..."

"Don't lie. Don't say you're sorry." His voice sounded heavy, slow, weary. "Don't say anything."

Robin took a deep breath, nodded and went to summon the boys.

By the time Brett came in, Craig had hidden whatever it was he felt—anguish, frustration because he'd failed to convince her, satisfaction because he might have driven in a wedge of doubt. She didn't know, couldn't guess. She was only glad for Brett's sake that he left her house with his dad's arm lying across his shoulders.

As for herself... She locked the front door after them, although she rarely bothered in the daytime, checked it again and realized that her hand shook. She balled it into a fist, then turned and smiled at her son.

"Homework?"

"Ah, jeez." His shoulders slumped. "I wish there was no school tomorrow."

"If wishes were..." She paused. This was a game they had always played. One or the other of them would make up something. The other had to finish.

"Tickets to the World Cup Soccer finals..." Malcolm supplied.

"We wouldn't be able to see a thing," she pointed out, "because the stadium would be so big."

He grinned at her. "You're supposed to say something good."

"Like, none of us would need TVs?"

"That's not good!"

She laughed with him, even though she still felt a chill inside. "I could argue about that."

Rolling his eyes, he said, "All right, I'll do my homework."

She went to the computer, turned it on, checked her e-mail—nothing worth getting—and then called up Chapter Seven.

But all she did was stare at the screen, the written words a gray blur. She heard again a man's deep, exhausted voice, as if she was replaying a tape.

...like she'd been possessed. Same body, same face, but even her expressions had changed.

And then she got pregnant and changed her ways. Women do.

We'd just moved here from Chicago.

No family, no old friends. Nobody who bridged before and after.

How could she believe him?

Closing her eyes, she thought, *Poor Brett.*

EVEN SHE HEARD the whispers. The police had talked to so-and-so's parents. What did they know about the Lofgren marriage? they were asked. Had Brett's mom ever complained of her husband becoming violent? Did she talk of wanting a divorce?

Brett went from cheerful on Monday to withdrawn and bristling with anger on Wednesday. Robin knew he'd gone to his first counseling session the night before. She'd hoped talking to a professional would help, not hurt.

When the class stood to crowd out the door of the portable for lunch on Wednesday, Robin said, "Brett, can you stay for a minute?"

He cast her a look as sullen as any he'd produced his first week of school, but shrugged and hung back.

She waited until everyone had gone, then strolled over to where he stood with a brown paper lunch bag in his hand. Half sitting on a desk, she said, "Tough week, huh?"

He hung his head and shrugged again.

"You've lived through this kind of talk before. You can do it again."

Brett lifted his head, eyes hot. "They don't know anything!"

"They know police officers have come to their homes and to them, that's exciting. They're not thinking about how this makes you and Abby feel."

"Abby cried on the school bus yesterday."

Robin winced. "Did you tell your father?"

"He's gone. Grandad's staying with us."

"Can you talk to him?"

"What can *he* do?" her student sneered.

"Listen?" She paused. "Your dad told me you were going to start seeing a counselor. That's what they're for, too, you know. They listen."

He bent his head again.

"Brett, don't play into the hands of gossips by picking a fight again. Promise me."

He didn't respond.

"Promise," Robin said more insistently.

Desperation twisted the face he lifted to her. "I'll try."

"Okay." She touched his arm. "Hang in there, kiddo."

"Yeah." He tried to smile. "Thanks."

"Now, go eat."

Brett nodded and left, walking so slowly Robin knew how little he wanted to rejoin his schoolmates.

Just after the last bell rang Wednesday afternoon, her classroom intercom screeched. The secretary said,

"Ms. McKinnon, Detective Diaz and Officer Caldwell are here to see you, if you have time."

Why did they want to see *her?* Nobody had interviewed her after Julie disappeared; they weren't that close.

Her pulse hammered, but she kept her voice calm. "Send them to my classroom, please."

She'd left the door open in hopes of acquiring some cross-ventilation. These portables froze in winter and roasted in hot weather. She had to raise her voice above the whir of two fans she kept running all day. Now she sat down behind her desk and closed her gradebook.

Were they here because Brett was in her class, or because of her casual friendship with Julie?

Footsteps sounded on the wheelchair ramp leading to her door. "Ms. McKinnon?"

"Come in." She stood, assessing the pair who entered.

Neither wore a uniform. The man, dark-haired, dark-eyed and strongly built, perhaps in his thirties, wore a short-sleeved white dress shirt and tie, pulled loose at the throat. The woman was young, younger than Robin, for sure. Her brown hair pulled tight in a bun, she wore blue slacks and a plain cotton blouse that tried to disguise a voluptuous figure. No makeup. Perhaps as a woman in a man's field, she tried to downplay her femininity.

They held out badges and introduced themselves. She waved them to chairs and sat again herself.

"How can I help you?"

The woman officer spoke first, her voice quick and

aggressive. "We're investigating the disappearance of Julie Lofgren. We understand you and she were friends."

"That may be putting it too strongly." Robin felt an urge to distance herself from Julie, which dismayed her. Had Craig actually driven a sliver of doubt into her mind? "Our sons played on the same sports teams, became casual friends. We often sat together to watch practices and games. We didn't socialize otherwise."

"I see. Did you discuss personal matters at all?"

"Well, of course!" Robin gave a little laugh. "Haven't you ever been to a Little League game? They go on for hours. We had plenty of time to talk."

"Do you mind telling us whether she raised the subject of her marriage?"

"We…touched on almost every subject you could think of." Noticing her gradebook sat crooked on her desk blotter, she aligned it. "I went through a divorce several years ago, and Julie listened to some of my troubles. We particularly talked about the impact on my son."

The male detective sat silent, watchful, letting his partner ask the questions. Because a woman might succeed better with another woman? Robin wondered.

"Did she confide in turn any problems with her own marriage?" Officer Caldwell asked.

Dismayed to discover how torn she was, how little she wanted to participate in this investigation, Robin made herself say, "The last year—especially the last six months before she disappeared—Julie did talk about…strain in her marriage. She complained about Craig's long absences."

"Do you know whether she planned to ask her husband for a divorce?"

"Yes." Robin cleared her throat. "Yes, I believe she did."

"Did she ever suggest that he was abusive or had threatened violence toward her?"

Robin shook her head.

"Did you know Mr. Lofgren?"

"Distantly. He came to games, of course."

"And your impression of him?"

"He, um, seemed very nice. Supportive of Brett. He often spent the entire game with Abby riding on his shoulders. To be honest, I wondered if Julie wasn't magnifying small problems out of proportion. Compared to my husband—"

The police officer's smile struck Robin as condescending.

"In other words, in public, he presented himself as a devoted father."

"And husband." Why did she feel compelled to say this? "He never let Julie carry anything heavy, he took care of Abby whenever he was there, and he—" Again, she stopped. Wetting her lips, she said without expression, "He touched Julie. Smiled at her. He did the little things that keep a marriage happy."

Oh, how jealous she'd been! Just pangs. Cramps of longing, but powerful enough that she'd been ashamed. *Don't covet thy neighbor's husband,* she had reproved herself, but it wasn't him she was coveting, not really. It was the glint in his eyes, the sexy, crooked smile he gave his wife, his gentleness and humor toward his small daughter. Okay, it was also his broad shoulders and clear eyes and easy, athletic way of moving, but mostly she felt the way she did because he seemed to represent an ideal to her.

"Were you surprised to hear about Mrs. Lofgren's disappearance?"

"Yes." If she sounded clipped, she couldn't help it. "Very surprised."

The officer closed her notebook. "If you think of anything that might shed light on what happened to Mrs. Lofgren, please call."

"Yes, of course." Robin rose with them, shook hands, then watched from the doorway as they went back through the breezeway and into the school building proper.

Her stomach churned as she wondered whether she'd helped or hurt Craig. She hated feeling like a snitch, when she'd done nothing but tell the truth. If he hadn't had anything to do with Julie's disappearance, wouldn't Craig *want* her to help the police?

Uncomfortably, she remembered how hostile he had sounded about them. The stress of being a suspect for a year and a half must be enormous—but shouldn't he be glad these two police officers seemed to be starting all over?

Robin frowned at the nearly empty playground. Or were they starting over? Every single question they'd asked had had to do with Craig. They hadn't probed a single other possibility. What if Julie had been having an affair, for example? What if she was depressed about something that had nothing to do with her husband? Robin would have had to volunteer that kind of information. She didn't actually know anything—but they hadn't asked.

And that bothered her. Somebody else *might* know something and might not think to volunteer it.

Sick to her stomach now, she wished Julie hadn't told her she wanted a divorce. Robin hated her awareness that she'd confirmed what the newspapers had hinted was Craig Lofgren's motivation: he'd kill rather than see his wife leave him.

The last stragglers abandoned the slides and climbers and wandered out open gates in the chain-link fence. Robin still stood in the doorway, fans blowing behind her, the late afternoon air hot and still out in the schoolyard, and thought, *I don't believe it.*

She'd seen him friendly and relaxed, and she'd seen him guarded and even hostile. But she simply could not imagine the man who cared so much about his children murdering his wife. Murdering anyone.

But she didn't let relief wash over her. Because wasn't that what the neighbors and coworkers always said? *He's always been so pleasant. I can't imagine…*

She didn't believe he was a murderer. But she didn't dare trust her instincts.

What must it be like? Robin wondered with a painful twist in her chest. To know that no one at all believed unreservedly in you?

Not even your son?

CHAPTER SEVEN

THEY WERE BACK AGAIN, not because they had any
new questions, but because they intended to push,
push, push until he cracked. What Craig hadn't figured out was what they expected him to do. Start
sobbing and admit he'd done it, saying his wife's
body was under the patio?

Or start shooting?

"We've received confirmation from several friends
of your wife that she intended to ask for a divorce."

Craig gripped the back of an armchair and repeated
in a monotone. "She didn't ask for a divorce."

"A separation?"

"Not even that." Tension squeezed his temples.
"Who told you that?"

"I'm not sure I should..." Detective Ann Caldwell, his nemesis, looked down at her notes with what
he took to be uncertainty. Or maybe she was just
stringing him along.

This time he'd made note of her first name. Ann.
It sounded gentle, girl-next-door. Deceptive.

"I have a right to know who is making accusa-
tions." He fought to keep his voice level, unemotional.

She lifted her head and met his eyes, hers chilly

with disbelief. "I wouldn't describe that as an accusation, Mr. Lofgren. Your wife spoke freely to half a dozen people. Abby's second grade teacher, Mrs. Cathey. A neighbor of yours with whom she apparently had coffee on occasion." She glanced down. "Sue Colvin. A couple of mothers who often sat with her at Little League games. Barb Nownes and Robin McKinnon."

Shock held him immobile for a long moment. "Robin McKinnon?" He sounded hoarse.

"That surprises you?"

Don't let her see weakness. He swallowed, relaxed his grip on the back of the chair and straightened. "I wasn't aware you'd spoken to her. Brett's in her class this year."

A flicker of something showed in Ann Caldwell's eyes. "She didn't mention that."

Good. He was glad to have unsettled her, if only briefly.

"Robin McKinnon said that Julie intended to ask me for a divorce?"

"That's right." Caldwell closed her notebook and stood. "Apparently a good part of the community knew she wanted to leave you. And yet you claim not to have had any idea."

His jaws ached. Relaxing them, he said, "It doesn't occur to you that she might have simply left me?"

Her nostrils flared. "Without the children?"

Therein lay the rub, as the saying went. He didn't blame her for her doubt. Despite his uneasy awareness that his wife wasn't quite what she seemed, that she could shed identities the way other people abandoned a golf swing that didn't work, Craig still had trouble imagining Julie taking off with no intention of ever seeing Abby and Brett again. She had to have loved them.

"What if she was leaving with someone? Maybe a married man who had no intention of breaking up his marriage?"

Ann Caldwell raised her brows. "Was she having an affair?"

Defeat washed through him. "If she was, I wasn't aware of it. But then—" bitterness lending acid to his voice "—I don't seem to have had a clue what she was thinking, and possibly doing."

"To this point, there has been no indication that Mrs. Lofgren had an affair." She nodded and left, her silent partner following.

Craig braced his arms on the chair again and let his head fall. With his eyes closed, he took slow, deep breaths. In through the nose, out through the mouth. The kids would be home any minute. He didn't want them to see him like this.

Would he never have peace again? Had he appreciated the days when he could mow his front lawn on Sunday afternoon and wave at the neighbors? When he drove home from SeaTac eager to see his wife and kids? Or had he taken them for granted, thinking his family would last forever despite Julie's increasing unhappiness?

The rumble of the school bus and the screech of its brakes brought his head up. Thank God the two police officers hadn't repeated their threat to interview the kids again. He dreaded seeing Abby with a pinched face and huge, bewildered eyes, Brett with simmering anger and a fierce need to defend his father.

Craig couldn't forget much of that horrific couple of weeks after he came home to find Julie's van in the garage, her purse on the kitchen counter, but no Julie. But one of the worst moments had involved Brett.

About a week into the nightmare, Craig had thought the cops were about to handcuff him when his son burst into the living room. His hands knotted into fists, his eyes wet, he'd confronted Sergeant Caldwell.

"You don't know what you're talking about!" He thrust his jaw out. "Mom said she was going away. She told me!"

Craig remembered turning, his mouth dropping open. In his memory, he'd moved in slow motion, a mime reacting with shock.

That bastard, Caldwell, laid a hand on Brett's thin shoulder. "Now, son, is this true?"

Brett bristled. "Yes!"

They made him sit down, where he told his story with a combative air, as if he expected to be disbelieved.

She'd come into his room to say good-night a couple of weeks before. She'd stroked his hair back from his face and said, "I'm going to have to go away soon, Brett. You'll have to be a big boy and help your dad and sister."

"You didn't ask her what she meant about going away?" Caldwell had asked.

Brett shook his head. "I just thought...you know. That she had to be gone for a few days or something. But she looked...funny. Weird. You know? It kind of scared me, but I was sleepy and she was there in the morning, so I just forgot about it."

They couldn't shake him, although they did try. Craig had sat silent, noticing the way Brett avoided meeting his eyes.

That night, long after the cops had gone, he'd tried talking to Brett. "What you did today took courage. I know you're scared for me."

Brett had hung his head and shrugged.

"If the police are going to find your mom, it's important they not be misled. Brett, if you made that up to protect me, you have to tell them the truth."

Brett had shot to his feet. "It did happen! She said goodbye! And even you don't believe me!" He had raced from the room.

In the following weeks, the boy stuck to his guns, although Craig noticed small shifts in the story. She whispered, "Goodbye," although he hadn't mentioned that the first time. Sometimes she said more, telling him not to say anything to Abby until she was gone. "Because she'll cry, you know," he reported her saying.

Was he remembering more? Embroidering the truth, to give it more texture?

Or making up a story whole-cloth?

Craig had never been sure. Still wasn't sure. He wished he had a better idea what Brett was thinking. If he'd manufactured the incident, had he done so because he really believed his mother had gone away?

Or was he prepared to protect his dad no matter what he'd done?

Craig had lived for a year and a half now with the knowledge that his own son might fear his father had killed his mother.

He hated waiting for Brett to be put back on the spot again, forced to struggle to remember what he'd said then, forced to make what might be fiction believable again. All of this out of fear that he'd lose his dad, too.

Craig had never told a soul, not even his father, that he suspected Brett might be lying. He hoped Brett's story didn't make any difference one way or the other, that in the end the police would find Julie, or she'd call one day, or…

Or what? he asked himself with a flare of anger. He'd wake up and discover this had all been a dream?

The front door opened, book bags thudded to the hall table and Abby called, "Daddy?"

She still wondered—would probably always wonder—whether Daddy would be here when she got home.

He put a smile on his face and went to meet his kids.

Not until evening, when he'd tucked Abby in and Brett was finishing his homework, did Craig let himself think about the fact that the police had interviewed Robin.

Loading the dishwasher, he pictured her the other day when she'd invited him in for coffee.

She'd been barefoot. That was the first thing he noticed. Her nails were unpainted, her feet narrow and her toes long. Khaki capris had left bare her smooth, slim calves. He had already lost his breath before he lifted his gaze far enough to see that she wore only a shell-pink tank top and no bra. She looked comfortable and unbearably sexy.

With his foul mood, he hadn't wanted to notice. He just wanted to pick up his son and go home. He should have known she wouldn't let him.

No, check that. How could he have known? Women didn't casually invite him in for a cup of coffee. Not even Summer's mother, who was always pleasant, ever suggested he step inside her house.

He was a wife-killer. What woman in her right mind would risk being alone with him?

But Robin had surprised him. With her stern look and order to sit down when he'd tried to stalk out, she'd cracked a dam holding too much inside. He didn't expect her to believe a word he said, but he'd found himself talking anyway.

Sitting there looking at her, with her feet curled under her, her forehead creased as she listened, her candid eyes fixed on his face, he had realized how badly he wanted her—this one person—to believe he would never have hurt his wife.

He'd known she didn't, that the weight of popular opinion and innuendo in the newspapers and fondness for Julie had sunk any chance he had. But still, she'd listened. She treated him like a human being, not a pariah, a monster. She might keep listening. Smiling with what appeared to be genuine friendliness when she saw him.

But now he knew what she really thought. His

pretty, petite wife wanted a divorce and he'd gone into a rage and killed her.

What else had she told the cops? It seemed that his son's sixth-grade teacher knew one hell of a lot more about his wife's state of mind in the months before she'd disappeared than he did. And she was apparently happy to confirm Officer Ann Caldwell's favorite scenario.

He was a fool to have expected anything different. To have let his guard down, to have imagined that under other circumstances she might be interested...

Craig swore, the harsh sound of the single word somehow shocking in the quiet kitchen. He wanted to punch something, throw something, put his fist through a wall. He felt as violent as he'd ever felt in his life.

He felt betrayed, even though Robin McKinnon owed him nothing, had promised him nothing, was unlikely even to suspect that the sight of her shimmering hair and gentle face and narrow feet made regret tear at his guts.

But, despite the wrenching anger, all he did was turn on the dishwasher, turn out the lights and head upstairs to say good-night to his son.

ROBIN DIDN'T SEE Craig again until Saturday. He was apparently dropping Brett off for practices but not staying. Saturday's game was away. Robin parked in the unfamiliar lot, grabbed her small cooler and lawn chair and followed her son, hoping he knew where he was headed. This vast complex must have eight fields.

Games were going on in most, warm-ups off to the sides, parents blocking the sidelines.

"Excuse me. Excuse me," she kept having to say, making her way along one sideline or another.

Apparently Mal knew what he was doing, though, because she spotted familiar faces ahead. The day was...not misty, but *damp* feeling, with gray skies. September had been dry and hot, but today hinted at fall. Leaves were turning, she'd noticed on the drive today. She always forgot in September how miserable the games got by November, but today she remembered. Other autumns, she had huddled under her umbrella in gales, frozen in snowstorms, taken a blanket to cover the car seat because Mal would be muddy from head to toe by the end a game.

Even he'd worn a sweatshirt today, which he was dropping to the grass along with the net bag that held his soccer ball.

"Hey," he said, looking past her.

Robin glanced over her shoulder to see Brett approaching, his father not far behind.

"Hey," Brett said. "Hi, Ms. McKinnon."

She smiled. "Hi, Brett. I hear you might start today."

"Yeah, Josh wants to play forward."

He dumped his stuff and the two boys joined the five or six others who'd already arrived.

Greeting other parents, Robin wasn't really paying attention to the boys until she heard one of the players say, "Brett, you know the cops are talking to all our parents about your dad, don't you?"

Her head whipped around.

In profile to her, Brett froze.

In a startlingly adult voice, her son said, "His dad's here, you know."

"Oh, jeez…" All the boys looked toward the parents, expressions guilty.

"It's crap, anyway," Malcolm continued. "So shut up about it, okay?"

That silenced them. Or maybe it was the arrival of the coach, who ordered them to drop to the grass for calisthenics.

Robin couldn't bear to look toward Craig. But after a moment she realized she couldn't *not* look—the normal, friendly thing would be to greet him.

But he wasn't nearby. He'd taken up a stand twenty-five yards away, a solitary figure despite the spectators packing up after the game that had just ended. Robin saw the way other parents eyed him surreptitiously, as if to check that he was staying where he belonged, a safe distance from them and their children.

Robin's heart ached with sympathy. For Brett, she tried to believe, but she knew better. If Craig hadn't had anything to do with Julie's disappearance, what must it be like, living with whispers and stares and backs turned when you neared? She hated even imagining.

Brett played well again, with such intensity and even aggression that the ref warned him once, unusual for a goalie.

After the team's victory, between glugs of orange juice, Mal asked, "Can Brett come home with us again?"

"Sure," she said, even though she felt a ripple of worry. Craig would have to pick up his son again. What had she started?

Brett ran over to ask his dad, who looked at her for the first time, his brows raised.

She nodded and smiled.

His face expressionless, he spoke to his son, who ran back. "Dad says he'll drop off my stuff later."

"Cool." The two boys started toward the parking lot. "Mom, can we stop for lunch on the way home? I'm starving."

One of the other mothers heard. Laughing, she said, "Are they ever *not* starving?"

Robin laughed, too, if ruefully. Her grocery bills had been climbing and climbing. "Not so's I've noticed."

Madeline Pearce fell into step beside Robin. Her son, who played defense, was walking with some other boys.

Lowering her voice, she said, "I feel so sorry for Brett. This situation must be awful for him."

Craig was gone, lost in the crowd of arriving and departing parents and players.

Robin nodded. "I know it's hard. He's in my class this year, you know."

"I'm glad you suggested he rejoin the team. I wish his father wouldn't come to games, though. It takes nerve, don't you think?"

"But how would Brett feel if his dad didn't come?" Robin pointed out.

"Well...that's true. Still."

"You know, he's never been arrested." Robin

knew darn well she wasn't going to boost her own popularity by defending Craig Lofgren, but innate fairness insisted she do it anyway. "What if he didn't have anything to do with Julie's disappearance? He's been ostracized!"

Madeline hoisted a slipping tote bag. "But the police seem to be so sure."

"Then why haven't they arrested him?"

"I've read it's really hard to convince a jury when no body has been found."

"Or blood, or even signs of violence. Wouldn't you think they would have found *something,* as hard as they've been looking at him, if he'd killed her?"

For a moment, the tall brunette looked thoughtful. Then, quashing Robin's flare of hope, Madeline shook her head. "Tell me one thing. Where is Julie?"

Robin had no answer.

"Can you imagine any woman running away without her purse? I mean, I feel naked without mine!"

"I do, too," Robin admitted. "But there could have been a stranger, or…"

Madeline gave her a pitying look. "You want him to be innocent, don't you?"

Gazing at the two boys ahead, Robin asked, "For Brett's sake, don't you? And for his little sister's sake?"

"I do feel sorry for them." Madeline's son caught up to her and amid calls of "See you Tuesday" and "Good game!" parents and kids separated.

In the car, Robin heard herself saying brightly, "Good game, boys."

"Yeah, you were awesome," Mal told his friend.

Brett fastened his seat belt. "You're the one who scored two goals."

"So, we're good." Mal poked the back of his mother's seat. "Can we go out to lunch?"

She succumbed with only a twinge of worry about her budget. "Why not? Where shall we go?"

They stopped for pizza, the boys taking off their cleats in the car, Brett going in with just socks and shin guards.

She even produced a few bucks worth of quarters so the two could play video games, which seemed to induce odd sound effects from the back seat on the way home.

Laughing, she left them to their own devices and began, for no particularly good reason, to clean house. That's what weekends were for, she told herself self-righteously. The fact that she attempted to tidy as well as mop and vacuum and dust had nothing to do with the fact that Brett's father would be stopping by not just once but twice this weekend.

And she was certainly not disappointed, she told herself later, to find out that while she was scrubbing the toilet bowl, Craig had come and gone. She hadn't even heard the doorbell. It wasn't as if she'd have invited him in anyway; she was busy.

She made spaghetti for dinner—mountains and mountains of spaghetti. By the time the boys were done, a modest hill remained. There might be enough left for her to have for lunch tomorrow, she thought with a sigh, cleaning up later.

She was grading a social studies test the next afternoon when she did hear the doorbell. No thunder of feet responded, so she got up.

In jeans and a corduroy shirt open over a gray tee, Craig was so handsome Robin felt that familiar twist of longing. *Not for him,* she told herself. He just… triggered something in her. A memory, maybe, of romance and sexual desire and…

She gave up, knowing she was lying. *He* attracted her. He always had. And that admission scared her a bunch, because it opened the possibility that Madeline was right. She did want him to be innocent, but not only for Brett's sake.

Maybe, in even giving him the benefit of the doubt, she was ignoring good old-fashioned common sense. Women left their husbands; they *didn't* leave their purses.

"Um, hi." She managed a smile. "Mal's got music blasting. I guess the boys didn't hear the doorbell. Come on in."

He hesitated, then gave a brief nod and stepped over the threshold.

"Coffee?" she heard herself asking.

"Maybe I should just take Brett."

If any other father had said that, she'd have gone down the hall to hammer on Malcolm's bedroom door.

Because Craig had said it, in that utterly blank voice, she crossed her arms. "So as not to stain my reputation by being in this house too long?"

He blinked. After a pause, he inclined his head. "Something like that."

"Not because you're really in a hurry, or you hate my coffee, or..."

He almost smiled. "I'm not sure I actually drank any of your coffee last time."

"You really can snatch your son and leave if you want."

"I wouldn't mind a cup of coffee. If you're offering."

"I wouldn't have said it if I didn't mean it." Leading the way to the kitchen, she thought, *Dear, God, what am I doing?*

Flirting with the impossible, she answered herself. Or maybe worse.

She poured coffee, chatting about the game.

She was pausing for breath when Craig interjected. "You have a remarkable son."

Robin knew exactly what he was talking about. Her spoon suspended above the sugar bowl, she said, "You heard."

"I heard."

"Did you know..."

"That the cops were talking to everyone? Yeah."

She concentrated on putting the spoonful of sugar in the coffee cup and stirring. "They even talked to me."

"I know that, too."

Robin lifted her head in surprise. "How?"

His mouth twisted. "They told me."

"But...why?"

Craig sighed. "I asked."

She felt her forehead crinkle in bewilderment. "Who they'd talked to?"

"Something like that." He nodded toward the table. "Can we sit down?"

"What? Oh." Feeling dumb, she picked up the two cups of coffee. "Of course."

Thanks to her industrious weekend, the clutter on the table was confined to two more-or-less tidy heaps. Craig sat in Mal's usual place, nodding his thanks when she handed him his coffee.

Neither of them took a sip.

After a moment, he said, "When they told me several friends of Julie's insist she intended to ask for a divorce, I said I had the right to know who those friends were."

"And I was one of them." The enemy. His betrayer.

As if reading her mind, Craig said, "I know you were friends. I wouldn't want you to do anything but tell the truth. I just, uh, was surprised."

"That they'd talked to me?"

"Yeah." His long fingers traced the rim of the mug. "And that she was apparently telling the world she wanted a divorce. Everyone but me."

"She really hadn't even raised the subject?"

He shook his head. "I knew she was unhappy. I wasn't sure it was so much with me as with her life. We'd reached a point that—" He stopped. "Oh, hell. I shouldn't even say this."

Robin lifted her hand, then curled it into a fist, shocked to realize she'd been about to touch him. "Say it."

His eyes, crystal clear, met hers. "I hoped she'd ask. I was miserable, too."

"Then why didn't you ask for one?"

"Because of the kids. I didn't want to be just a weekend dad." The muscles in his jaw spasmed. "That's supposed to be my motivation for... I wanted the kids."

She nodded, avoiding his gaze. "I know."

His voice sounded raw. "I would never have hurt her."

"I'm...starting to believe that, too." Robin was stunned by what she'd said, stunned to realize she meant it. She was crazy! She couldn't know him, not really. She couldn't know what he might do. *Would* do, if he was angry enough.

But...not that, Robin thought again. Killing. Hiding the body. Lying all these months, despite the intense pressure on him. She just couldn't believe it.

He had gone completely still, only his eyes were fiercely alive. "Except for my father, you're the only person ever to say that to me."

Captured by that glittering gaze, she whispered, "You must have friends."

"I had friends." He cleared his throat. "I thought I had friends."

"They...abandoned you?"

"They avoided the subject. They called less often. Started being busy." He let out a ragged sound and then muttered a profanity. "I'm sorry. I try not to descend into self-pity."

"It's okay." She bit her lip. "It sounds as if you need to talk."

"Why? Why do you believe me, when no one else does?"

Because I'm crazy? Because I have a crush on you? God help me, she thought, *neither are good answers.*

"I don't know," she said honestly, because that, too, was true. She didn't understand. "When I called you to talk about Brett, I suppose I did think..."

"That I'd murdered my wife."

After a pause, she gave a jerky nod. "What I read in the papers didn't sound good."

His face looked stark. "It still doesn't."

"I used to watch you with her." She sounded so odd. Reflective, far away. "The way you'd turn even when you were down at the dugout and smile right at her, as if she were the only person in the stands. Sometimes, she didn't even smile back. She'd keep talking, as if she didn't see you. Or..." She swallowed. "As if she was deliberately ignoring you."

"Julie was a strange woman. Stranger even than..." He clamped down on whatever he'd been going to say when they both heard the bedroom door open and the voices of their sons.

"Hey, Mom, has Brett's dad called or..." The boys stopped in the doorway. "Oh."

"Hi, Dad." Brett's wary gaze went from his father to Robin and back. "I didn't know you were here."

"That," Robin said, "is because you're both going deaf from music played at an excessive volume."

"Get your stuff." Craig pushed back from the table.

As the boys retreated, she shook her head in mock disappointment. "You still haven't tasted my coffee."

A real grin spread on his face, one that was slightly rakish, very sexy and yet also…sweet. "I can remedy that." He lifted the cup and took a long swallow. "Manna."

"Seattle's Best, actually."

"You could have given me instant. I'm not a connoisseur."

She laughed. "Next time, we can skip the coffee and go straight to talking."

At the front door, he turned to face her, his eyes serious. "Will there be a next time?"

Crazy. Reckless.

Robin ignored her inner voice. "You have to finish that thought."

He nodded, lines seeming to deepen and age him. "You were her friend. If I can convince you, there might be hope."

"Where do you think she…" Even whispering, she couldn't finish.

Mal and Brett had emerged, one of them bumping the other so that they both ricocheted off the walls, laughing raucously. Watching their clumsy, heavy-footed approach, she couldn't believe they were athletes.

They thundered out the front door.

Craig cleared his throat. "Have you thanked Malcolm's mother for having you?"

Flushing, Brett turned. "Thanks, Ms. McKinnon. I had a good time."

"You're very welcome." She smiled. "I'll see you bright and early tomorrow."

He made a face. "Yeah."

"Jeez," Mal said in a stage whisper as they continued down the walk, "I can't believe my mom is your teacher."

Craig hadn't moved. "During practice tomorrow, if I can find somewhere for Abby to go, can we go get a cup of coffee?"

Her heart skipped. "More coffee?"

"It's a good excuse."

She nodded. "Sure." Her voice squeaked, and she repeated, "Sure. I want you to finish."

He hesitated, gave a brief nod of his own, and left, following his son. Robin stayed on the porch, watching as his dark blue Lexus pulled away from the curb.

She was crazy.

Crazy, scared…and exhilarated.

CHAPTER EIGHT

"ARE YOU SURE you don't want to come to dinner tonight?" Craig asked his father. With the phone crooked between his shoulder and ear, he was checking the freezer. "I put together a lasagna last night. We have plenty."

"Nah, I have my Internet class tonight. I'll be over afterward. Nine-thirty, ten."

"Okay." Craig let the freezer door swing shut and leaned against the counter. "Listen, Dad. I told you the cops have been here again. They mentioned wanting to talk to Brett and Abby."

His father fired back, "Over my dead body."

"That's the spirit. I want to be here if I have to let this happen. You tell them they're not seeing the kids without me being present. If they try to insist, call Riordan. His number's in the address book here in the kitchen."

"I can hold 'em off without the help of any attorney," his father said.

Craig relaxed. Thank God his father had retired up here to be near his son and grandkids. Craig didn't know what he'd have done without him in the wake of Julie's disappearance.

"All right. There'll probably be enough lasagna left over for tomorrow night...."

"I can cook, you know. You don't have to plan dinners."

Craig thought of the neatly labeled dinners stacked in the freezer. "But I feel less guilty this way."

"Brett and Abby are my grandchildren as much as they're your son and daughter."

Surprised at his father's anger, Craig began, "I do know that..."

"What is it you think I should be doing instead of spending time with those kids? Hitting a goddamn little white ball into man-made lakes?"

Craig tried again. "No..."

"I consider myself a lucky man to be needed instead of having to fill my days however I can."

"Dad..."

"Which is not to say I'll object too much to being turned back out to pasture when you find the right woman."

"There won't be any other woman until Julie's found."

"Won't there?" his father said, then, "Don't wait up for me tonight." *Click.*

Where in hell had that come from? Craig wondered, setting down the phone. Had his father just decided it was time for him to find a girlfriend? Or had he met Robin at soccer practices and jumped to unwarranted conclusions?

Unwarranted? Hadn't her face jumped into his mind the minute his father said "the right woman?"

Wanting and having were two different things. He

didn't have to remind himself of that. Under other circumstances, he'd be pursuing her.

But as things stood, he'd meant what he said. He couldn't let himself even think about something like that until the mystery of Julie's disappearance was resolved. He was a married man, and one whom no woman in her right mind would consider getting involved with.

Even one who had said she was starting to believe in his innocence.

If he had been standing when she told him, he thought he would have crumpled to his knees. He'd almost quit hoping anyone would ever say those words. Robin McKinnon, Julie's friend and confidante, was the last person he'd ever dreamed would utter them.

He was torturing himself, taking her out for coffee this afternoon as if they were friends—or more. But he found he was starved for conversation with someone who would actually listen, someone…impartial. His father got combative; he was incensed that those fools would think for a minute that his son would even raise his hand to a woman, never mind kill her in cold—or hot—blood.

Dad had never liked Julie, a fact that had irritated Craig during his courtship. But Dad had also, to his credit, shut his mouth the minute the wedding took place. He had watched her with worry on his face after each of her sea changes, commenting quietly to Craig that Julie seemed…different.

Oh, yeah. She was different.

Craig went upstairs and packed his small bag, not

having to think about what he put in or how he folded it thanks to his many years' experience. He never took much: a change of clothes for the layover and the basic toiletries, a book or two—hanging out in bars in any country didn't interest him.

He zipped it closed and carried it down to the car when he realized that he had to pick Brett up at school in fifteen minutes. The night before, Craig had called Summer's mother and asked if Abby could go home with Summer after school.

"No problem," he'd been assured. "The girls can do their homework together."

Brett was waiting at the curb when Craig pulled over. He hopped in, said, "Hi, Dad," tossed his book bag in the back seat and grabbed the bundle of soccer gear and clothes he had put in the car the night before.

Two blocks from the school, safe from the possibility of being seen by classmates, he wriggled out of his jeans and pulled on shorts, shin guards, socks and cleats that were caked with dirt from Saturday's game.

"You staying for practice?" he asked, the transformation complete.

"Not today." Craig'd decided it was better to mention casually what he was doing today during practice. "Robin and I are having coffee."

"Robin…" Understanding, closely akin to horror, transformed Brett's face. "You mean…Ms. *McKinnon?*"

Craig pretended not to notice his son's shock. "That's right."

"Why... I mean, does she want to talk to you about *me?*"

"Actually, no. We were having an interesting conversation when the two of you came barreling in yesterday, and we decided to continue it."

"Conversation."

"I *am* capable of having one."

"Yeah, but... Ms. *McKinnon?*"

Exasperated, Craig said, "Would you quit saying her name in that tone of voice? Is it so impossible to believe I'd want to talk to her? Or that she'd want to talk to me?"

Brett kept stealing looks at him. "You're not..."

"Not what?"

They pulled into the parking lot, gravel crunching under the tires, the car bouncing in and out of the potholes that seemed to develop during every sports season.

"Never mind." Brett grabbed the door handle before the car had come to stop, and leaped out as though eager to escape.

Not seeing Robin's car, Craig turned into a parking spot and waited. Two minutes later, she pulled in next to him. Malcolm was out of the car and hurrying across the field as quickly as his own son had.

When Craig gestured, she got out, locked her car and got in his. "Afraid to ride in my heap of junk?"

Backing out, he couldn't help noticing the scrape along the side where her elderly Subaru had been keyed. Or the rust corroding the trunk. "It's not that bad," he said.

She laughed. "Yeah, it is. Bless its heart, it has

216,000 miles on it. And it runs. What more can I ask?''

Now he was going to start worrying about her car breaking down when she was by herself.

''A new car?'' he suggested in response to her—probably rhetorical—question.

''Not unless I win the lottery. And since I never buy tickets…''

He stopped before turning onto the road. A van was just turning in, and he saw the woman driver's head turn in their direction. One of the other parents.

''Damn,'' he muttered. ''I was hoping nobody would see us.''

''Why? They know I talk to you.''

''Being civil in public is not the same thing as getting in a car with me,'' Craig said grimly.

''I will not let other people tell me who I can and cannot talk to.'' She gave him a severe look. ''Understand?''

''I just don't want you to suffer because you've been decent to me.''

Genuine puzzlement crinkled her brow. ''Craig, people aren't that unreasonable.''

''Aren't they?'' Stopped at a red light, he turned his head. ''I've had rocks thrown through the windshield of this car twice, both times wrapped in notes that told me not very nicely I deserve to hang. I've changed our phone number twice because of the hateful messages that filled our voice mail.'' He gritted his teeth and made himself stop. ''You have no idea.''

She stared at him. ''I…no. I guess I don't. Oh, Craig…''

"I shield the kids as well as I can. But they're not deaf or blind. They're well aware that their friends—assuming they have any—can never play at our house, or that neighbors don't wave anymore. I can't remember the last time anybody but the cops and my dad stepped inside my house. Brett isn't reacting just to the way he's treated at school, you know."

The light changed. He started forward.

"I had no idea. I am sorry. I wouldn't have thought people like that…"

"Lived in a nice town?" he asked, with irony. "They live everywhere, Robin. They're us."

"I wouldn't…"

"No." He let out a breath. "But you're the exception. They're the rule."

Her forehead creased again. "I can't believe that."

"I didn't used to, either." They'd reached the outskirts of town. He wished he'd thought ahead of time where he could take her.

She gestured at an espresso stand that had sprouted a year or so before in a vacant lot. "Why don't we just get something to go?"

Grateful, Craig put on the turn signal. A teenager who apparently had no idea who he was cheerfully made their orders and took his money. A moment later, he turned back toward the soccer fields.

"Why don't I park by the river?"

Robin nodded.

The soccer fields were part of the city park, which also included a walking trail along the river and a picnic area. On a gray Monday afternoon like this, they had it to themselves.

At her suggestion, they carried their steaming cups to a picnic table at the edge of a ten-foot bluff above the river. It was more of a creek in this season, meandering along a rocky bed. Fallen leaves floated slowly on the surface.

They sat side by side on the table, their feet on the bench. It made it harder to look at her, to see her changing expressions, but easier to talk.

They both sipped, the silence more comfortable than he had any right to expect.

It was Robin who said finally, "Tell me what you meant about Julie. About her being strange."

He watched a clump of sodden brown leaves lodge briefly on a large rock, then swirl around it to continue with the current.

"I told you we're from Chicago. When we met, Julie was a potter. A good one. Did she ever talk about that part of her life?"

He wasn't surprised when Robin shook her head. His kids ate their breakfast cereal out of bowls their mother had thrown, fired and glazed, but he wasn't sure they knew she'd made them, either. The truth was, he sometimes wondered if Julie remembered. Not that long before she'd disappeared, he'd lifted one and said, "These really are beautiful bowls," and she'd looked at them with puzzlement before saying, in the tone of someone humoring a crazy person, "They're nice."

"She was arty. Wore her hair in a braid down her back. She potted in overalls and a tank top. I don't think she ever put on makeup. She sold her stuff at art fairs and a few galleries and took custom orders. She was natural, warm, funny.''

He felt Robin's gaze, but kept his own on the river. It was easier this way to talk about a past that felt like someone else's.

''I fell hard. She laughed at the idea of getting married. Maybe when she was ready to have kids, she said.''

The idea of Julie, beautiful in the way of a wild-flower, carrying his child, had made him hard. That particular marriage proposal, like most of his others, had ended in passionate lovemaking.

''But suddenly one day she agreed. I remember being…startled. I was half teasing, and she looked at me with this serious expression and said, 'Yes.'''

He could see her face to this minute. She'd been cleaning up her studio and still wore those bib overalls caked with dried clay. She was wiping her hands on a rag when she answered the doorbell. Red clay streaked one delicate cheek. Dried particles flecked her pale hair.

Yes. I'm ready.

''She…changed that day. She was tired of potting, she said, with this irritated shrug. Next thing I knew, she'd found a job as a rep for a clothing line. The ones that go around to stores. She dressed for the job. Great suits, elegant pumps. She got her hair cut—in a chin-length bob that she styled every morning. Even on days off she kept the look. Her jeans were suddenly name brand, looked ironed. Cute shirts, this shining hair that always turned under just so.''

"Maybe…maybe she just grew up. Or was trying to please you."

Craig made a sound of agreement. "I told her she didn't have to turn into someone else for my sake. She looked at me like I was nuts."

What are you talking about?

"She wanted to get married right away. I was fine with that. I'd been trying to persuade her for months. We did it and she moved in with me. She brought hardly anything. Even though my place had room, she got rid of her kiln and potting wheel and most of her pottery. I asked her to keep some of her best work. Then one day I was dragging the garbage can out to the street and checked to see why it was so heavy. It was full of shards. As if she'd stood there and smashed piece after piece."

With deep pain he'd recognized bits of beautiful bowls and tall, graceful vases. She'd made a teapot and set of cups, then sculpted comical faces on the sides. Those, too, had ended up in the garbage can. She'd missed the cereal bowls he and the kids used to this day, maybe because they were mixed in with the everyday functional dishes.

"I asked her about it, and she said, 'They weren't that good. I'd rather have new stuff.' 'Have' she said, as if the things she'd broken had no more connection to her than store-bought dishes."

Robin listened, taking an occasional sip of her latte, her eyes wide, those lines crinkling her forehead as they always did when she concentrated.

"Julie got ambitious. Pretty soon she supervised other reps, was in charge of a multistate territory. In those days I flew for a regional carrier, but she urged me to apply to the big airlines. Reminding me how much more money I'd make, what cool places I'd see.

"After a couple of years, I suggested we start a family. 'Don't be ridiculous,' she said. That would mean taking time off. What about her career? She didn't like kids anyway."

Her expression had been disdainful; she'd glanced around the living room of their lake-view condo, decorated in cream and taupe and glass, and said, "Kids are messy, loud and hell on a woman's figure." She'd smiled seductively at him and twined her arms around his neck. "I *know* you like my figure."

"She insisted she'd never wanted children. Talked as if we'd discussed it before we got married and I'd known."

Of Julie's incarnations, that was the one he'd liked least. She had been witty, elegant, passionate in bed, but more interested in shopping and entertaining and rising the next step at work than she was in having fun or talking about anything that mattered. She had become…hard.

Craig fell silent while a pair of joggers passed, a man and a woman who might be in their fifties, their strides synchronized as if they always ran together.

"Six months later," he continued, "I came home from a flight to Paris. She flung herself into my arms and screamed, 'I'm pregnant!'"

"She was upset."

"Hell, no. She was thrilled. Dancing around the living room." He shook his head, still confused. He remembered standing there with his mouth hanging open watching this bright, cheerful woman celebrating the start of a family.

"Enter the Julie I knew." Hands wrapped around her cup, Robin looked out at the river and the trees along the bank.

"Julie Number Three. It was the strangest damn thing. The airline wanted to move me out to Seattle, and she'd thrown a fit when I mentioned the possibility. Now she could hardly wait to go. Our yuppie condo was no place to raise children. We needed to buy a house in a small town."

With a yard, she'd said dreamily, *and a patio in back.* Oh, and the schools would have to be good.

"'Children?' I said in a daze. 'Plural?' Well, of course we'd have to have more than one, Julie scolded me. No child should grow up an only."

"So you moved."

"We moved. Got rid of most of our furniture rather than bring it. She didn't like it anymore." Hell, he'd *never* liked it. "As she went into maternity clothes, the expensive suits disappeared. Maybe she shredded them. I don't know. All of a sudden, she was Suburban Mom. Pretty but natural. That's when we sold her sports car and bought a station wagon. 'They have side air bags,' she told me. 'I want the very safest car we can have. For *their* sake.'" He shook his head. "Brett hadn't even been born. Abby not imagined. It was…"

"Weird," Robin concluded. "I can see that it would be."

"When I told you that our moving from Chicago meant we'd left friends behind…" He hesitated.

"She'd already ditched her friends. They were career women. She wasn't. She did the same when she married me. Her artist friends didn't interest her anymore. They didn't fit."

"That does happen to all of us as our lives change…"

"But slowly. We don't wake up one morning and say, 'I'm going to cut off everyone I've ever known.' Some friends change with us, or stay close even if our lives diverge."

Robin nodded, her ponytail bouncing. Craig noticed the way she held her arms close to her body and wrapped both hands around the coffee cup.

"Are you cold?" he asked.

"What? Oh. No." She frowned. "Not…cold cold. Chilled, maybe. I think you've given me the creeps."

He set down his own coffee on the picnic table beside him and braced his elbows on his knees. "Yeah, this Julie gave me the creeps, too. She was a nice woman, if over the top. Whatever she did, she had to be the best at. Motherhood was a competition, too. She had to be Mother of the Year."

Robin actually did shiver. "Everyone thought of her that way." She pushed out her lip in a meditative way. "What was *her* childhood like?"

"You know, I don't really know." Craig sighed. "It…took on different interpretations. Supposedly, her parents had been killed in a car accident. When I first knew her, her eyes would get misty as she talked about her mom sitting on the floor with her doing art projects. During Julie's career phase, she didn't want to be like her mother who was just a housewife. By the time we moved out here, her mother had gone back to being a model parent. The thing· was, she didn't actually talk about them much. Especially her father. Even when I first knew Julie, I wondered if she'd really *had* a father at home. Mentions of him were always an afterthought. An 'Oops, I should put him in the picture.'''

"And she had *no* friends from her childhood, or college, or…?"

"Zilch."

There had been times after Brett was born that Craig had looked at the woman in bed beside him and thought of the Stepford Wives. Could somebody really be possessed? Could it happen a couple of times? Who was the real Julie?

Come out, please.

"That's the story." Craig gave a smile that probably looked ghastly. "Pretty bizarre, isn't it?"

Robin was thinking again, not listening to his summation. "She was trying to change again, wasn't she? Is that what you're suggesting?"

Hearing it put that way, he felt a chill walk over his skin like unseen fingers.

"Yes," he said slowly. "But this time…she was stuck. Other times, nothing was stopping her. I was the only accessory that had to fit into each new scheme. But the kids, they weren't adaptable. What was she going to do with them? And this *is* a small town. What if she suddenly abandoned the Mother of the Year thing, maybe went into business, became an absentee mother? In the past, when she'd shed her old friends and acquaintances, she hadn't had to keep seeing them.'' Somehow, he'd never defined it for himself this clearly. But now he understood her struggles, her cries that she was smothering. ''First she felt uncomfortable.'' He was quiet for a moment. ''Then trapped.''

''So you think she just…left one day.''

He shook his head, still baffled. ''I'd have sworn, despite everything, that she loved the kids. The look on her face sometimes…'' Craig grimaced. ''But, yeah. I can imagine her shedding this life, too. Most women wouldn't leave their purse, but in her case…''

''It was Suburban Mom. And she wasn't anymore.''

''Something like that.'' He rubbed a hand over his face. ''But I have trouble believing she'd never contact us again. So I've wondered if something didn't go wrong. If she hadn't found someone she was leaving with…''

''And he murdered her.''

''Yeah. I guess that seems the likeliest scenario to me.''

Now was when she should say politely, *Well, that's interesting. I'll have to think about it.* Because, God help him, the whole story sounded ridiculous. Far out. Like science fiction.

Robin *knew* Julie as warm and motherly. How could he expect her to buy his tale of multiple women in the same body?

In the beginning, he'd tried to explain her bizarre changes to the cops without sounding crazy himself. *No, Officer, I didn't kill my wife. She became someone else and left.*

Uh-huh. Sure.

Sergeant Caldwell and his sidekick had just looked at him with contempt and he knew what was going through their heads: *Does he think we're stupid?* Eventually, he'd given up.

Beside him, Robin was quiet for a long time. Craig struggled not to fidget while he waited.

"Do you have any idea *who* she wanted to be next?"

The question was the last thing he'd expected her to say. It skipped right over the "Gee, that's a really weird story but I can buy it" bit.

"Who?" he echoed.

"Yes. Who." Robin pursed her lips at him as if he were being exceptionally dense. "Maybe the other times she was able to change almost overnight, because nothing was stopping her. But this time she had to keep on with one role while she was aching to assume another. She must have showed flickers of who she was becoming. So, who was she trying to be?"

He still gaped. "You don't think my whole story is the equivalent of 'this little alien was in my closet last night, see, and he ate my homework'?"

She shook her head. "No. I *liked* Julie, but... Hmm." Her face was almost comical as she struggled for words. "You've put things that I noticed about her in context. Things that always bothered me a little, I guess."

"Like?" He sounded hoarse, but doubted she'd notice. She was too involved in her own internal replaying of remembered scenes to guess how stunned he was.

Nobody had believed him in so long. Why her?

"I always felt like we should be better friends than we were. But she was either incapable of some kind of deeper relationship or she didn't want it. I couldn't decide which. Women share their histories. They talk about their mothers and their first boyfriends and dreams that didn't come true along with comparing notes on new dishwashers and last year's fourth-grade teacher. The dishwashers and teachers she'd talk about, but the other stuff... Julie just...evaded anything about her past. I realized one day that I knew absolutely nothing about her. Not really. So, while I liked her and we connected about our kids, that was it."

"But she talked to you about me."

"Oh." Her cheeks turned a little pink. "Yes, those last few months. But...something about that bothered me, too. Isn't that funny?" He sensed she was talking to herself now. "Then, I thought it was because nothing she said seemed to jibe with *you.* I mean, the you I saw at practices and games. She'd grumble about you never doing anything with the kids, and I'd look down at the field and there you were with Abby on your shoulders as you cheered Brett on. My husband—" Robin apparently thought better of what she'd nearly said, because she stopped so quickly she almost gulped. "Well, I sat there wondering if you were putting on an awfully good show, or whether she was crazy." She made a face. "I didn't actually mean crazy in the sense you're talking about. Not then. I just thought…well. If she wanted to see a man neglect his kid, she should have met my ex.''

Beneath her flippancy, Craig heard pain. ''Does he see Malcolm?''

''No. He did the every-other-weekend thing, more or less reliably, for the first year. Then, to prove to a woman he was seeing that he was Devoted Father— hear the capital letters?—he actually went back to court and claimed I was keeping him from seeing Malcolm as much as he wanted and that Mal should live with him. I was scared to death. What if some male-chauvinist judge thought a boy needed a father's influence more than a mother's?'' She shuddered and hunched her shoulders. ''It was the worst few months of my life. I'm sure Glenn enjoyed hurting me. When he lost, he shrugged and went on his way. He and the woman he was trying to impress parted ways. Now he calls once in a while. Mal doesn't see him more than every few months.''

Craig's eyes narrowed. ''That's what you were going through a year and a half ago, isn't it? Why you let Brett drop off your radar, as I think you put it?''

Robin nodded, her eyes filled with regret. ''I was so terrified, I let my world narrow to my own problems. I can't tell you how sorry I am.''

''No. You have no reason to be sorry. You've done a huge amount for us now. Even with the new pressure on us, Brett's able to hold on to hope. You gave him that.''

''I don't deserve that much credit,'' she protested. ''All I did was make a phone call.''

''You know better than that.'' Somehow he'd set

down his coffee and half turned to face her. Their knees bumped. "You—and your son—invited Brett into your home. You made him feel like any other friend."

"But…he's a nice boy. None of this had anything to do with him."

"No." His throat felt thick. "But I have everything to do with it, and you invited me into your house, too."

"I…" Her eyes were huge pools of a thousand emotions. Her lips were soft, parted, as if…

He made a guttural sound and realized he was staring. He wanted to kiss her. God, he wanted to kiss her.

He swung back to face the river. "You're a good woman, Robin McKinnon. Most people would say too good. Foolish. Credulous. But I…" He had to clear his throat, and even then heard the raw feel of it in every word. "I'm grateful. You treated Brett like any other kid and me like a human being."

"Craig…" she whispered.

He couldn't look at her. He'd do something he couldn't take back. Something he had no right to do.

"Practice is going to be ending. We'd better get going."

"Oh. Oh!" She jumped from the picnic table. Voice as artificially bright as the Superdome on game night, she said, "I'm so glad you were watching the time! Gracious, I try to be so careful never to be late."

She chattered some more on the short drive back

to the soccer fields, trying—he guessed—to restore some normalcy, to regain distance.

But he couldn't let it go at that. When he'd pulled into the still-open slot next to her car and she reached for the door handle, he said, "Robin."

She went still, then turned very slowly, as if reluctant to face him.

He couldn't help himself. He reached out and touched her cheek. He meant to stop at that, but the satiny texture of her skin eroded his self-control. His fingers slid to her mouth. He felt a tiny vacuum as she drew a quick breath, then the quiver of her lips before he snatched his hand back.

"Thank you," he said, voice husky.

Her teeth closed on her lower lip. She gave him a panicky look, nodded, and fled.

HOURS LATER, he remembered her question and realized he'd never answered it.

Julie must have showed flickers of who she was becoming. So who was she trying to be?

It was a question he'd never asked himself. With quickening excitement, he saw that this answer might give him others.

He lay in bed, moonlight building a silver ladder where slivers slipped through cracks in the blinds, and let himself fully remember a woman who had become a mystery to him, even before she disappeared and left his life in chaos.

CHAPTER NINE

ROBIN HAD FORGOTTEN the upcoming state-wide teacher in-service day until Malcolm reminded her that evening. There'd be no school on Thursday—except for the teachers.

"Oh, dang," she said, pausing with her hands in dishwater. "I know you'd be okay by yourself, but... would you rather go to a friend's house?"

Her son put away the pan he'd just dried. "I was thinking Brett could come over."

"Sure. Or..." Okay, was she nuts here to actually be suggesting this? "Why don't you go to his house? I could drop you off in the morning. If his dad isn't home, his grandfather probably will be."

"You think we're going to play with matches or something if somebody isn't supervising us?"

She laughed at his indignation. "Sorry. I didn't mean to imply that you aren't mature, responsible and completely adult. But you *are* only eleven years old. And Brett has had a few problems at school. He may not be quite as mature, responsible..."

"And completely adult as I am." Mal rolled his eyes. "Okay, okay!"

"So why don't you check with him?"

"Can I quit drying?" he asked hopefully.

"You may."

"Cool!" He whipped the damp dish towel around the handle on the fridge and had the phone off the cradle before she could blink. "Is Brett there?" he was asking as he left the kitchen.

Robin sighed. Why was "May I speak to…" an impossible phrase for kids to learn? Or, better yet, "Hi, Mr. Lofgren. This is Malcolm McKinnon. May I speak to Brett?" She knew her son wasn't alone; his friends all said the exact same thing when they called. "Is Mal there?" Occasionally, just for fun, she said, "Yes," and let the silence dangle. She loved to hear them fumble. "Um…well, uh…like, can I talk to him?"

Mal came back a minute later. "His dad says sure. He won't be home, but Brett says his grandad will."

They arranged for Malcolm to take his soccer gear and for her to pick him up after practice. With a chilly rain falling, she wouldn't have watched anyway.

When she arrived, the boys were already trailing toward the parking lot. Soaked to the skin and muddy, they squelched across the wet grass, their shoes undoubtedly caked. They laughed and yelled insults back and forth, apparently delighted with the chance to play in mud sloughs.

Brett and Malcolm were the worst, she saw with a sigh. Of course. She flipped open the trunk, a signal Mal understood. He grabbed the old comforter from atop the spare tire, slammed the trunk and spread it on the seat before gingerly climbing in.

"I wish I could hose you off," she told him. "Did you have fun?"

"It was *great*." He grinned at her, looking about two years old. "Brett played goal. We dueled."

"Which apparently involved going face first in the mud."

Despite the groundskeepers' best efforts, the grass always disappeared in front of each goal. By the time the rains began in October, the bare, worn ground was ready to become a mud puddle. No, not puddle—pond.

"Yeah!" her son said enthusiastically.

"Did you have a good time at his house?"

"Yeah. Wow! He has, like, ten thousand Nintendo and computer games. His bedroom is bigger than our living room. We set up goals and played soccer with a hackey sack."

Dryness crept into her tone. "Did you."

"His dad's in Montreal. Did you know he flies to Paris and Tokyo and places like that?"

"Yes, actually I did."

He didn't care what she knew. "Can I spend tomorrow night? I'm only at level three on…"

She held up a hand. "Has he asked his father?"

"Brett says he'll be cool with it. We don't have a game Saturday, remember? So can I?"

"Let me think about it," she prevaricated. "No, don't argue. I just want to get home and peel these panty hose off before I make any decisions. Okay?"

"Okay," he said, confident that she wouldn't be irrational.

Or would it be rational to say no? The Lofgren house was the most notorious in Klickitat. Julie had vanished from there, as if aliens had beamed her up.

Brett's father was suspected of having chopped her up in little pieces and put her down the disposal— although the newspapers had assured readers that not even trace blood was found in the disposal. Still…

She parked in their cluttered garage and went to her bedroom, where she kicked off her hated pumps, took off her panty hose and reached for her sweats.

Still… How on earth could she say no? She'd *encouraged* Mal to revive his friendship with Brett, to invite him over, to defend him and his dad against all comers. Now how could she say, ''But I don't quite trust Brett's dad?''

Anyway, she did. Didn't she?

Trudging downstairs, Robin sighed, half her mind on what she could make for dinner and half on her dilemma. Faith was one thing—but putting her son at risk to test her faith was another.

She wrinkled her nose. Oh, for Pete's sake! Even if Craig *had* murdered his wife, he wasn't going to hurt Mal. Why would he?

''Yes,'' she said, the minute she saw Malcolm. ''You can go.''

He let out a hoot and dashed for the phone, calling, ''What's for dinner?'' as he grabbed it.

''I have no idea,'' she admitted, and opened the refrigerator.

Faith, she told herself. Common sense.

The fact that Craig might invite her in for coffee, might look at her again as if he wanted to kiss her— well, that hadn't even entered her thinking.

ROBIN WAS A LITTLE intimidated Saturday when she pulled into the driveway of a house that must have cost four or five times what her little bungalow had. The development was new, the houses all in that $350,000–$500,000 range. All huge, by her standards, dwarfing their lots. Craig's was shingled and stained a deep brown, river rock facing below the front bay window. A few half-grown fir and cedar trees, mulched in beds with the standard rhododendrons, were circled by immaculate lawn. The house would have looked better set in the woods.

His car sat in the driveway next to hers; a blue sedan was parked at the curb in front. His dad's, she thought vaguely— Mr. Lofgren usually drove Julie's red van when Robin saw him.

A next-door neighbor was edging flower beds. Feeling his stare when she got out of her car, Robin waved and called, "Hi."

He gave a curt nod and turned away.

Friendly, she thought, then remembered what Craig had said. Did the man disapprove because she was visiting at the Lofgren's?

On the porch, she rang the doorbell. Craig answered the door almost immediately, his face as blank of expression as she'd ever seen it. She felt tension emanating from him in waves.

"Robin."

"I'm, uh, here to pick up Mal?"

He muttered something under his breath, then squeezed his eyes shut. When he opened them, they were bleak. "I'm sorry. I'd forgotten…" His jaw muscles flexed. "The police are here. I'll call Malcolm down. You'll want to get him out of here."

"Get him out of here?" Robin echoed. "Before… what?"

"They want to interview Brett and Abby again."

"Oh, no," she whispered. "Why? It's been so long!"

"They want to shake Brett's story, of course. What else?"

"Oh, dear." How inadequate! she thought, mad at herself. Mad at that woman cop who apparently didn't care what she did to a sensitive boy.

He shook himself. "Let me get Mal. You don't even have to come in."

"Don't be ridiculous!" she snapped, and darn near pushed past him. "Why don't I stay? Maybe I can talk to Brett afterward." She saw Craig's face and flushed. "Unless…"

His voice dropped a notch. "I'd be grateful. If you're sure…?"

"Of course I am." She crossed the vast parquet entry to a pair of French doors that were open to a living room as big as her whole house. The two cops she'd already met were there, as she'd suspected, the man with his back to her looking out the front window, the woman sitting on a brocade sofa with her notebook open on her knees.

"Detective Diaz." Robin nodded. "Officer Caldwell."

She was glad to see that she'd startled them.

Diaz recovered first. "Ms. McKinnon. You didn't mention that you were friendly with…Mr. Lofgren." The significant pause told her what he'd been going to say, or wanted her to know he was thinking: the suspect. She was friendly with the suspect.

Conscious of Craig behind her, Robin reminded them, "Our sons are friends. That's how I knew Julie."

"You used only past tense talking about Mr. Lofgren," the woman cop said sharply.

"Then I must have mixed up my tenses." Robin met her stare for stare. "My son spent the night with Brett. I'm here to pick him up."

"Then we won't keep you." Her nod was dismissive.

"Craig tells me you intend to interview Brett again. You do understand how traumatized he's been by losing his mother and by the suspicion pointed at his father?"

No hint of regret showed on Officer Caldwell's face. "Nonetheless, we need to take his statement."

"Surely you can find a copy of the statement he's already given."

Craig's hand wrapped around her arm. "Robin…"

Simmering, she subsided.

Robin knew the two officers would discount anything she said from now on, after finding out she was on first-name terms with their suspect.

"I'll get Abby first," Craig said, his voice dead.

Robin waited right where she was. She turned, though, when she heard them coming down the stairs. Abby looked heartbreakingly small and scared, her face white and her eyes huge.

Robin mustered a smile that Abby's panicked gaze didn't seem to register. The two passed Robin and went into the living room. Glued to her father's side, the eight-year-old faced the pair of police officers.

The woman cop said, "Abby, we need to ask you some questions. Will you please sit down?"

The child lifted pleading eyes to her father. He smiled, nodded and gently pushed her forward.

Diaz cleared his throat and in his deep, quiet voice, said, "Don't worry, Abby." He smiled, transforming his impassive face into a gentle one. "You know we're trying to find out what happened to your mom."

She nodded.

He rounded the couch, ignoring his partner, and crouched in front of the little girl. "Do you remember the last time you saw her?"

Her head bobbed.

"Can you tell me about it?"

"She woke me up," Abby whispered. "Just like always. She said, 'Upsy daisy.' So I got up and I got dressed and she made me go back upstairs 'n change, 'cause she said my favorite purple shirt didn't go with my red pants."

He nodded, grinning at her as if he agreed that her mom had been silly; of course red and purple went together!

"Then?" he prompted.

"I had cereal. I didn't like milk back then." Her tone implied it was a long time ago. "So she let me put chocolate milk on my Kix. Sometimes she did, and sometimes I ate them dry."

Robin watched Craig, who was listening to his

daughter with so much emotion on his face, it shattered her heart.

"After, Mom said…" Abby's soft voice cracked. "She said…" Tears shimmered in her eyes.

Craig jerked, as if only pure will was keeping him ten feet from his daughter.

Abby sniffed. "'Bye, Punkin. Be good." A tear rolled down one cheek. "That's what she said. 'N she hugged me."

Craig made a sound, but stood rigid.

Quietly, the police officer asked, "Is that what she said every morning?"

Abby shook her head. "Usually she just said stuff like, 'Do you have your homework? Lunch? Hurry, you're going to miss the bus!'" She'd mimicked adult tones well enough that Robin heard herself as much as Julie.

"Did that seem strange to you at the time? Your mom saying goodbye that way?"

Abby shook her head.

"Do you think now she was really saying goodbye?"

After a brief hesitation, she nodded.

He asked other questions, in that quiet way, eliciting from her the information that Mom hadn't seemed "'specially different" in the days leading up to her disappearance, that she'd never said anything about going away, that she'd been grumpy "'cause Dad wasn't there to do stuff like—" She didn't quite remember what.

"…like drive Brett and me places," she finished uncertainly. "You know."

"Yeah." His smile was unexpectedly charming. "I do know."

"'Cause you have kids," she said with a nod.

"That's right," he agreed.

He glanced at his partner then, for the first time acknowledging her presence. "Any more questions?"

She shook her head.

He smiled at Craig's daughter again. "Okay, Abby. You did great. Thank you."

"Can I go?"

"You sure can."

She sniffed, swiped at her cheek, hopped from the couch and raced to her father. He swung her into his arms and held her tightly until she squirmed in protest.

Setting her down, he said, "Will you tell Brett we need him?"

She nodded and left.

"I'm not sure Ms. McKinnon should be present," Officer Caldwell said in her stiff voice. "Perhaps you'd wait in another room?"

Her face tight with anger, Craig stared her down. "She stays."

She got to her feet. "Mr. Lofgren, you fail to understand. *We* set the terms of interviews, not you."

"No. I may have to let you ask your questions, but *I* control the environment you ask them in. Ms. McKinnon—Robin—is someone Brett trusts."

She looked mad, but when her partner laid a hand on her arm she clamped down on a rejoinder and finally gave a short nod.

Footsteps in the entry made them all turn. Even

Robin, still standing by the doorway, hadn't heard Brett come down the stairs.

Unlike Abby, he did meet her gaze. His eyes dark with turmoil, he looked scared but controlled.

"It'll be fine, Brett." She touched his arm.

He nodded, passed his father without a word and sat down on the couch facing the two police officers.

Once again, Diaz took the lead, although this time he sat on the coffee table, posture relaxed, expression sympathetic.

"Brett, you're aware that the officer who originally investigated your mother's disappearance died recently in a car accident."

The boy nodded.

"So we need to ask you to repeat a lot of the same stuff. Sergeant Caldwell took notes, but he didn't write down everything you said. So it helps us to hear it again."

Another jerky nod.

Diaz leaned forward. "It's very important that you tell us the truth. Sergeant Caldwell thought maybe you were trying to protect your dad. But I think he'd be the first to tell you that he doesn't need you to do that."

The boy stole a scared look at his father.

Craig nodded at his son. Robin could only guess at how much effort it took him to look calm and confident.

"So, let's go back to the night you said your mom told you she had to leave soon." He lifted a brow and asked, as if offhandedly, "How long before she disappeared was that?"

"I don't remember exactly." Brett's voice squeaked and he flushed. "It was, like, a week before."

"Did she take you aside?"

He shook his head. "She always came in after I was in bed. I'd leave my lamp on, and she'd say good night and turn it off."

"But this time she didn't just say good night."

He shook his head, but he also ducked it so he didn't have to meet anybody's eyes. His voice just audible, he mumbled, "It was…I mean, I'm confused, because…because I think maybe I was asleep. Sometimes I think I was dreaming, but I know I wasn't."

Nobody moved; the room was absolutely quiet.

"She sat on the edge of the bed. I could feel it give, you know? And she took my hand. And she said, 'I'm going to have to go away. You'll have to be brave and help your sister and…'" He took a deep breath. "'And do what your dad tells you. Remember, I love you, but…'" Brett drew a couple of shuddery breaths. "'But I have to go.' That's what she said. I mean, that's what I remember."

They led him through the last morning: had his mother said anything unusual? Seemed different? Had the telephone rung? Had he seen any cars he didn't know outside? He shook his head to everything, except he said she'd hugged him goodbye, too.

"Only the bus came, so I pulled away and ran." His face worked. "I didn't know…"

"Of course you didn't." The big cop laid a hand on his shoulder. "How could you have?"

"Because she did tell me. If...if I'd asked Dad about it..."

"If your mom was leaving me," Craig said, "she would have just denied saying anything like that to you."

Brett nodded, his head down so he wasn't looking at anyone.

"Okay, Brett," Diaz said. "I think we're done."

He stood and walked out, pausing for his father to clasp his shoulder.

Officer Caldwell, who had been flipping through her spiral notebook with a frown on her face, said suddenly, "Wait!"

The boy turned. Everyone stared at her.

"Your mother didn't drive you to school that morning?"

He shook his head, his expression bewildered.

"But she did sometimes."

"If she had to go somewhere, or had errands or something, she'd take us on her way. Like, maybe once a week."

"Did your mother say anything that morning about having errands?"

He gnawed on his lip while he thought. "Uh-uh. She was still in her bathrobe."

"Okay. Thank you, Brett." She still looked dissatisfied, Robin saw with interest. Brett had told her something unexpected, something that didn't jibe with what she thought she knew.

Nonetheless, she flipped her notebook shut and stood. "Mr. Lofgren, thank you," she said formally.

He nodded, then gave Robin a distracted look. "Will you show them out? I want to talk to Brett."

"Sure."

Robin accompanied them to the front door. Detective Diaz went down the front steps and started toward their car at the curb. The policewoman turned to face Robin.

"I hope you know what you're doing here."

Robin stared at her in astonishment. "What?"

"This is a man who may have murdered his wife."

Anger stirred. "Only, in a year and a half, you've never found the slightest evidence to support that belief."

In a stiff, supercilious tone, Officer Caldwell said, "His wife, who was universally popular, did disappear."

"After apparently saying goodbye to her kids."

"The boy admits himself that he may have dreamed the entire scene. He's trying to find closure for himself. Assuming," she added, "he isn't lying to protect his father."

Enraged now, Robin snapped, "And Abby? She's lying, too?"

"She said nothing like this in her initial interview. Of course she wants to believe her mother at least said goodbye to her."

"Is it possible nobody asked her the right question back then? Or listened to what she told them? If your father—he *was* your father, right?—had his mind made up, as you clearly do, maybe he ignored anything that didn't condemn Craig."

Temper flared on the other woman's face. "My

father was respected as one of the best. You don't know what you're talking about, Ms. McKinnon.''

Robin tried to soften her voice. "Even well-meaning people jump to conclusions.''

"Or ignore what's right in front of them.''

Robin's hand tightened on the doorknob. "What's that supposed to mean?''

"Either you are being very foolish, Ms. McKinnon, or you're getting your kicks from flirting with a killer. For your own safety, please think about it.'' The policewoman nodded and walked away, leaving Robin gaping after her.

Robin felt as if she'd been dunked in the Sound. Goose bumps sprang up on her arms. She had been foolish. He was a suspect. Julie had vanished without a trace, and his only excuse was…what? She had multiple personalities?

Without thinking, she stepped onto the porch and called, in a voice that shook, "Maybe I need to think, but you do, too. Has anyone ever seriously *looked* for Julie?''

The woman cop, almost to the curb, turned. Her partner looked at Robin over the top of the car. Then, without speaking, they both got in, slammed their doors and, after a moment, drove away.

Robin stood shaking on the porch.

Oh God oh God, she thought. *What if he killed Julie?*

If they didn't find her or her body, Robin would never know for sure. Given the creep her ex-husband had turned out to be, she sure couldn't trust her own judgment.

She should take her son and go home. Now.

But she couldn't do that to Brett. She just couldn't.

Her stomach churning, her chest tight, she turned and went back into the house from which Julie had vanished, never to be seen again.

CHAPTER TEN

DIAZ SAID ALMOST NOTHING on the drive back to the station. Ann stared straight ahead. He didn't have to say anything: he was thinking she hadn't been professional, that she shouldn't have gotten into some kind of personal spat on the front steps. He was thinking she was obsessed with this case and that maybe her father had been wrong.

She resented that most. Sergeant Caldwell had been almost a god around here! Now everyone who'd lived in his shadow was creeping out to whine, "He wasn't that great." Once, he'd been admired for clinging so tenaciously to this case, for insisting that Julie Lofgren not be forgotten. Now, they called it obsession?

They walked into the station side by side, still not speaking. Ann plopped in her chair, her jaw clenched so hard her teeth squeaked.

"I have some phone calls to make," Diaz said. "About the Berg case."

She nodded without looking at him. She heard the unspoken part of what he was saying, too: *we have other cases.* She knew they did! She was working on them, too. But this one mattered! It was the last thing she could do for her father. Her last chance to...

Ann jerked. She glanced around to be sure she

hadn't made a sound. Other detectives were on the phone or awkwardly hammering on keyboards. Nobody was paying any attention to her.

Warily, as if she were easing into a dark warehouse where she knew a hostage was being held, Ann circled back.

Her last chance to make her daddy proud.

That's what she'd been thinking. But Daddy was dead and she'd never know if he was proud no matter what accomplishments she bragged about to his headstone.

She frowned at her heaped desk. Still, this case *did* matter. For his sake to start with, but now because…well, because it was a puzzle. She liked puzzles; she was good at them. She'd become interested in the people, in the mystery, in knowing what had become of that pretty blond mom who had hugged her kids goodbye that morning.

Or had she?

Ann didn't know anymore. She still thought the boy might be lying, but if he was, she suspected the lie was to himself. Or maybe it started as an outright lie, but being a kid he'd convinced himself it was the truth. Or…

Scowling, she unearthed the fat manila folder that held her father's notes. *Had* Sergeant Caldwell asked the little girl what the last thing her mommy had said to her was? Having read through all of this at one time, she found his descriptions of early interviews quickly.

Youngest child unhelpful, he'd scrawled. *Doesn't know where mother went.*

That was it. If he'd elicited more, he hadn't bothered to write it down.

Having met most of these people now, Ann kept
reading.

Brett's story, as reported by Sergeant Caldwell, was
similar to what he'd said today, but not exact. So, he
hadn't memorized a lie word for word and was stick-
ing to it.

Boy upset, her father had written. *Keeps looking at
father.*

Brett, Ann thought, had been ten—no, nine—years
old then. A child. Scared, confused. Of course he kept
looking at his father, his anchor.

Sergeant Caldwell hadn't seemed very interested in
what Lynn Adams, the neighbor, had had to say. *Last
person to see J.L.,* he'd noted. *10:30 a.m. Heard no
disturbance thereafter except dogs barking because
of passing UPS truck. Was in backyard or her house,
never looked out front. Admits to napping—heavy
sleeper?*

Ann blinked. She flipped through the next pages to
find his follow-up, but either those notes had been
lost, or…he hadn't been interested in interviewing the
deliveryman.

Was it possible that he'd let a possible witness go
unquestioned? Why? And then, shocked, she realized.
The UPS truck had gone by too early.

Craig Lofgren hadn't left the airport until—she
checked—11:15, and therefore couldn't have made it
home until almost noon. Sergeant Caldwell had been
sure that the UPS driver hadn't seen anything, because he'd had only one suspect.

No. That couldn't be. He'd let a detail slip. That's all. Everyone made mistakes.

But as she read, she kept noticing discrepancies he hadn't jumped on, gaps where he should have asked questions.

Lynn Adams had assumed Julie was coming home after having driven her children to school. But she hadn't driven them; they'd taken the bus. So where had she gone? She'd have had to get dressed pretty quickly after her kids had gone out the door to get anything done and be home by the time Lynn and she had waved at each other. So why *hadn't* she dropped the kids at school on the way to do her errand, as was apparently her habit?

Maybe she just hadn't felt like it. According to her husband, she'd been unhappy about having to spend so much time with her children.

And yet, she'd said goodbye to them with unusual fervency.

Okay, maybe something came to her after they were gone. She needed—what?—tampons? To mail something? *Where had she gone that morning?*

Sergeant Caldwell apparently hadn't cared. Ann found no suggestion that he'd sent uniforms out to local businesses with her photo.

She kept reading, kept being bothered. He'd done a cursory search for a living Julie Lofgren. He'd checked airlines, bus terminals, Amtrak. Phone records—the only call all morning had been Craig's from the airport, when he left a message on their voice mail saying his flight had been cancelled and he was on his way home.

Sergeant Caldwell had issued a bulletin so that other law enforcement agencies would watch for her.

But what, Ann thought, frowning, if Julie's errand that morning had had something to do with her disappearance? What if she'd met somebody while she was out? What if she used a public telephone so her call wasn't traced? What if she bought supplies—the equivalent of a new purse to replace the one she abandoned?

Sergeant Michael Caldwell had been so certain Julie's husband had murdered her, he hadn't followed up on other possibilities. Not really.

Has anyone ever seriously looked *for Julie?*

Her heart drumming, feeling sick, Ann thought, *No. The answer was no.*

Still staring down at her father's familiar handwriting, Ann saw it as if through a camera lens. The dark scrawl was made tiny, distant and crystal clear.

Perhaps *she* was one of those people creeping out of his shadow to point fingers, but she realized that in the space of the past hour, he had become less godlike, more human. A man with prejudices and insecurities, who had seen in Craig Lofgren what he most despised—or perhaps, what made him feel most inadequate.

And here had been his chance to prove that wealth and success bred arrogance and immorality, that a well-to-do man used to having what he wanted would think nothing of smashing something rather than letting anyone else have it.

Here was his chance to prove that men who had advantages he didn't couldn't be decent.

No, she thought, already retreating from an understanding she didn't want to accept. If he'd acted on prejudice, it hadn't been consciously. Craig Lofgren *was* arrogant. She saw him again staring her down as he said, "No. I may have to let you ask questions, but *I* control the environment you ask them in."

Her father had been expecting to see fear and bewilderment when a wife and mother had gone missing. If he met irritation and disdain for the police instead, he might reasonably have taken that for a thin veneer hiding a killer who was sneering inside because he knew he'd get away with his crime.

Her father had focused on one suspect, that's all. Perhaps he'd done so too soon; perhaps he should have pursued other scenarios more aggressively, but that was an easy mistake to make when you caught a scent and *knew*.

Unfortunately, grocery store clerks wouldn't remember one face at the check-out counter on a particular morning a year and a half ago. Or would they? Ann stared into space, thinking.

Maybe, if someone had read in the news the next day that Julie Lofgren had disappeared, he or she *would* remember waiting on her the day before. If she'd bought seemingly innocuous items, contacting the police wouldn't have seemed important. Especially if news articles reported that she'd been seen arriving home later in the morning.

Energized, Ann opened her notebook. Okay. Time frame. Julie would have had—Ann calculated—one hour and twenty minutes, tops, to do her errand. So she'd likely have gone to Klickitat or Salmon Creek, both within ten minute drives. Unless she'd gone specifically to meet someone, or to pick up one item and make a quick turnaround... If that were the case, they'd never find out where she'd been. But closer to home, they might get lucky.

She had some calls to make before she went back to Klickitat, starting with UPS.

BRETT SLUMPED on the floor with his back to the bed, his knees drawn to his chest, his chin resting on them. Malcolm slouched on the bed looking uncomfortable. Robin had knocked and come in, leaving Craig talking to Abby in her bedroom.

"Hi, Brett."

He glanced up. "Hi. Um... You'd better watch out." He scooted crablike to the middle of the room to shove a heap of dirty clothes and soccer gear out of her way.

"That's okay. My bedroom looks like this half the time." She grinned at his expression. "Well, not really, but it did when I was your age. I've learned to make myself do the minimum to keep the floor cleared, but I still lose stuff constantly."

"Really?" She'd distracted him, at least; he obviously couldn't believe his teacher was admitting to a huge character defect. "I mean, your house is...well, not, like..."

She saved him from embarrassment. "Super neat? Nope. It isn't. I just have so much going on. Has Mal told you I'm writing a book?"

He shook his head. "What kind of book?"

"A novel for teenagers. It's actually my third. The other two haven't sold, but the second one came close and I think I'm getting better."

He scooted back to the bed. "That would be so cool."

"I think so." She nodded at his desk chair. "Do you mind if I sit down?"

Brett shook his head.

"I'm sorry you had to go through that. I mean, downstairs."

He ducked his head and mumbled, "Yeah."

"I just thought I'd see if you wanted to talk about it before I take Malcolm and go home."

He shrugged, his shaggy hair hanging over his forehead.

"That's really tough on you, knowing they suspect your dad."

"Tough on me?" he burst out, lifting his head. "What about Dad? What if they arrest him? Because of what I said about not being sure if it really happened?"

"Now, how can they do that?" Robin was careful to keep her voice calm, reasonable. She was very aware of her own son, listening. "Last I heard, they have no evidence whatsoever that your mom is even dead, never mind that your father had anything to do with it. They need evidence to arrest someone—dried blood, a weapon, a body. Something. They don't have any of that."

"But…" His voice shook with doubt. "Back when…when she first went away…I know they were about to arrest Dad! That cop Caldwell kept saying he was!''

''But he didn't, did he? He was just trying to shake your dad. In case he had a guilty conscience.''

''Oh.'' He picked at a loose thread on the hem of his T-shirt. With a low voice he asked, ''Do you think…I mean, you don't think Dad hurt Mom, do you?''

''Oh, Brett!'' If Malcolm hadn't been here, too, she would have dropped to her knees and taken the eleven-year-old's hands. Or even hugged him. But she didn't want to embarrass him. ''No! Of course not! I don't know what happened to your mom, but I don't believe your father had anything to do with it. If nothing else, he loves you and Abby too much to put you through this.''

Brett sniffed and gave a small nod.

Robin lifted her gaze to see Craig standing in the bedroom doorway. His eyes met hers for a long, silent moment, before he cleared his throat and stepped into the room.

''Hey.''

Brett swiveled and looked up at his father. ''I really blew it, didn't I?''

''Blew it?'' Craig crossed the room in a couple of strides and crouched in front of his boy. ''What are you talking about? You told the truth. How can that be 'blowing it'?''

''Because…because now I'm confused about what I remember,'' he said miserably. ''Witnesses are supposed to know what they saw or heard. Not think they might have been dreaming.''

"But if you're not sure, saying that is the best thing you can do." With his back to Robin, Craig clasped his son's shoulders. "We want the police to find your mom. If we lie, we might send them off looking in the wrong place."

Robin couldn't see Brett's face. He was hidden behind his father. But she heard his heartbreaking uncertainty. "But…you said you don't think they *are* looking. That's why you hired that P.I. back when Mom first disappeared. Right?"

Craig didn't answer for a moment. When he did, he sounded as if he was choosing his words carefully. "I think Sergeant Caldwell was so sure I'd killed her, he wasn't really looking. But then the P.I. didn't find her, either. Maybe I'm blaming Sergeant Caldwell for not accomplishing the impossible. I don't know. Brett, I could be wrong, but these new police officers seem to me to be trying to get at the truth. And they have resources a private investigator doesn't."

His son sniffed again. "They were okay to me. And they did ask a lot of questions."

"Yeah, they did. They asked Abby a lot, too. Some Sergeant Caldwell didn't. I think maybe these two believe that your mom *was* saying goodbye to you two. And if they start believing that, they'll have to look for her, because it means she chose to leave."

"Yeah," his son agreed, first with doubt, then more strongly. "Yeah, I guess so."

"You know it's getting on to dinnertime."

Startled, Robin glanced at her watch. Had she actually been here for nearly two hours?

"How would it be if we go out for pizza? Maybe Robin and Malcolm would like to go with us."

He glanced back at her in inquiry.

She bit her lip. In her head, she heard the police woman's voice.

Either you are being very foolish, Ms. McKinnon, or you're getting your kicks from flirting with a killer. For your own safety, please think about it.

Which was she being?

But neither she nor Mal would be in any danger at a pizza parlor. She could…well, think about this later. Decide.

She sounded like Scarlett O'Hara, Robin thought. Tomorrow was another day.

"Sounds good to me," she said. "Mal?"

Her son scooted toward the edge of the bed. "Yeah!"

"Okay!" Brett said. "Are we going now? I have to find my shoes."

"And I have to go tell Abby to get ready." Rising, Craig looked again at Robin. "Shall we all go in one car? Or do you want to follow us so you can go straight home afterward?"

"Depends where we're going."

"We like Luigi's in Salmon Creek. Unless you have a better idea."

"No, that's one of our favorites, too. We'll follow you." That would give her a chance to talk to Malcolm, too. She hoped she hadn't traumatized him by pushing him into a friendship with Brett again.

Since he was ready, they went ahead, leaving Craig helping his daughter find a second sandal. On the edge of tears, she was insisting she *had* to wear those sandals.

Robin and Mal did their best talking in the car. Conversation seemed to flow when the two people weren't obliged to look at each other. He could slouch in his seat and put his feet up on the dashboard. With such an old car, she had never objected.

"Hey, you okay?" she asked.

"Why wouldn't I be?"

Even her extra-mature son suffered from the male belief that he always had to seem tough.

"It's not every day you're hanging out with a friend who gets questioned by the police about an alleged murder."

"Yeah, I guess so." Most eleven-year-old boys would have decided that actually it was kind of cool being involved in a murder investigation. Heck, under some circumstances Malcolm would have. But this was different. He turned a troubled gaze on his mother. "You don't think Brett's dad *did*...you know. Do you?"

"If I really thought so, I wouldn't have let you go over there, never mind spend the night." Which was the truth, as far as it went. Robin weighed the pros and cons of sharing some of her worries and doubts, but went with the cons. Her son, however mature, *was* only eleven.

"I like Mr. Lofgren."

"I do, too."

"But why would Brett's mom have just...left?"

She hesitated.

Mal gave a shrug meant to be indifferent. "Dumb question, huh? Dad did."

"He did want you to live with him."

"Mom, I'm not stupid." This was one of those moments when Malcolm might have been twenty-five. His face had a wry twist that hid hurt. "I know he didn't want me."

She reached for his hand. "Do you wish he had?"

"No. I mean, not really." His face vulnerable, he met her glance. "I want to live with you. I never would have gone with him. It just…doesn't feel good, knowing my own father doesn't care."

She squeezed his hand again, then put her own back on the steering wheel. "I'm sorry."

"It's okay. Really. His loss, right?"

She'd told him that a million times. Now she smiled. "Big time."

Oh, how she wished Glenn would someday know how much he had lost! She liked to think of him suffering. Dying alone in a nursing home, telling a bored orderly in a creaky voice, "I had a son, you know. It's my fault he's not here."

That was one of her favorite fantasies. She'd have been ashamed to admit as much to anyone else, but every time she saw what rejection by his father had done to Malcolm, she rediscovered her vindictive streak.

Not on a major highway, Salmon Creek was maintaining a small town atmosphere better than Klickitat was. A few new houses had sprouted on vacant lots in town, but the large developments were springing up around Klickitat instead because the commute to

Tacoma and Seattle was shorter. Fast food outlets hadn't yet displaced cafés where old-timers sat for half the day over coffee, refilled with no complaints by white-aproned, middle-aged waitresses who unashamedly eavesdropped on gossip.

She had some qualms about the schools, which didn't offer the choices the Klickitat District could with its larger enrollment. Classes were overcrowded, too. Because she was an employee, Malcolm could switch to Klickitat. But so far, he was happy and she was leaving well enough alone. High school would be soon enough for them to make a change.

Luigi's had been on the main street as long as Robin had lived in Salmon Creek. Walking into the restaurant was like entering a cave. Apparently, Luigi—if there was such a person—thought darkness lent atmosphere. Candles flickered in red glass jars on each table. The pasta here was only okay. The pizza, though, was fabulous, with a thick, chewy crust and a mixture of cheeses that was a little different than usual.

"There'll be five of us," Robin told the hostess, who led the way to a corner booth with a red padded seat that curved in an arc.

Robin and Mal scooted in and looked at the menu while they waited. This was a treat for both. Her budget didn't allow for much eating out.

Craig and his kids weren't five minutes behind them. Brett sat next to Malcolm and Craig slid in beside Robin, a subdued Abby next to him.

Robin glanced at her and raised her brows. Craig shook his head in silent warning.

"Well, do we order a pizza together?" he asked.

They wrangled contentedly, even Abby finally joining in. They ended up ordering two pizzas, pepperoni for the kids, artichoke hearts and chicken for the adults.

When the waitress departed with their order, Robin groped for an innocuous subject of conversation. But Craig surprised her.

"Pretty crummy day, huh, kids?"

"Yeah!" his son agreed.

"Were you scared?" Malcolm asked.

"Um…" Brett fidgeted. "Kind of. Probably not as scared as Abby, but…yeah."

"I wasn't scared!" she flared. "The policeman was nice to me!"

"'Cause you're a little kid."

"I'm not!" she declared fiercely. Then, "You are, too!"

"I am not!"

"Are, too!"

Craig jumped in before the argument could descend further. "Brett, you and your sister are only two grades apart. And, actually, Detective Diaz did seem like an okay guy."

Robin might have been the only one who could tell how much even that admission stuck in his craw, but she admired him for making it.

"He said he had kids," Abby agreed.

"I don't like the lady cop," Brett chimed in. "She's the one who is that other guy's daughter, right, Dad?"

"Right."

"Do *you* like her?" his son asked.

Craig sat silent for a moment. At last he said, "In all honesty…no. I don't. But maybe I expected not to. Because of her father."

"And maybe," Robin suggested, "she expected not to like you, either. Because of her father."

His smile twisted, too. "The thought had occurred to me."

"Are you going to hire a private eye again, Dad?"

"I've been thinking about it." Craig's gaze touched Robin's, his expression unreadable. "I'll give Detective Diaz and Officer Caldwell a few weeks. See if they're really hunting for your mom. If not…yeah. We have to find out." He reached out and gripped Abby's hand even as he looked at Brett. "All of us need to know what happened to her."

Abby looked down and didn't say anything. His face solemn, Brett nodded.

For a moment, it was as if Robin and Malcolm weren't there. Craig and his children were a closed family circle, isolated by Julie's disappearance. They must know that nobody else would ever completely understand what they'd gone through. Robin doubted they even talked about Julie or the investigation or what they felt in front of most people. Perhaps she and Mal should be flattered.

The next moment, Craig forced a smile. "Looks like our pizza is coming. I forgot to have lunch today. I don't know about the rest of you, but I'm starving."

Conversation ranged widely while they ate. Strained at first, it came more easily with each slice of pizza. Maybe it was eating with their hands. How could talk be stilted when your hands were greasy?

Robin talked about a workshop she'd attended on how to recognize bullies and how to deal with the perennial problem for schools.

Craig told a funny story about a flight attendant whose air-filled bra sprang a leak at high altitude. "She was hissing when she brought us our dinners."

By the time they walked out to their cars, they were relaxed, the kids intermingled. Robin had almost— but not quite—forgotten her awareness of how acutely the Lofgrens had become isolated from the rest of the world.

Craig had parked right next to Robin, so he unlocked and let Abby in while saying good-night.

Just as Robin opened her door, he touched her arm.

"Thank you," he said, voice pitched low so that the kids wouldn't hear him. "I'm sorry to have involved you in our mess, but I'm glad you were there today."

"I didn't do anything. Except annoy that policewoman."

He flashed a grin that was only a little wry. "Oh, I do that every time I see her."

The kids had all gotten in, leaving the two adults talking. "I asked her if anyone had ever really looked for Julie."

His face sobered. "What did she say?"

"Nothing. She just drove away."

"At least she didn't lie."

Robin didn't know what came over her, but words crowded out. "She told me I was being foolish."

He went still. "Stepping foot in my house?"

"Something like that."

"Did she scare you?" His voice was low, gravelly.

With his back to the streetlight, his face was shadowed. He seemed…mysterious. Robin thought, *Yes. Yes, she scared me. Yes,* you *scare me.*

Or maybe, she scared herself, because she had the horrible feeling she was falling in love with a man who was married—if his missing wife was still alive.

"I haven't yet kept a tryst with you in a dark alley," she said, making light of the suggestion.

"Only in a deserted park on a gray day."

"We weren't alone," she protested. No—whispered.

"Weren't we?"

Despite herself, she saw the two of them, sitting on the picnic table side by side, thighs occasionally bumping, gazing out at the river. His car had been the only one in the small parking lot at the picnic area. The passing joggers had been the only other people they had seen. The soccer fields weren't far away, but a stand of trees put them out of sight.

With a taut, even angry voice, he said, "Maybe she's right. Maybe you are being foolish. There's a reason, Ms. McKinnon, that most people won't even let their kids come to our house."

She hated the way he said her name, with disappointment and anger and even contempt.

It was the contempt that made her bristle. "You're being an idiot," she snapped, and got into her car, leaving him standing in the parking lot looking down at her. "Good night." She half hoped he'd stop her from closing her car door, say he was sorry, thank her again.

He did none of the above. She couldn't see his expression as she nodded, started the car and backed out. When she drove away, he was still standing there, shoulders hunched, unbearably alone.

If not for Malcolm, she might have turned around and gone back.

If not for Malcolm and the sneering words that she heard over and over.

Either you're being very foolish, Ms. McKinnon, or you're getting your kicks from flirting with a killer.

Multiple choice. A or B.

Unless there was a C. Unless her deepest instincts were right, and she wasn't foolish at all.

Because he wasn't a killer.

A, B or C?

CHAPTER ELEVEN

THAT NIGHT, Craig slumped in an easy chair in the family room, ostensibly watching the evening news. In reality, the flickering images before him were just that—background. The flashing lights of a never-ending carnival.

He grunted at the imagery. Yeah, a carnival. That was life. Dirty and tawdry behind the glitter and hope. And he was stuck on a ride. Probably one of those damn things that twirled you upside down until you puked.

He took a swallow of the soda he'd been nursing—no booze for him, he had a flight tomorrow afternoon.

What a jackass he'd been tonight, reacting with anger because Robin had hinted that the cop's warning had made her a little nervous.

The miracle was that she'd been friendly to start with, willing to reach out to Brett, to treat Craig as if he were any other father. He and she weren't dating. He had no right to feel hurt.

Of course she felt doubt. She should, damn it. She had no reason to believe in him when no one else but his father did.

But he wished she did. She wasn't the fool. He was.

Despite his vows, he'd let himself feel things he shouldn't.

Staring bleakly at the television screen, Craig made himself butt up against reality. Again.

He couldn't have Robin McKinnon, couldn't touch her, had no business even asking whether she might feel the same attraction, until he knew what had happened to Julie.

Which might be never. Divorcing Julie wouldn't free him. Neither would declaring her dead after the seven years Washington state required him to wait.

Conclusion? Stay away from Robin.

ROBIN CAUGHT UP with him when he tried to drop Brett at soccer practice on Friday and make a get-away. He'd succeeded for a week, a victory of sorts. Today, she must have laid in wait, she appeared so immediately.

She smiled and greeted his son, then marched right up to Craig's side of the car, leaving him with no choice but to roll down the window.

She shouldn't have been beautiful in an outfit as ordinary as a red turtleneck, jeans and a navy blue polartec vest, but she was. Just the sight of her, slim, energetic and shining with ideals, made his gut tighten.

She skipped the pretense. ''You've been avoiding me.''

''I was away.''

''You've brought Brett to practice three days in a row.''

He thought about asking coolly if they'd had an appointment. But, damn it, she deserved better.

"Staying away from you seemed like the best thing to do. For both our sakes." The minute the last few words left his mouth, Craig knew he should have kept his mouth shut.

Robin's eyes widened. "Both our sakes? Am I bad for your reputation?"

He scowled at her. "You know it isn't that."

She was as stubborn as a bomber pilot who had his eyes only on the target. "Then what is it?"

She had no idea. He'd be sure it stayed that way.

"I'd like to be friends with you, Robin." *Friends.* That so tepid, he doubted she'd buy it. But, if he was lucky, she hadn't noticed that he was having trouble keeping his hands off her. "But I'd be putting you in one awkward position after another. It's not fair."

She rocked on her heels and considered him, her eyes narrowed now. "Isn't that my decision?"

Increasing desperation made his voice hoarse. "I can't let it be."

"So you're just going to be noble and friendless, even while you push your kids to get back to normal lives."

"Whatever choices Julie made doesn't have anything to do with them. They're kids. They have a right."

Robin nodded as if understanding. "And you don't." She let the silence grow before frowning thoughtfully. "No, we'd better back up a step here. You don't have a right. Instead, you have to live in some kind of...uh..."

He supplied the word from between gritted teeth. "Purgatory."

She blinked, then recovered. "Purgatory. You have to exist forever in purgatory because…"

His knuckles were white where he gripped the steering wheel. "Because I'm married. Because I'm under suspicion of having murdered my wife."

"Even men in prison for *having* murdered their wives have friends."

The first frost might not come tonight, but it would soon. Her nose and cheeks were pink from the bite in the air. Her lips would be cold, too, her breath warm between them.

"Robin, don't push." He sounded harsh.

"I thought…" She bit her lip, nodded and stepped back. "I'm sorry. It's one of my failings."

His chest burned. "No," Craig said roughly. "It's one of your strengths."

Her gaze flew to his then. "Then?"

She wouldn't give up. He was either going to have to be a son of a bitch or he was going to have to bare himself.

Of course, he didn't really have a choice. He couldn't let her walk away feeling…unwanted.

Unwanted. What a joke.

"You…tempt me."

She didn't move, but her pupils contracted. Because he'd startled her? Or because… No. Damn it, he wouldn't even let himself dream.

Raggedly, he continued, "You make me want things to be different. But they can't be. Not until I know what happened to Julie."

"What if…" Her voice was small, husky. "What if you never do?"

With raw honesty, he said, "I don't know. If it weren't for the kids…" Even drawing a breath hurt. He looked away from her. "I try not to think about that possibility."

Robin didn't speak for a long time. When she did, her few quiet words made him feel like he'd just driven into a telephone pole.

"You…make me want things to be different, too." She gave a small painful smile. "I hope they find her, Craig." She hesitated, nodded and walked away, toward the field where their sons practiced.

Watching her go, her back straight, her hair shimmering with every color from wheat to amber in the late afternoon light, he half wished he *had* just gone head-on into a telephone pole. What was the splintering agony of a few broken bones compared to knowing he couldn't go after her? Not now. Not ever.

HE MISSED Saturday's game. Robin feared that was her fault, until she saw Brett's grandfather apparently returning from the concession stand with a steaming cup of espresso after the teams had already lined up.

Robin waved at him and he came over to her. Pretending to puff, he said, "I cut that short. At least I didn't miss the save of the game."

She laughed. "No, that hasn't happened yet."

His grandson was the goalie. Gradually, he'd taken over the starting position while Josh most often played forward.

Oh so casually, she asked, "Craig off somewhere exotic?"

"Montreal again. He claims airport hotels look the same the world around."

"They probably do." She made a face. "Isn't that sad? Surely he does some sightseeing!"

"Oh, I'm sure." He clapped when the other team kicked off and called out encouragement to Brett, then continued, "He brings little things home to the kids. They don't look like duty-free gifts. I'm sure he ventures out. You know, on his international flights, he has at least a day layover. You have to do something to fill the time."

"Mmm," she agreed, then gasped as a blue-shirted player booted the ball toward the corner of Brett's goal.

He made the save and kicked the ball back over the heads of the cluster of boys around the goal, but the game was as fast and aggressive as any they'd played. Within minutes of the second period beginning, Brett allowed a goal. The only goal, as it turned out. His teammates couldn't match it and he walked off the field with his head down.

The other boys slapped him on the back and each said a few words, but after they lined up to congratulate the opposing team, he went off by himself and yanked off his goalie gear, throwing each piece to the ground with violent bursts of frustration.

Malcolm talked to him, then shrugged and came over to his mother. "I'm ready."

"Brett's not coming home with us?"

Her son shrugged. "He says he's too bummed."

Worried, she saw the sulky-faced boy who had first walked into her classroom. The young James Dean, simmering with repressed anger.

Was it just the game that had gotten to him? Or was the renewed investigation and suspicion of his father more than he could handle?

She smiled her sympathy at Mr. Lofgren, who muttered, "Thanks," before going to his grandson and saying, "Ready?"

Robin thought about e-mailing Craig that evening. Online, she typed a few beginnings but erased each and finally closed Microsoft Explorer. Brett was competitive and he felt as if he'd let down his teammates. That was all. She was looking for an excuse, and she should be ashamed of herself for even thinking about using Brett.

Sunday she worked on lesson plans and graded papers. She was a human being and she'd come to terms with the fact that she sometimes had favorite students—so long as she was sure in her heart that she never showed that favoritism. Brett was the student she wanted most to see thrive. She agonized when she had to give him a bad grade and was thrilled when he did well.

Even in his journal, Robin hadn't seen any more violent fantasies—only anger and frustration that seemed more age-appropriate. If he still seethed with rage, he was hiding it well. But she didn't really believe it was there.

On Friday they had peer-graded a vocabulary test, and he had been the only student in the class to get 100%. Today, she was equally pleased to read a short story that was a funny takeoff on *Harry Potter*. He used fanciful imagery remarkably well, especially for a boy determined to display a tough facade to the world.

Ryan, on the other hand, had written about a teenager accused of murdering a teacher, whose body was never found. He got off, but in the last paragraph slyly admitted he'd done it. Robin was not amused. She was also very glad this assignment hadn't been peer-reviewed, and that she hadn't asked students to read their stories aloud without having seen them first herself.

On Monday she asked Ryan to stay in during recesses and start work on a new story. "One that makes use of your creativity, not your desire to humiliate another student."

He pretended not to know what she was talking about, but mumbled and flushed and finally, sulkily, sat down at his desk and went to work. Robin only hoped she hadn't made things worse for Brett.

On her way to pick up Malcolm at school that afternoon, she realized she felt a faint thrum of excitement, just because she might see Craig Lofgren. In fact, she was already dreading the end of soccer season in early November. The boys had gotten to be good friends, but at best they weren't likely to get together more than once a week.

Maybe, she admitted to herself, when she pulled up to the curb and watched her son separate himself from a cluster of other boys, it would be just as well if she *didn't* see Craig so often.

Even if she was absolutely, positively certain he'd

had nothing to do with Julie's disappearance—and she was *almost* sure—but even if she was, she had to respect his decision not to let their friendship grow.

Or had it been an excuse? Had he guessed she was attracted to him and he didn't feel the same?

At this point in her brooding, Malcolm hopped into the car, tossing his book bag in the back seat. "Hey."

"How was your day?" She put on her turn signal and waited until a school bus passed.

He shrugged. "Okay."

"Is this a no-news-is-good-news report?"

He grinned. "Something like that."

"Better get changed," she advised.

His eyes widened. "Oh, no! I forgot my shin guards! Remember? You washed them?"

"And they're still hanging up to dry. Darn." She pulled out. "Well, we go home first then. If we're late, we're late."

He changed as she drove, then ran into the house to grab the shin guards while she waited in the car. They made it to the sports field in the nick of time.

She deliberately didn't look to see whether Craig's car was in the parking lot. Only a couple of parents hung around the sideline today. She had brought her walking shoes, determined to take advantage of the huge field and the paths to the river. She'd felt like a slug lately; she should *use* this time to get some exercise herself.

Robin laced her shoes, locked the car and pocketed her keys. Deciding on the trail for the river, she stepped over the concrete curb, lifted her head—and saw that she wasn't alone.

Craig stood a few feet away, his hands in the kangaroo pocket of a gray sweatshirt. "You look purposeful."

Her heart gave an uncomfortable bump. "I was aiming to get in at least three miles before practice ends."

"Mind company?"

"Not at all." She strode away, arms swinging, as if she didn't care one way or another whether he came. "Although I seem to recall that you intended to avoid me like the plague."

Keeping pace without visible effort, he glanced down at her, expression embarrassed. "I'm sure I didn't put it that strongly. I promise, you don't make me think bubonic plague."

"Oh, good. My ego is rebounding a little bit."

His mouth quirked at her dry tone. "I don't think the woman who marched up to my car last week to demand an explanation of why I was avoiding her is suffering from a deflated ego."

Hiding a smile, Robin sniffed. "I think I could take offense at that."

In a deep, lazy voice, he said, "But you won't."

The trail was just wide enough for the two of them to walk abreast. It curved through a dense stand of trees and emerged to follow the river bank for half a mile.

"I'm actually a coward, you know," she confessed. "I'll do anything to avoid confrontation, unless it's with an eleven-year-old. And that's because I can always win with them."

He laughed. "Bully those sixth-graders, do you?"

"Has your son been complaining?"

His voice became serious. "You know he worships you."

Startled, she glanced at him. "Brett?"

His gray eyes met hers. "You are the coolest."

"Wow. I'm flattered. That's funny, because I was just thinking this weekend that I shouldn't have favorites in a class, but I always do. This year, Brett is hands-down the kid I most enjoy and want to see succeed."

"I don't suppose I can tell him that."

"Don't you dare!" She stopped. "Oh! Look!"

Bald eagles were a common sight soaring above the river; farther upstream were nesting trees. But she rarely saw one this close. White-crested, with cold eyes, a full-grown eagle sat on a lower limb of an old maple not fifteen feet from the trail. In one taloned foot, he held a half-eaten fish.

"I wish Brett could see him," Craig murmured.

She nodded.

The eagle contemplated them with those unsettlingly emotionless eyes, then apparently decided they were inconsequential and tore a piece off the fish. Craig and Robin stood rapt for a good five minutes before she whispered, "Do you think he'll mind if we slip by?"

"He looks as if he's decided we're beneath notice."

She gave a muffled laugh. "Well then, let's just saunter on, shall we?"

The eagle raised his head and watched as they walked by, then returned to his feast.

When a bend of the trail took them out of sight, Robin exclaimed, "That was incredible!"

"It was."

Craig's grin was open, youthful, making her realize how much strain she'd become used to seeing on his face. He'd aged more than he should this past year and a half. Sidelong, she noticed a few gray hairs threading his dark head.

They got back to the soccer fields just as practice ended. The coach sent the boys off to run a lap and called, "Parents, can I talk to you?"

Glances were exchanged, and they gathered around, Craig hovering on the outskirts.

"I haven't mentioned this to the boys, because I didn't want to get their hopes up. You know this weekend was to be another bye."

Nods.

"I got a call last night inviting us to participate in a tournament this weekend in eastern Washington. Most of the teams are select—we're really lucky to be asked. It's last-minute because there was a drop out. Now." He held up a hand to silence the tide of questions and babble. "I know this is short notice. Talk it over tonight. Call me. Majority rules."

"Where is the tournament?" one father asked.

"Walla Walla. It's a four- to five-hour drive."

"Will hotels be available?"

"They're holding the block of rooms reserved for the other team at the Best Western."

"It actually might be fun," Josh's mother ventured.

"Unless the boys get annihilated."

"You know, they're good. I think they can hold their own."

This time he let voices rise and interweave like a dozen rivulets. The first game, he said, was eight o'clock Saturday morning. "We'd need to go over Friday night. Remember, we can carpool. Not every boy's parents have to go."

Robin asked Craig in a low voice, "Are you out of town? I could take Brett."

"Actually, I'm flying out tomorrow morning and will be back Thursday evening. I can go."

She nodded. "It does sound like fun, doesn't it?"

Looking at the other parents breaking into small clusters to chatter, he said, "Maybe."

Robin felt a pang, realizing she'd forgotten for a moment that he wouldn't be a welcome part of the group. He could never forget.

The boys were coming around the back of the goal, those in the lead sprinting. Malcolm, triumphant, threw his arms in the air when he beat Josh and Brett by a stride or two.

"Yes!"

He'd no sooner collected his ball and water bottle and joined his mother than he said, "What did Coach want?"

"Want?"

He gave her his almost-teenage look. "We're not stupid. He talked to you guys about something."

She told him about the tournament and restrained his enthusiasm. "It's okay by me, but the whole idea may get voted down."

"That's not fair! Just because parents don't want to go…"

"You know, it will be an expensive weekend," Robin reminded him. "Two nights in a hotel, lots of meals out, a couple of tanks of gas. I can swing it, but barely. Some families might not feel they can."

That silenced him, although he listened intently when she phoned the coach later that evening.

"You know," he said, "I think your vote puts us over the top. Looks like we're going to Walla Walla."

She grinned at her son and gave a thumbs-up. He let out a whoop.

"Are any of the boys not going to be able to come?"

"So far, Tanner has a conflict. Dylan is going to ride over with Josh and his family."

"Great! We'll look forward to it," she told him.

She'd barely hung up than Malcolm was snatching the phone. "Can I call Brett?"

"Yes, you may."

"This'll be radical!" he declared, and disappeared.

Robin assumed Craig would let his son go. But she found herself secretly—okay, not so secretly!—hoping he would make the trip, too.

ANN WAITED with scant patience while the dark-haired young man in the brown uniform flipped through pages and pages of delivery records.

"April ninth?" he asked, for what seemed the fifth time.

She was losing hope that he would have any memory of a day so long ago. She was surprised he had the IQ to find addresses so that he could deliver packages.

As it was, she'd had to wait until he returned from his honeymoon on Kauai to interview him. Heck, maybe two weeks of surfing and sex had befuddled him.

Striving for an encouraging tone, she repeated the date. "That's right."

"Wait!" He frowned at the columns. "Yeah. This is it. See? 5914 North Tillicum."

She bent forward, as if she could decipher upside-down the multiple abbreviations and notes. "Can you tell what time of day you would have delivered to that address?"

"Yeah. Let's see." He frowned in deep concentration, his square face earnest. "It was my fifth delivery. So, let's see…like, ten-thirty."

She scribbled down the time, then asked the undoubtedly hopeless question. "Do you remember that delivery, by any chance?"

His pleasure faded and he gaped at her. "Remember?"

"I know it's asking a lot. That was a long time ago. But there must be days that stick in your mind for some reason."

"Stick in my mind."

Or not, she thought uncharitably.

"Say, an oddball item you're delivering." She smiled at him as if to say that of course this would happen. "Or a woman invites you in for…a cup of coffee."

"Yeah." He gave her a smile he probably imagined to be rakish. "Yeah, things like that happen."

Ann nodded at the records in front of him. "Is there anything there that triggers a memory of that day?"

"Triggers a memory."

If he repeated what she said one more time, she was going to scream. After a moment, she released her jaw to say, "That's right."

"Oh. I get ya." Frowning again, he read with excrutiating slowness.

She saw no flicker of memory or for that matter, evidence any other kind of brain activity. His lips actually moved when he read a few names. Her minimal store of hope shrank.

"Wait," he said.

She hadn't actually started to go anywhere, but she leaned forward again.

"Wait." His finger was stabbing—she could read that much upside down—the address on North Tillicum. Half a block from the Lofgren house. Could she get this lucky? "That woman yelled at me. She was, like, a real…" He turned red. "Um, you know."

"What was she mad about?"

"The box was dented. I mean, it was. But I didn't do it. I finally told her I'd have my supervisor call her. Because I don't have time to talk. I have to run to get everywhere."

Ann nodded. The UPS carrier who came to her house always tore into the driveway, grabbed her package and half ran to her door. He was always cheerful and always brisk.

On the other hand, weren't boxes dented often and customers irked?

"I take it this woman was more than just irritated."

"Oh, yeah." He shook his head. "I don't know what was in the package, but she got so mad I thought she might have a stroke or something."

"Any of the neighbors around to hear her?" Ann asked.

"I don't know if he was a neighbor, but there was this Volkswagen bus parked—I don't know—a couple of houses down. Just at the curb. This guy was leaning against it, like he was waiting for someone. He laughed and asked if I needed a joint. To decompress. Or something like that."

Ann hid her excitement. "Which direction was this Volkswagen bus parked from the house where you made the delivery?"

"Uh…" He closed his eyes, as though visualizing. "It was off to my right when I was coming down the driveway, so it would have been north." He opened his eyes and grinned. "Yeah! Like 5924, 26. Something like that."

He was placing that Volkswagen bus right in front of the Lofgren house. Maintaining a calm voice took an effort.

"Tell me about this bus. What color was it?"

Blue, he thought, but really faded. Maybe dented. And it had something painted on the side. "You know, like this guy was a hippie or something."

"Did he look like a hippie? How old would you say he was?"

"I don't really remember his clothes or anything.

But he seemed like an aging hippie. You know? I mean, he had to be, like, forty. Or maybe older. But he still had long hair and a goatee.'' He fingered his own chin.

If he didn't remember the clothes, they presumably hadn't been striking.

When she asked about the license plate, he ruminated, but finally shook his head. ''I'm sorry. I didn't have any reason to notice it.''

''I know you didn't. One more question. Did you see anyone else? Did anybody come out of any of the houses while you were there?''

He shook his head with certainty. ''I was surprised the woman was home where I took the package. That neighborhood, people usually aren't. You know? They're all at work.''

He went on to explain that the long-haired man was still leaning against his Volkswagen bus, looking as if he had all the time in the world, when the young UPS driver turned the corner and lost sight of the street.

''I did wonder.'' He looked apologetic. ''I mean, whether I should call the cops or something. Because...he didn't *fit*.''

''You've been invaluable,'' Ann said, rising. She almost hated to admit it. ''If you remember anything else, here's my card.''

''Yeah.'' He jumped to his feet. ''I will!''

Ann went out to her unmarked squad car, but didn't start the engine immediately. A witness not interviewed at the time had now placed a vehicle and an individual who ''didn't fit'' at the curb in front of the

Lofgren house, right about the time Julie Lofgren disappeared.

The direction of this investigation had just changed. But pursuing this lead was going to mean admitting to Diaz and to her lieutenant that Michael Caldwell had screwed up. Had worn blinders, because he didn't like the husband.

Ann had kept her own doubts about the way her father had conducted this investigation to herself. Her habit and instinct was to protect him. Even his memory.

But this time…she couldn't. After a moment, she reached for the key in the ignition. If she was going to figure out what happened to Julie Lofgren that April morning, Ann couldn't hide her father's mistakes.

"I'm sorry, Daddy," she murmured, and started her car.

CHAPTER TWELVE

OH, HE WAS BEING STRONG, Craig mocked himself. One minute he was too noble to taint Robin by association with him. The next thing he knew, he'd seen her set off for a walk and leaped out of his car to join her. Never a hesitation. Not until he saw her face when she was watching the eagle did he think, *Oops, shouldn't be here.*

Because, damn it, she was beautiful when her face went soft with wonder. Would she look like that after a first kiss? He'd pictured her lashes fluttering up, her lips parted, her cheeks rosy.

Forbidden territory.

And now he was about to be an idiot again. He'd dialed half her number, stopped, started again, stopped.

If he was going to this tournament, how could he cruise across the state in his air-conditioned Lexus, wondering whether her old car had broken down somewhere out beyond Ellensburg, where the country got dry and bleak?

Either he shouldn't go, or he should offer her and Malcolm a ride. Even with Abby along, they could drive the van and have plenty of room.

Craig groaned and started dialing again. Maybe

he'd get lucky and find out Robin and Malcolm were already riding with someone else.

"Hello?" She sounded curious. It was after nine, probably too late for most people to call. Craig had waited deliberately until the kids had gone to bed.

"Robin, this is Craig Lofgren."

There was a momentary silence. "Craig," she said finally, in a tone he couldn't interpret.

He cleared his throat. "I got to thinking. Unless you've already hitched a ride for you and Malcolm, I wondered if you'd like to come with us to Walla Walla."

"I'd intended to drive."

"How many miles did you say your car has on it?"

Sounding defensive, she said immediately, "It's been reliable." When he just waited, Robin sighed. "About 216,000."

"I don't like the idea of you breaking down out there somewhere."

"It *is* a major route, you know. Other motorists would be passing constantly."

Okay, he was hearing a loud "Thanks but no thanks" here.

Trying to tell himself he wasn't disappointed, that it would be just as well if she wasn't right next to him for the ten hour round trip, he said, "If you'd rather drive, can we at least caravan? For my peace of mind?"

Again, she was silent for a long moment before saying, "You're confusing me."

He knew the way her forehead crinkled when she was bewildered or thoughtful. Her phone was in the kitchen; chances were, she'd be leaning against the counter, perhaps in her nightgown or pajamas. Pajamas, was his guess. Flannel, with cartoon animals on them. Something cheerful and utilitarian. She wasn't a black lace type.

"Yeah." His voice sounded a little rough. "I can see why." He paused. "I was running scared, Robin. I guess you could tell that. But…I miss having coffee with you."

"Even if you never actually drink the coffee."

Hearing her smile, he found his own mouth curving into a matching one. As crappy as his mood had been lately, the smile felt stiff. "Right."

"Okay," she said. "Malcolm and I would love to ride with you. Actually, my car does need new brakes and I was debating whether I could afford them before next weekend."

"How badly does it need them?" he asked in alarm.

"Not an emergency, I promise! But I don't mind saving five or six hundred miles. *If* you'll let me help with gas money, at least."

For the sake of her pride, he'd take her ten bucks. "Okay."

When he hung up the phone after making plans with Robin, Craig wondered what Officer Ann Caldwell would think if she knew he was falling for another woman before his missing wife had been found.

Or had she guessed?

"I'D LIKE TO DEVOTE more time to the Lofgren case," Ann told her lieutenant.

Balding, with his gut hanging over his belt buckle,

Lieutenant Wilson was an old crony of her father's. She'd never be anything but Caldwell's little girl to him, she was willing to bet.

She'd heard he had recently quit smoking. Now he stuck a toothpick in his mouth and sucked on it while he scrutinized her in unnerving silence. Finally, without taking his eyes from her, he said, "Diaz?"

Her partner, lounging in the office doorway, shrugged. "It's cold. It doesn't justify more than an occasional poke to see whether any stench rises."

Anger at the betrayal tasted like bile in her mouth. "I have new developments. I've been working it on my own while he…"

"Did the job I assigned?"

"We split up our forces," she said stiffly.

"You know, your father had a bug up his ass about Lofgren." The toothpick twirled. "Appears it runs in the family."

"You know this case meant a great deal to him." Her jaw tightened. "Sir."

Lt. Wilson spit the toothpick into his trash can and pulled a bottle of antacids from his drawer. Popping two, he chewed. Ann stood waiting with her shoulders back like a recruit on inspection.

"What new developments?"

"Yeah?" Juan Diaz committed himself to coming into the room, grabbing a straight-backed chair and straddling it backward. "You ever plan to share?"

She leveled a stare at him. "I didn't think you were interested."

"You mean, you know I'm not obsessed."

"I'm not obsessed!" She glared at both men. "I just want…"

"To finish what your father started?" The lieutenant didn't sound altogether unsympathetic. He reached for another toothpick.

Almost embarrassed that it had begun that way, Ann shook her head. "To know what happened to Julie Lofgren. I, uh, I'm beginning to think Dad was wrong."

The toothpick froze an inch from Wilson's mouth. Diaz lifted his head, eyes sharp.

After a moment, the lieutenant stuck the new toothpick in his mouth. "Why?"

She told them what she had learned from asking questions her father hadn't.

"You think this kid really remembers one delivery from a year and a half ago?" Diaz asked.

"I checked records. The neighbor filed a complaint the next day about the damaged parcel. So I went and talked to her. She remembers it and thinks she was perfectly justified in 'dressing down' that young man. He throws packages onto doorsteps. She's seen him, she insisted. She was quite certain he was at fault. And—here's the best part—she remembers him exchanging a few laughing remarks with some guy 'hanging around' outside. Apparently she boiled after hearing them laugh at her, as she interpreted it. Unfortunately, she didn't notice the vehicle."

"Okay," the lieutenant said. "So we've got a young delivery driver who places a vehicle on the street near the Lofgren house. Could've been a boyfriend of some teenage daughter."

Ann shook her head. "He was too old. The driver put him in his thirties, at least. Anyway, I've asked. No teenagers on the entire block. No one has a friend who drives an old VW bus."

"Have you followed up on where Julie went that morning?" the lieutenant asked.

She shook her head. "I haven't had time."

The toothpick bobbed up and down while he thought. "Diaz? You okay on your other cases?"

"Sure."

The sharp brown eyes zeroed in again on Ann. "Okay, then do it. I can't let you off the Gossen murder, but when you can spare an hour, show her photo around."

Ann's shoulders relaxed. "Sir, thank you."

"Know better than your father, huh?"

She froze again. "Not better. I just…have a fresh eye."

The corners of his mouth twitched and incredulously, she came to the conclusion that he was smiling.

"Go." The lieutenant nodded toward the door. "Both of you."

Diaz lazily rose and restored the chair to its proper place. Nodding at Wilson, he sauntered out after Ann.

"Traitor," she growled, the minute they were out of earshot.

He grabbed her arm and stopped her. "He asked for an honest opinion. I gave it."

"You knew this meant a lot to me."

His eyes narrowed. "So I should have lied?"

"You should have supported me!"

"This isn't the playground." He let her go. "Grow up."

She found herself gaping at his broad back as he walked away.

Grow up.

"Jerk!"

ROBIN LOOKED ill-at-ease from the start and Craig knew it was his fault. Why had he ever opened his mouth? In his I-must-suffer-alone dramatics, he'd given away too much.

She'd hinted that she felt the same attraction. Which was nice to know, but he almost wished he didn't, because it made resisting her harder.

The price he'd paid was that she might never treat him again with the same relaxed, friendly warmth she once had. If he had a goal this weekend, it was to erode the wall she'd built. Coax her into forgetting what they had both revealed.

Malcolm had bounded out of her house when Craig and Brett pulled up in their van. After dropping his duffel bag on the sidewalk and leaning a lawn chair against the side of the van, he poked his head in the sliding side door. Spotting the small TV monitor poised between the front seats, he proclaimed, "Awesome! I'd forgotten you had a TV in here."

"We can play video games." Brett opened the box at his feet. "See? I brought…"

Craig didn't hear what he brought. Didn't care. Dressed in chinos, Robin was locking the front door, a suitcase at her feet and a carry-on slung over her shoulder. He hurried up the walk.

"Let me get that."

She turned a polite smile on him. "Don't be silly. It's on wheels."

"That one looks heavy." He reached for the bag over her shoulder.

"Well…thanks." She trailed him, pulling her small suitcase. "Mal, are you sure you have everything? Uniform? Shoes? Shin guards?"

Her son rolled his eyes. "You've asked me, like, three times. I'm not that stupid."

"So I fuss." She lifted her own suitcase into the back of the van. "Oh! Where's Abby?"

"At a friend's," Craig said. "She wasn't excited about spending the entire weekend watching soccer game after soccer game."

"The hotel does have a pool."

"But I couldn't leave her at it." He put her lawn chair in with his, then added Malcolm's bag to the heap. "She wrangled an invitation from her best friend."

"That was probably smart."

Malcolm and Craig's son had both buckled in and were huddled over the shoe box full of video games. Robin shook her head, climbed in herself and fastened her seat belt.

"Julie loved having that TV in the van."

Hearing constraint in her voice, Craig raised a brow. "You don't approve?"

"Mal and I do our best talking in the car. I think kids watch enough TV without taking it on the road."

"I agree." Out of the corner of his eye, he saw her

surprise. "Julie and I had a mild argument about it. She won."

Robin stroked the seat and looked around. "Have you been tempted to…" She hesitated.

"Sell Julie's van?" He kept his voice low. "Damn straight. But when's the moment to decide she's not coming back? I keep thinking about what the cops would think, and what the kids would think. They still say, 'Can we take Mom's van?'"

Robin nodded and folded her hands primly in her lap. "I have to admit, when I saw your dad pull into the parking lot with it the first time, I thought, oh, there's Julie."

"I should have driven the Lexus."

"No, this is okay. The boys'll have fun. Besides…"

"She's not coming back?"

Emotion battled on her face, ending with a sad twist of her mouth. "I suppose that's what I was thinking."

"It's roomier. I thought it would be more comfortable for this trip."

Robin nodded. "Really. It's fine. This is so nice of you."

When she said things like that, he was conscious of the formality in her voice. It made him grit his teeth.

"I figured we could stop in Ellensburg for dinner, if that works for you."

"Sure." She smiled brightly in his general direction. "I've actually never been to Walla Walla. Have you?"

The conversation for the first hour stayed at about that level. They discussed scenery, alternate routes, traffic and the hope for heavier snowfalls this winter to fill the reservoirs for summer. Once, near the Snoqualmie summit, an SUV owned by one of the other families passed and Craig beeped while the boys made horrible faces at each other out the windows.

The ski area atop the pass was still bare of snow.

"I'm sure they're hoping to open by Thanksgiving," said Robin, gazing at the brown slopes and ski lifts marching up the slope.

More weather. Hoping to get slightly more personal, Craig asked, "Do you ski?"

"Hmm? Oh, I used to. Malcolm took the school ski bus up last year and started lessons. It's gotten so darn expensive, though." She looked wistful. "Do you?"

"A couple of times a year. The kids started young. Abby loves it, Brett hates being cold."

Robin laughed. "Did you learn as a child?"

Glad she was curious, he told her about his family's annual one-week stay at Lake Tahoe.

"So you're a Californian?"

"Bay area. Dad owned an office supply store in San Mateo, just south of San Francisco. The chains were getting to be heavy competition about the time he decided to retire and sell out, but he hears his store is still hanging in there." He told her about his mother, who had designed and sewed children's clothes, which she sold in small boutiques. "She'd have loved to dress Abby now." Silent for a mile or two, he said finally, "She had a stroke. It was a real shock. She was just starting rehab to get back full mobility when she had a second one that killed her.''

"I'm sorry," Robin said softly. "Had the kids been born yet?"

"Yeah, Brett remembers her. Abby was only two when she died. Only a couple of years later, Dad sold his store and moved up here to be near me and the kids." He shook off the memory. "What about you?"

"I'm a Washington girl, born and bred. My parents moved a couple of times when I was growing up. We lived in Spokane until I was eight or nine, then came to the west side of the mountains. I graduated from high school in Marysville, just north of Everett, went to Western Washington University in Bellingham, and then got my first teaching job in Tacoma. That's where I met Mal's dad."

Craig had been itching to know what her ex-husband was like and why her marriage had failed.

"How long have you been divorced?"

"Two-and-a-half years." She nibbled on her lower lip.

Craig had to tear his gaze back to the freeway, curving ahead down from the mountains toward the dry, open country of eastern Washington. He doubted she had any idea how sexy she was.

She sighed almost inaudibly and glanced over her shoulder at the two boys, whooping as Brett took a turn with whatever bloodthirsty game they were playing.

In a low voice, she said, "I told you about the nasty custody battle. Glenn didn't actually want to raise a son. Even Malcolm knew that."

"You were given full custody?"

"Oh, he has visitation rights, which he rarely bothers to exercise." Under her breath, she added, "Thank heavens."

"What went wrong in the first place?"

"We got married." She laughed at his expression, although her mouth had a sad twist. "It was just…a mistake. I don't know what we ever saw in each other. He liked hanging out at bars with his buddies. He bowled once a week, he drank beer and watched football games when he was home and a *Terminator*-type movie was his idea of a great night out. As it turned out, he had old-fashioned views of gender roles, too. One of those things you don't learn when you're dating. Housekeeping was my job. I was supposed to have dinner on the table at an hour that suited him and he never touched a diaper."

Reflecting on his own mistakes, Craig said, "We don't use our heads when we're young and in love."

"Apparently not. The truth is, Glenn and I were married eight years too long. But I can't regret a thing. If not for him, I wouldn't have Malcolm."

"Yeah." Craig looked at his son in the rearview mirror. "I think the same thing sometimes."

They were silent for five or ten minutes, but comfortably so. After a while, he was the one to ask, "If *Terminator* wasn't your idea of a good time, what is?"

They were deep in a discussion of movies and theater when they reached Ellensburg. The boys voted for pizza and Craig took the exit that seemed to have gas stations and fast-food restaurants clustered around it. He found a Godfather's, where they ordered, got drinks and salads and gathered at a table.

"Can we go swimming when we get there?" Brett asked eagerly. "Huh, Dad?"

Craig shrugged. "I don't see why not. We have a long ways to go, though. I doubt we're halfway."

"That's okay. We're having fun."

"Yeah!" her son agreed. "We can drive all the way to New York, if you want. I don't care."

The two boys thought that was funny. The adults had to laugh, too. Craig had the fleeting thought that he wouldn't mind, either. Driving on and on, Robin beside him, intimacy growing.

Malcolm looked at Craig. "It must be so cool to be a pilot. Do you feel, like, *powerful?*"

"No. I flew a fighter plane in the Navy, you know."

Awe transformed the boy's face. "Really?"

"It's...exhilarating. But if you're smart, you learn some humility, too."

With Robin's encouragement, he told them about his early fascination with airplanes and flying. His father had paid for lessons in a two-seater, probably assuming he'd outgrow the phase, but instead he had become single-minded.

"All I wanted was to go into the Navy. I saw myself launching from an aircraft carrier." He smiled and shook his head at his youthful determination.

"I still love to fly. There's a serenity and freedom up there, with the earth so small below, that I've never found anywhere else."

"Could you have applied to the astronaut program?" Robin's son asked, expression avid.

"Yes, but I didn't consider it. I like flying above the earth. Not leaving it."

Malcolm nodded. "But imagine walking on the moon. Or Mars. That would be totally awesome!"

Robin looked less than thrilled at the idea of her son rocketing into space. Craig remembered his mother having a similar, slightly horrified expression as she listened to him dream aloud.

"It would be," Craig agreed. "Seems these days, though, after budget cuts, the NASA pilots are mostly glorified delivery men."

"Satellites." Malcolm nodded. "But they go out on tethers to fix stuff. They get to, like, *float*. I'll bet they feel really heavy when they land on earth again."

"I didn't realize you were so interested," Robin commented.

"Remember that space unit we had in school last year? I've been reading more about astronauts and astronomy ever since."

Craig cocked his head. "That's our number. Boys, do you want to go get our pizza?"

"And plates," Robin called after them, as their chairs rocked in their wake. "An astronaut," she muttered.

"You know, this too will probably pass," Craig pointed out.

"But your passion for flying didn't."

"No, but it was a little more practical than aiming for space travel. Getting into the astronaut program is…'' He broke off when the boys returned, Brett triumphantly carrying the pizza and Malcolm the plates.

Night had fallen by the time they left the pizza parlor. The lights of Ellensburg quickly fell behind them. The boys put in a movie and talked more quietly. Craig and Robin alternated periods of silence with relaxed conversation about everything and nothing: favorite foods, the worst movie they ever saw, the scariest teacher they could remember having, the friendships that endured from childhood. In the middle of telling Robin about his disastrous high school prom, Craig broke off.

"You know, it just struck me. This is the kind of thing Julie and I never talked about. I know her favorite food, but nothing about her high school friends or the first guy she ever kissed."

"Will Calpeno." Robin let out a low, delicious chuckle. "Oh, dear. You probably didn't want to know that."

"Yeah, I did," he said, smiling even though she wouldn't see. "Was it exciting?"

"It was awful! I was…um, twelve, I think." Amusement laced her voice. "I didn't know he had a crush on me. I felt sorry for him because he was short and his mother used to hug him right in front of God and the whole school when she picked him up afternoons. Anyway, he cornered me at a middle school dance, stood on tiptoe and pressed this wet mouth on mine." She made a gagging sound. "I don't think I was nice to him after that, although I felt guilty for being so repulsed. The funny thing is, by our junior or senior year in high school, he'd shot up and was actually pretty cute.''

"But no second kiss for you," Craig guessed.

"Heck, no! I don't think he ever looked me in the eye again." She laughed, shaking her head. "Okay. Your turn."

"I was a late bloomer. I was thirteen before I worked up the nerve to kiss a girl. Rita Wills. Her friends had asked my friends if I wanted to go out with her, and I sent word back that sure, why not? Which meant I danced with her and we hung out together while we waited for the school bus. The pressure built, though, and I knew I had to make a move. I was self-conscious about braces." He felt old, remembering. Kids were different now. More sophisticated. Probably half of them were sexually active by fourteen or fifteen, not shy about a mere kiss. Not an idea he liked in connection with his own two.

"Tell me she didn't wear braces, too."

"No, although a friend of mine did get his tangled with a girl's when he kissed her." Craig grinned. "The father had to pry them apart."

"Killed that romance, I'll bet."

"I think the girl's father did use the word 'kill' at some point."

She giggled. "How awful!"

"No, my first kiss was entirely unmemorable. A peck. No fireworks, no desire to prolong it. She scared me. She broke up with me a few days after that."

He loved the sound of her laughter. It was soft, bubbly, almost musical. Pure joy, expressed.

Perhaps a mile passed in easy silence. Craig caught

a few lines of dialogue from the movie the boys were watching. *Shanghai Knights,* he diagnosed. About their level of humor.

"You know," Robin said, "Glenn and I never really talked like this, either. It hadn't occurred to me before. I'd laugh at myself, but he always bragged. He told glorious stories about triumphs on the football field, or showing up a teacher, or bagging the head cheerleader. He could be funny, so when we first met I thought…" She gusted a sigh. "I actually thought his stories were tongue in cheek. Silly me."

"Is he good-looking?"

"Obviously, *I* thought so." She sounded disgusted, but then laughed again. "He is handsome. He really was a good athlete. He'd have been drafted by the pros if he hadn't wrecked his knee. I think in a way that broke his heart. That was his dream, and he was so close…" She fell silent again.

But the idiot had thrown away an incredible woman and a great son. Craig had no sympathy for him.

"Tri-Cities," he announced loudly enough for the boys to hear.

They peered briefly at the lights reflecting on the Columbia River as they crossed it for the second time today. Seeing a mileage sign, Craig said, "It shouldn't be more than about forty-five minutes to Walla Walla."

The boys cheered and went back to their movie.

"I'm glad you offered us the ride," Robin said suddenly, when the highway had become narrow and dark. "The drive has gone really fast."

"Yeah," he said with regret. "It has."

He couldn't let the silence last. Craig felt this hunger to know everything about her. "Tell me about the book you're writing."

This was her dream, he realized immediately when she started talking. Her voice gained animation, hope. She talked about her first efforts and then this young adult novel, a coming of age story set in the early days of logging in the Pacific Northwest.

"I really love it," she concluded with a small laugh. "I guess you can tell."

"Having something you love rejected must sting."

"I sulk for days." She paused. "But I've gotten better with each book and each revision. The editors have been right. I think this might be the one."

"Would you quit teaching if you started selling?"

"Heavens, no! In the first place, not many authors of childrens' books actually make a living, from what I can gather. Anyway, I love teaching, too. I'd probably run out of inspiration without being surrounded by kids all day. I can do both. I'll bet I could write a book every summer."

Not many people had two gifts. "I'll be rooting for you."

"Thank you." Her voice had a tiny hitch, as if he'd actually moved her. Maybe she hadn't had too many people rooting for her.

Not likely, he told himself. She must have plenty of friends. For all he knew, she dated regularly. He hadn't figured out a way to ask that yet. How could he, when he had no right to care about the answer?

"Boys," he said over his shoulder, "I do believe we're here."

CHAPTER THIRTEEN

THE ROOMFUL of grocery clerks shook their heads. One contributed, "I've seen her picture in the paper. But she never shopped here that I know of."

"Thank you." Ann nodded at the manager, who had gathered the crew that had worked the morning Julie Lofgren disappeared.

Outside, she crossed another business off her list. She'd started two days ago with the stores where Julie had been a regular customer. Nobody who worked at any of them remembered seeing her the morning of her disappearance. Now Ann was moving on to stores where Julie might have hoped not to be recognized.

The whole idea was a long shot. In a year and a half, people moved, changed jobs. The one clerk who'd waited on her might have gone to join her boyfriend in Sacramento by now.

Ann might find the right one, who wouldn't recognize Julie. Or she might not have read the newspapers about the missing housewife, and therefore might not have pinpointed the day in her memory.

Heck, it might turn out that Julie had run to the store for milk and eggs so her family didn't have to grocery shop for a couple of days. She might have gotten a pedicure so her feet were sexy for her lover.

The possibilities were endless, and most would offer no clue to where she'd gone.

Nonetheless, Ann moved her car to the main street, parked and went into the first small store, a gun shop. Hey, you never knew.

The bearded, tattooed, potbellied proprietor looked wary at the sight of a cop but took the photo and studied it. He handed it back, shaking his head.

"Never seen her outside the *Times*."

Two hours later, she'd seen a lot of heads shaking.

"Nope. Sorry, ma'am. I mean, Officer."

On that last morning, Julie Lofgren hadn't bought a gun, an ice-cream sundae or a new windshield for her van. She hadn't bought dog food for a nonexistent dog, vitamins from the health food shop or a cholesterol-laden breakfast at the café.

She hadn't gone to the farmer's supply, the bakery or the furniture store.

A few of the proprietors knew her. She apparently did shop at the health food store occasionally, for example, and had taken troops of kids into the Taste Treat for ice-cream cones.

But, "Not that day." More head shakes.

Half a dozen antique stores later, Ann was down to the AM/PM market and the side streets. Nobody at the AM/PM had the slightest idea who had worked there a year and a half ago. Ann couldn't think of anything—except maybe a map—that Julie might have bought there that would shed any light on her whereabouts anyway.

Ann checked with several dental offices—no cigar—and a place that gave karate lessons. The consignment shop that sold baby and children's clothes seemed like a long shot, given Craig Lofgren's likely income, but Ann asked at every single open business. No, Julie hadn't felt compelled to snap up a used playpen or toddler-size overalls.

The Volunteers of America thrift store occupied an old house. Ann climbed the steps and went in, ignoring the miscellany of battered and cheap furniture that filled the front porch.

She'd have to give up for the day soon; she shouldn't have spent this long. Knowing that Diaz was working twice as hard to make up for her absence was an itch she couldn't ignore. Ann didn't like owing him in any way.

A sweet-faced, elderly woman with blue hair sat behind the glass counter filled with costume jewelry. "Oh," she said brightly, after finding her glasses to peer at the photo. "Mrs. Lofgren gave to us regularly. Bags and bags of children's clothes, always in wonderful condition. We were so grateful to her!"

Ann explained her mission, concluding, "Is there any chance she brought in a donation that morning?"

As if it would do any good to find out she had.

"We felt so dreadful when we read about her disappearance. Oh, dear, let me think. Was it Edith…? Or Myrtle…?" She pushed herself to her feet. "Myrtle!" she bellowed, in a voice that had Ann's eardrums quivering, like a trampoline recoiling from a bounce.

Myrtle was even older, surely not five feet tall, her face a mass of wrinkles. In her starched blue apron, orthopedic shoes and polyester slacks, she made her way between racks of women's dresses and men's sports coats.

"Did you call me?"

"Do you remember us talking about Julie Lofgren? Her being in here right before she disappeared?"

"Right before" would probably turn out to be a week before, Ann thought with resignation. Nonetheless, she had to follow up.

"Yes, but it wasn't me who was here." Myrtle pursed her lips, which had the effect of making them disappear. "Let me think. Was it Lavinia? Or Edith?"

Both women were reasonably certain Edith was the one who had excitedly told them about seeing Julie. They called her and explained. Edith Safford—a widow, they murmured confidentially—said she'd be glad to talk to Ann, who thanked the two women and walked five blocks back to her car.

Edith lived up the hill, in a tiny house with a white picket fence that was collapsing. Yet her garden was carefully tended, with bright, spiky asters and dahlias in fading bloom in beds along the fence.

Edith was a little younger than her fellow volunteers, but not by much. She was developing the hump of osteoporosis, and had to peer up at Ann when she answered the door.

"Why, you don't look like a policewoman!" she exclaimed. "Come in, come in."

"In major crimes, we rarely wear uniforms."

"Oh, it's not that. You're just too young and pretty!" She chuckled. "But I do realize women don't wait to join the force until they're plump and forty."

Actually, they were more likely to have left it by

then, Ann reflected. Starting a family often brought about a change in career.

"Thank you for the compliment," she said. "Now, about Julie Lofgren…"

"Oh, that was so terribly sad!" At a shuffle, Edith led the way into her minute living room, where a love seat took the place of a couch, the arms covered with crocheted doilies. "Would you care for a cup of tea? Or coffee? I only have instant, but…"

"Thank you, but I'm afraid I don't have time."

She had to make time to hear all about that sweet Julie Lofgren—wasn't she so pretty? and so young to have something so awful happen to her. She even heard about the darling baby clothes—they didn't even look worn!—that she'd donated.

"Why, I remember one exquisite midnight blue velvet dress with lace trim that must have cost $100, and she admitted her little girl had worn it only once, for a photography sitting! She even showed me the picture. Her daughter was so cute!"

Ann felt her eyes glaze. She guessed Abby Lofgren was cute enough, as children went.

"I understand you saw her…"

"Of course, her little boy was so handsome, too! Just like his father. She showed me his photo, too. A fine-looking man. I was shocked to hear that he might have hurt her."

"We haven't determined whether he was involved in any way in his wife's disappearance. We're still pursuing our investigation."

"But she's been gone for so long!" Edith gazed at her with watery, disappointed eyes. "I've read that with the Internet and all, tracing people has become easy. And if she were dead, wouldn't her body have… well, floated up or something by now? Like that horrifying case in California?''

"Yes,'' Ann said with eroding patience. "I would have expected to find her body by now. That's why we're once again investigating Mrs. Lofgren's last few days, to see if we can't find a clue to what happened to her.''

"But nobody talked to me before.''

"Can you please tell me when you saw her last?''

"Why, I thought you were here because you knew! It was that morning.'' She bent forward. "I would have called 911, but I read in the paper that a neighbor saw her arriving home after she shopped at VOA. So I wasn't the last person to see her.''

Excitement charging her, Ann asked, "You're certain?''

Edith's face crumpled in confusion. "That I wasn't the last person?''

Deep breath. *We all get old.*

"No,'' Ann said. "I meant that she was in the thrift shop the morning she disappeared.''

"Oh, yes! We all discussed it the next morning, after we heard the news. Yes, I'm quite sure.''

Shopped. She hadn't donated, she'd shopped.

Carefully, Ann asked, "Mrs. Lofgren didn't bring in a donation that morning?''

"No, although she assured me she had some bags almost ready to come. 'Brett is shooting up,' she said. 'He outgrows clothes as fast as I can buy them.'

Her patience getting thin again, Ann tried to steer her back to the facts. "Did she buy something that morning?''

"Yes, indeed! She said she'd gotten involved with community theater. You know there's quite an active one in Salmon Creek. Why, they just did a lovely job on *Crimes of the Heart.*"

Ann unclenched her teeth. "What...did...she... buy?"

Looking startled and even affronted at her brusqueness, the elderly VOA volunteer said succinctly, "Hippie clothes."

"Hippie clothes?" Her mind was racing, connecting the dots. Volkswagen van, long-haired man waiting. Husband unable to tell police what clothes might be missing from his wife's closet.

Edith gave a stiff nod.

Ann leaned forward. "This could be very important." She paused while Edith unbent. "Can you describe what she bought?"

The elderly volunteer couldn't describe every item, but she did remember there were a couple of pairs of low-cut jeans frayed at the hems, a black crocheted shawl, a man's shirt and a purse. A drawstring suede one with fringe.

"Oh, and sandals. Used Birkenstocks. She seemed quite delighted with them."

Craig Lofgren's wife had bought an entirely new— well, secondhand—wardrobe only an hour or two before vanishing.

"Thank you," Ann said, rising. "Thank you very much. You have a remarkable memory, Mrs. Safford."

She blushed and disclaimed, but was clearly

pleased with her part in an ongoing police investigation.

Ann departed with her notes and vindication.

"Wow!" Robin touched her throat. "I think I'm hoarse."

"Wouldn't be a shock." Across the dinner table from her, Craig grinned. "You should have heard yourself screaming, 'Kick it! Kick it!' The way your foot was going, I'd have had bruises if I'd been standing in front of you."

She made a face. "I get excited."

"I noticed."

"Mom always screams." Malcolm licked the last ice cream from his spoon. "I barely hear her, though."

"Oh, great," she muttered. "I'm wasting my voice."

"Yep."

"Brett?" she asked hopefully.

Craig's son shook his head. "When I'm playing, Coach is, like, the only person on the sidelines I notice."

"Me, too," Mal agreed.

Robin threw her hands in the air. "I'll shut up from now on."

"I'll believe that when I see it," Craig teased.

"Yeah." With regret, Malcolm set down the spoon. "I bet you can't."

"What?" she exclaimed in mock—and maybe real—indignation.

Looking extraordinarily handsome in a heavy navy blue Polo shirt, Craig cocked a brow. "If I were you, I wouldn't let this go any further."

She sniffed, "If I choose to accept a bet from my own son…"

"You'll spend tomorrow sitting on your hands. With tape over your mouth. During the semifinals." He paused for effect. "And maybe the finals. Where's the fun?"

Dang it, he was right. Whatever they said to the contrary, she *could* sit placidly watching the game, if she had to. She just didn't want to.

"I enjoy cheering you on. Is there anything wrong with that?"

"Nope." Her son gave her a sunny look. "Are you guys done eating? 'Cause Brett and I are ready to go back to the room."

"You can't swim for a while."

"We know. But we can watch TV, can't we?"

"Well, sure." She looked at Craig. "Are you ready?"

"Why don't we stay and have another cup of coffee? Sitting on a hotel bed watching television on Saturday night doesn't appeal to me."

"Me, either," she admitted. "Go ahead, guys. Here." She bent and rummaged in her purse. "Take my key. Just don't go anywhere until we get back, okay?"

They agreed and shoved their chairs back with the social aplomb of mountain gorillas invited to the Plaza.

"Oops!" Malcolm said, when a waitress had to dodge with a tray of dinners. "Sorry!" he added hastily, before bolting.

Robin turned her head as if she didn't know them.

After a day spent at the soccer fields—the boys had

won three games—she and Craig had decided to eat at Jacoby's, a restaurant across the parking lot from the Best Western hotel. Jacoby's was in what appeared to be an old railroad depot, with one dining room in a railroad car. The boys had turned pleading eyes on the hostess, who had laughed and seated them in the narrow car.

Several of the other families were here as well, some at tables next to each other in the main dining room. Madeline had called to Robin when they walked in.

"Robin! Won't you join us? Oh!" She pretended to surprise at the sight of Craig and Brett. "Are you two already…"

"Yes, I'm joining the Lofgrens." Robin had managed a smile for everyone.

Not a soul said, "Sit with us." They always nodded civilly at Craig, and would never be outright rude, but he made them uncomfortable. He knew it and they knew it.

"The boys want to eat in the railway car," Robin said.

There were smiles and murmurs of relief. Her chest felt tight with distress when she continued after the hostess, Craig behind her.

"If you'd rather join them…"

She had shaken her head. Because of the boys, Robin had let the subject go.

But now, with just the two of them at the table, the candle guttering low, the light dim, she said, "I wonder what would have happened if we'd just joined the rest."

She wished she hadn't said anything when his face became expressionless.

"Nothing." He shrugged. "They're nice people. For Brett's sake, they would have been pleasant."

"How can you be so calm about it?"

"Practice." His mouth twisted. "At least these families are willing to be decent for Brett's sake. Not everyone is."

"So much for a nation founded on the principle of innocent until proven guilty."

He actually let out a low, rough laugh. "Public opinion has never been that restrained, Robin. You know better."

"I guess I didn't," she admitted. "I understand why people who don't know you would be wary, but this is a public place. They're safe."

His long fingers toyed with his coffee cup. "I doubt it's literal fear, as least in their case." He nodded toward the other dining room. "More a level of discomfort that shuts down conversation."

She hated his acceptance as much as she did his impassive expression, which must hide a cauldron of bitterness and anger and humiliation. "Cowards!"

"Maybe." Craig's mouth relaxed. "You're the abnormal one, Robin."

She sniffed.

Now he was almost smiling, but his eyes were watchful. "Are you so sure I'm not a murderer?"

"Yes!" she snapped without thinking. Surprise—no, not even that—*confidence* came in the wake of her instinctive response. Not even a thread of doubt remained. She knew this man would never have hurt his wife, no matter what.

He blinked and sat back. "I wish..." He cleared his throat and said more clearly, "I wish I'd met you in other circumstances."

"Why?" Her heart was pounding and she knew what she wanted him to say.

"Because..." Craig stopped. A muscle twitched along his jaw. "No," he said, with a ragged edge to his voice. "If the circumstances had been different, I'd never have known..."

"Known?" she whispered.

"How extraordinary you are." He reached across the table and took her hand. "I hadn't realized how bitter I'd gotten until I met you. You've made me believe almost anything is possible."

Her throat clogged, and she had to wait a moment before she could say—as lightly as she could manage, "I can't promise 'anything.' I don't do miracles."

His mouth crooked into a painful smile. "Is finding Julie a miracle?"

Feeling his grip relax, she withdrew her hand from his. "Wouldn't it be? In a way?"

Robin watched his face closely. Despite everything he'd said, she wondered if he didn't still love Julie. She remembered the way he'd smiled at his wife in the stands as if she were the only person there. The only one who mattered, to him.

"Yeah." He moved his shoulders as if they ached. "It would be. The kids need to know what happened to her. For me..." His chest rose and fell with a long breath. "You know there'll be mixed feelings, especially if something terrible happened to her. I'll mourn. But mostly, I've alternated grief with hate for so long, I think I'm done with both. I'd be grateful for closure. Freedom. I'd feel like a man who's been in prison for a crime he didn't commit, and suddenly he's being ushered out into sunlight with everyone apologizing.''

She hoped he couldn't see the tears trying to sting her eyes. ''They would apologize, wouldn't they?''

''Some people would.''

''Will you...accept?''

He was silent, candlelight casting the lines of his face deeper, aging him, accentuating the bitterness he still carried.

''I'd nod and thank them and say I understand. But you can't go back from this kind of thing. It would...lie between you forever.'' For a moment he was quiet again. ''When this is over, one way or the other, the kids and I need to start afresh, somewhere else. I'll ask the airline to transfer me.''

Was he warning her? Telling her that, as nice as she'd been, he'd be packing up one of these days, so she shouldn't get any ideas?

''Dad intends to go, too.'' Craig's smile wasn't quite successful. ''He's been sprucing up his house to put it on the market for the past year. That's what he keeps saying.''

''Then...'' Her voice caught. ''Then he'll be all set.''

''Robin...'' He closed his eyes, then opened them and shook his head. ''I'm getting ahead of myself. Way ahead of myself. I'm still waiting for a second miracle.''

Surprised, she said, ''Second?''

''Your...faith is the first.'' He held out his hand again, palm up, and waited until she laid hers in it.

Then, his voice low and husky, he said, "Thank you, Robin."

She was unable to look away from his shadowed gray eyes. "You're welcome," sounded inane, but what else could she say? *It was nothing? I stand in defense of the accused every day?* She'd never even *met* anyone suspected of murder before.

He let her hand go, but she felt reluctance—*imagined* reluctance—in the way he lifted one finger at a time.

"Maybe we'd better get back," she said.

He took out his wallet and laid a pile of bills on the table. When she opened her purse, he shook his head. "My treat. No. Don't argue."

"You always say that." He'd insisted on paying for breakfast, too. She had bought lunch for herself and Malcolm only because she'd stood in line at the concession stand ahead of Craig.

"You were willing to sit at the same table with me. If you at least let me pay for the food, that restores my sense of balance."

She puffed out a sigh. "I sat with you because I wanted to."

His glance was cool. "Still…"

Robin made a face and muttered, "Fine."

Craig laughed, the amusement reminding her of carefree days, of the man who had always made her heart flutter just a little, even though he belonged to someone else.

"I didn't play fair, did I?"

"No, but I'll forgive you."

She was relieved to see that the other team parents had already left the restaurant. When she and Craig started across the dark parking lot, she became conscious of how alone they were. His arm brushed hers, and she felt a quiver in her belly. *If only,* whispered in her mind.

If only Julie hadn't disappeared. If only she and Craig had gotten the divorce that Julie had hinted at.

No. Robin didn't care. She ached for a different *if only.* For him to suddenly grip her arm and stop her, to say, "Will you kiss me, Robin?" For his mouth to descend onto hers, his arms to close around her and pull her against him. She ached for him to groan, for the kiss to deepen with desperation and passion, for...

She must have made a sound, because he turned his head. "Did you say something?"

Grateful for the darkness, Robin shook her head. "No."

No, he wouldn't do any of that. Not even if he was attracted to her, not even if he cared.

If he was falling in love with her, as she was with him.

Because he was a good, principled man who would not touch her, no matter how he felt, until he was free.

Pain pierced her. If Julie wasn't found, he would never be free. And Robin would never know whether he reciprocated all of the joy and tumult and hunger she felt for him.

But perhaps he was right, and it was better this way. If he never did find out what had happened to Julie, he and Robin might hurt less if they'd never spoken their hopes aloud, never shared a kiss.

EVEN THOUGH she'd heard the doorbell ring inside—twice—Ann hammered on the door. She'd stopped by

Lofgren's house yesterday afternoon, called a couple of times during the evening, come by this morning, too. Where in hell was he?

Maybe he'd taken his kids and fled.

Maybe he just wasn't answering the door.

She glared at the paneled door with shiny doorknob and deadbolt and wished it was flanked by sidelights. If this were a weekday when she could feel confident she was unseen, she'd have peered in a few windows. As it was, a man two doors down was edging a flower bed and a woman across the street was sweeping out her garage.

In exasperation Ann marched over and asked whether she had seen the Lofgrens depart.

The woman didn't even glance at the shingled house across the street. "I'm sorry. I'm afraid I don't pay any attention to his comings and goings." She put faint, sneering emphasis on "his."

The neighbor working on an already razor-sharp divide between dark earth and velvet lawn shook his head, too.

"Haven't seen 'em today."

Which would suggest they genuinely weren't home. Ann climbed back into her car and stared with intense frustration at the blank face of the house. Now that she had some leads, some important questions to ask, he had to make himself unavailable.

Well, she had other things to do. Like stop at the grocery store and pick up something for dinner. Or grab fast food. Ann didn't like going into a restaurant for a sit-down meal when she was alone and therefore pathetic in the eyes of others.

Her best friend was a cop, too, working tonight. Ann hadn't dated in... She couldn't remember.

On impulse she called her partner on her cell phone.

"Diaz," he answered.

Voices and laughter and music murmured and swelled in the background and Ann heard the clink of glass against glass.

"Sorry," she said. "I didn't mean to interrupt."

"You're not if you have something important."

"Not important. It can wait until Monday. Have fun." Without waiting for a response, she pressed End.

Starting the car, Ann willed herself not to think about the party to which she hadn't been invited, and thought, *pizza.*

And ice cream. She'd pick up a pint of Ben & Jerry's. The more sinful the better. She could eat pizza and then ice cream in front of the TV at home and tell herself she was having fun, too.

CHAPTER FOURTEEN

HE WISHED HE HADN'T suggested they go swimming with the boys. Last night Robin had barely taken a dip before wrapping herself in a thick beach towel and announcing that she was going to take a shower and read for a while, if he didn't mind waiting for Malcolm and Brett.

But tonight...

Tonight she floated with her arms outflung, her hair spread in the water like kelp, her eyes closed and her expression serene.

Craig couldn't look away even though a part of him was saying, *The boys will notice. They're going to wonder if you keep standing here staring.*

Brett and Malcolm were at the other end of the pool taking turns diving to the bottom for something.

If only she hadn't worn a bikini. Modest, compared to what teenage girls paraded in, but revealing enough to strike him dumb.

Her legs were long and pale and shapely, her hips curvy, her waist as small as it must have been before she had her son. Her breasts were creamy swells barely covered by scraps of coral colored fabric. The tie floated between them. Craig looked at the innocent bow and imagined giving it a tug. She might squeak and put her feet to the bottom, maybe clasp her hands over her breasts, but too late. He'd have seen them in all their glory, pink-tipped from the chilly water.

He groaned and at last wrenched his gaze away. He had a hard-on and two eleven-year-old boys were present to notice if he wasn't careful. Craig dunked, hoping the water would slap some sense in him, but when he surfaced for a breath, he was looking for her even before he'd blinked to clear his eyes.

She'd rolled onto her stomach and was doing the breaststroke toward the boys. Away from Craig. His gaze went straight to her bottom, rising as the kick pushed her higher in the water, sinking as she glided.

He turned his back to them all and swore under his breath. *Think about something else,* he ordered himself. What if she came over? What if she suggested getting out and going over to the hot tub?

As if he'd planted the notion, she called, "Hot tub, anyone?"

Powerless, he turned just in time to see her climbing the ladder. Her hair streamed over her shoulders and back and water sluiced over her bare skin. His body tightened further as she turned, laughing at something one of the boys called, and lifted her arms to wring out her hair.

He had never in his life wanted a woman as much as he wanted this one. Right now.

And he couldn't touch her, couldn't kiss her, couldn't even *hint* at what he felt.

Because either his wife was dead and the world would continue thinking he'd murdered her, or he was still married. How many times did he have to remind himself?

"What are you doing, Dad?" Brett swam toward him.

Lusting after your friend's mother. Not an appropriate response.

"Being lazy." He forced a smile and dove deep, coming up under Brett and grabbing an ankle.

They wrestled and chased each other around the pool, Malcolm joining the fun. Craig was only grateful Robin didn't jump back in and grab him.

Eventually he had enough confidence to pull himself from the pool and casually step down into the hot tub with Robin, who smiled at him through the steam.

"Hi." Her cheeks were pink now, her eyes sleepy.

"Hi to you."

"They're having fun." She yawned.

"Mmm." He sank lower and closed his eyes. He didn't dare look at her, her wet hair seal dark, her throat pale, the curve of breasts just rising above the bubbling surface. "You look ready for bed."

Poor choice of words. No, wishful thinking.

"I guess I am. It's been a long day." Her jaws made a cracking sound as she yawned again, then laughed. "All that yelling."

"Right."

He must have sounded clipped, because she sat up and looked at him. "Is something wrong?"

"No."

Her eyes, big and warm and gentle, searched his face. "Are you sure?"

"Sure?" He heard himself give a harsh laugh. "I'm not sure about much anymore."

"Craig…" Robin's voice was as soft as the steam.

He ached with wanting the impossible. Why had he thought this weekend would be a good idea?

"I'd better get out of here. Can you wait for the boys?"

She started to stand, water sloshing. "Something *is* wrong."

He could have touched her. They faced each other, both standing hip deep.

"I should have kept avoiding you."

Her eyes widened and her lips parted.

"Now you know what's wrong." His voice was guttural. "I'm either a murder suspect or a married man. Take your pick."

As quiet as a breath, she said, "I don't care."

In the act of turning away, he stopped. "What?"

"You can't…stop your life because she's gone."

"I don't see that I have much choice."

She slipped back down in the hot water. Tiny waves lapped at his thighs.

"Go ahead, Craig. I'll wait for the boys."

He couldn't move. "What did you mean?"

She was quiet for so long that he faced her. Her teeth were worrying her lower lip.

At last her lashes rose and she met his gaze. Color bloomed on her cheeks. "If you were to ask for…for almost anything, I'd say yes. And it's incredibly immodest of me to tell you that, I know. So let's just both pretend I didn't."

Pounded by a tsunami of desire, he took a step toward her.

"Hey, Mom!" Malcolm hoisted himself from the pool, Brett behind him. "Can I do a cannonball into the hot tub?"

"You may not," she said automatically. Still blushing, she seemed glad of an excuse to look away from Craig.

He turned, left the hot tub and grabbed a towel, wrapping it around his waist. "I'll see you upstairs."

At the moment, he didn't care what the boys thought. He had to get out of here before he made a fool of himself.

He didn't even see her when she followed half an hour later with the boys. Brett let himself into the room. "Coach kicked us out of the pool and told us to go to bed," he reported, sounding disgruntled.

In bed, Craig looked up from his book. "The semi-final game is at nine in the morning. I'd say the coach is right."

His son made a face and disappeared into the bathroom. Craig heard the sounds of a hasty toothbrushing, the flush of the toilet and then Brett appeared in pajama bottoms. "Are you going to keep the light on?"

"Nope." Craig closed the book. Hell, he couldn't remember a word he'd read anyway. "Just waiting for you."

Climbing into the other queen-size bed, Brett said, "We get this *huge* trophy if we win. The team does, I mean. Did you see it, Dad?"

"Yep." Brett knew he had. "Let's get through the first game before trophies dance in your head."

His son chuckled, his voice already slurring. "Like sugar plums."

Craig turned out the light and they exchanged good-nights. Lying in the dark, he knew sleep would be a long time coming.

He heard Robin's shy admission: *If you were to ask for...for almost anything, I'd say yes.*

Did she trust him that completely? What if he'd asked for her love? What if he'd said, "Will you marry me when I'm free?"

He gave a soft grunt. Didn't he mean "if I'm ever free?" What kind of an SOB would he be to lay that kind of proposition before a woman?

What he'd really be saying was, "We can sleep together now, but as for the rest...well, maybe someday I can marry you."

As if marriage to him was any kind of prize. At best, he'd have to ask her to pull up roots, leave her job and her friends to join him in making a fresh start somewhere far away.

At worst...

No. There wouldn't be any "at worst." He wouldn't ask her to join him in his special purgatory. She'd endured enough stares and whispers just because she was befriending him.

No, he thought again, his eyes burning. He was unbelievably lucky to have found a sexy, kind, gutsy woman who was apparently willing to trust him despite all evidence to the contrary.

He wouldn't abuse that trust.

BACK TO SCHOOL.

Robin's classroom looked much as it did every Monday morning, the desks in neat rows, courtesy of the janitor, the blackboard clean, the hooks and cubbies for book bags and coats empty.

She should be doing something more useful than standing here staring at the empty classroom, but she couldn't seem to regain her usual beginning-of-the-week energy.

Instead, depression hung over her like a too-heavy cloak.

One more regular soccer game and the season would be over. Robin doubted that Mal and Brett's friendship would end, so she'd still see Craig once in a while.

She could see it now. Pleasant hellos, awkward conversation made on the doorstep while they waited for the boys to appear. Conversation couldn't be anything *but* awkward after her unprompted offer of her body and soul to Craig.

The drive home had offered a sample. The boys' ebullience had been dampened by their loss in the semifinals of the tournament to a select team from Vancouver. In the front seat, road conditions and weather had been the primary topics. Heaven knew *she'd* been devoid of ideas. What was she supposed to say?

So, what do you think? Do you want me?

Sure he did; she'd seen his arousal as he fled the hot tub. That meant nothing. Less than nothing. He'd likely been celibate since his wife disappeared. Robin was the first woman he'd spent any appreciable time with. She wasn't bad-looking. She'd flaunted herself in front of him in the bikini she should have left in the drawer at home. So he'd become aroused. That didn't mean he hadn't been scared to death by her admission that she was in love with him.

Because that's what it was. Not the light "just want you to know I'm interested" she'd intended. Of course not. Lacking any gift for flirtation, she'd ripped open her chest and offered her heart instead.

Robin let out a huge sigh and sank into the chair behind her desk. The bell would ring any minute, the kids would pour in. And she hadn't even looked at her lesson plan.

Forget it, she ordered herself. Most people had managed to humiliate themselves utterly at some point in their lives. Okay, so most did it when they were gauche and fifteen. Maybe sixteen. She could consider herself a late bloomer.

And yes, her heart was cracking, but she still had a job to do and a son to raise. And she still nursed a tiny glow of hope that Craig hadn't responded to her offer, hadn't commented on it later, not because he was taken aback by it, but because he believed he had no right until Julie was found.

The bell rang. She glanced blindly down at her lesson plan.

Where are you? she silently asked a woman she'd once thought she knew.

MONDAY MORNING, Craig Lofgren answered his phone. "Hello?" He sounded cautious, as though nobody called him on a Monday morning with good news.

Ann identified herself. "May I come over to speak with you?"

"Was that a question?" He waited a beat. "I don't know what else I can tell you."

"I'd like to talk to you anyway."

Again he was silent for a moment. "All right," he said at last, even warier.

When she arrived, he answered the door immediately and gestured her ahead of him into the living room. No offer of coffee. He simply waited until she sat, then chose the chair facing her.

In jeans and a plaid flannel shirt with the sleeves rolled up, he was a good-looking man. He would have been a better-looking one without bitter lines etched in his face, without shuttered eyes and the rigid posture of a man waiting for another blow.

"I have discovered evidence that makes me think your wife may have left voluntarily."

He jerked. His eyes came vividly alive. "What evidence?"

She told him about the Volkswagen van and the long-haired man waiting for someone or something at the curb in front of his house that April morning, about the clothes his wife had bought from the Volunteers of America thrift shop just before she disappeared.

"Was she ever involved with the community theater, Mr. Lofgren?"

He shook his head in bewilderment. "No. No. We never even saw one of their shows. I..." His Adam's apple bobbed and he bent his head. "God. A purse. She bought a purse?"

"That's right."

"But her wallet, her driver's license…she left everything."

"Did you look for her birth certificate?"

He nodded. "They asked me to at the time. I couldn't remember ever seeing it, though. I don't even know if she had a copy. I couldn't find it."

"We've talked about it before, but maybe you've given more thought to how much money she might have taken."

"Uh…" He looked so stunned, she could tell he was struggling to focus. "There wasn't any in her wallet."

"According to Sergeant Caldwell's notes, she had made a $300 withdrawal from an ATM the day before."

"Yeah. He dismissed the idea she was planning ahead. Wasn't it routine for her to make withdrawals? he asked."

"Did you check for other withdrawals in the weeks leading up to her disappearance?"

"There were quite a few. More than normal. Not so many I had any reason to notice at the time, but she might have squirreled away eight hundred, a thousand dollars."

"What about other, more personal items from her purse?"

"I still have it. I never took anything out. Do you want to see it?"

"Yes." Ann struggled to hide her elation. She should have asked sooner. "Yes, I would, if you don't mind."

He shook his head and left the living room. She heard footsteps on the stairs. Not two minutes later he returned with an elegant embossed black handbag that had probably cost a week of Ann's pay. Craig Lofgren set it on the coffee table and sat down.

Ann removed every item and laid them out. Wallet—credit cards, driver's license, a few ATM withdrawal slips, a clear plastic photo holder with school pictures of Julie's kids and one of her husband in his navy blue airline uniform. No bills. Half a dozen coins. No...miscellany.

Ann thought with some chagrin of her wallet, bursting with notes scrawled on corners of paper napkins, deposit and withdrawal slips from the bank, dog-eared business cards and phone numbers of people whose names she'd forgotten. Julie Lofgren must have been exceptionally tidy.

Address book. Date book. A container of tissues. Car keys. Checkbook.

Period.

No clutter, no wads of coupons never used, no breath mints disintegrating on the bottom, no... Ann's rueful list slammed to a stop.

"Did your wife usually carry a hairbrush?"

He stared at the things she'd laid out on the table as if they were unfamiliar objects. "Yes. Yes, she did."

"Lip gloss or lipstick?"

"Lip gloss." Now he stared almost feverishly at the scant row of items. "And hand lotion. She bought some special kind. Emu oil. She always had it with her." He let out a shuddering breath. "How is it that I didn't notice?"

How was it that Ann's father hadn't asked these questions? she thought on a surge of anger.

"You were in shock. And you're a man. You don't carry a purse. The obvious things are here—her wallet, her checkbook, her car keys."

"But not the really personal things." Craig Lofgren's mouth twisted. "Not a birth certificate and not the things she would have taken even if she planned to assume another identity."

"No. Not those."

His shoulders had sagged and his face looked slack. He rolled his head as if his neck ached. "Now what?"

"Now," Ann said, leaning back, "you have to think hard. Where might she have gone? What name might she have assumed?"

He shook his head. "Where would she have met this man who was waiting for her?"

Now, that was an interesting question. Where *would* a suburban mom meet a scruffy, long-haired man and get to know him well enough to run away with him?

"A craft fair?" she suggested, thinking aloud. "A farmer's market?"

"She did go to things like that. I told you she was a potter when I met her. She never seemed interested in using her artistic talent, but she did buy jewelry, artwork…'' He shrugged. ''Julie probably went to half a dozen arts fairs a summer.''

They threw around ideas, people Ann could contact to discover what artists and craftspeople had displayed wares at any of the fairs Julie might have attended.

''The farmer's markets are more casual, though,'' she said. ''I doubt any organizers would have records.''

''She might have sought this guy out,'' Craig said. ''If she wanted to run away from her life. It might not have been a casual meeting.''

''What are you suggesting? She posted her name on an Internet bulletin board?''

''Maybe. God. I don't know.'' He had aged in the past half hour.

''We've done routine searches for her under her married and maiden names, which you provided. Can you think of any other names she might have used?''

He shook his head. ''She was Julie Gibbs when we met. That's the only name she used until she married me.''

''Do you know where she was born?''

''Uh…'' He obviously had to drag his thoughts from somewhere.

''Waterloo, Iowa. Or so she said. But her stories about her childhood never seemed substantial. I've gotten so I doubt everything I thought I knew about Julie.''

Ann closed her notebook. ''If you think of anything, Mr. Lofgren…''

He nodded and rose with her. Gruffly, he said, "I owe you an apology. I assumed you'd try to vindicate your father's belief that I was guilty. I've probably been rude."

She couldn't—wouldn't—apologize in return. She didn't yet know what had happened to Julie. Maybe all of this was a dead end. Maybe Craig Lofgren was lying through his teeth and he knew damn well why his wife had bought some thrift store clothes. Ann didn't think so—but until she was sure, she had to stay professional. Dispassionate.

"You've been cooperative. I appreciate that."

He walked her to the door. She was aware that he watched her until she was behind the wheel of her car. Ann prayed that she hadn't given him unfounded hope.

WHILE SHE CLEANED the kitchen, Robin sang along to Christina Aguilera on the radio. She kept her voice low both because Malcolm was asleep and because she wouldn't want the neighbors to hear her tuneless drone. She sounded fine to *her* ears, but she knew from sad experience that she was her one and only fan.

When the phone rang, she turned down the radio with one wet hand before reaching for the receiver. "Hello?"

"Robin, this is Craig." He paused. "Craig Lofgren."

As if she hadn't known instantly whose voice his

was. She tucked the phone between ear and shoulder and reached for the dish towel to dry her hands.

"Hi, Craig. What's up?" She was proud of her casual, friendly tone.

"Malcolm in bed?"

Surprised, she said, "Half an hour ago. I'm just washing the last few dishes."

"I'm flying out in the morning. But I had to talk to somebody."

Fear snatched her. "What's wrong? Is it Julie?"

"Officer Caldwell was here this morning." His voice was charged with some emotion, repressed but powerful. "The woman cop. She's discovered some things that make her think Julie left on her own."

Robin groped for a stool and sank onto it. "What did she find?"

He talked about a hippie van and a long-haired man and the clothes his wife had bought at a thrift store. Robin tried without success to imagine the fastidious, elegant woman she'd known buying a fringed suede bag and secondhand clothes. Julie had been the only baseball parent who had always brought a plastic seat pad to every practice so she didn't have to come in contact with the scarred, dirty benches.

"Is it possible?"

He said more, telling her about the items missing from Julie's purse and the multiple withdrawals in the weeks before her disappearance.

"I should have noticed before what was missing from her purse."

"You're a man."

"That's what she said. The policewoman."

"Well, it's true. Men never understand why a woman can't walk out the door with no more than her wallet in her hip pocket."

"Until he has to ask his wife for something."

"Exactly." She drew a shaky breath. "Now what? Are they any closer to finding her?"

"I don't know." He was quiet for a moment. When he spoke again, his voice had been stripped bare of the excitement and hope. "Maybe not."

She was sorry she'd asked. "But at least the police are looking elsewhere."

"That's something." After a moment he said, "I shouldn't have called so late. I'm sorry."

"I'm glad you did," Robin said softly.

"Robin, what you said Saturday night, in the hot tub…"

She held her breath.

"If things were different…" He was having trouble finding words. Kind ones, to let her down easily. "If they become different…"

Tears burned her eyes. "No. Don't say anything. You don't have to. Really. I don't know why I did. We're friends. Let's leave it at that."

"Leave it at that?" His voice was quiet, raw. "I wish it was that easy. Good night, Robin."

Stunned, she realized he was gone. She could hardly breathe; her chest felt as if it were filling with helium that might lift her gently into the air until her head bumped the ceiling. At the same time, her vision blurred and her sinuses stung.

Once again, he'd implied that he might care. Care! What an anemic word. Be falling for her. Feel something of the same turmoil that was making her realize she would happily, without the slightest hesitation, uproot herself and Malcolm to go anywhere at all with Craig.

If only he asked.

If only he someday became free to ask.

CHAPTER FIFTEEN

NO INFANT named Julie Gibbs had been born in Waterloo, Iowa, or in any surrounding county. Somehow Ann wasn't surprised.

Could she have lied about her age? There were no records of an earlier birthdate, either. Julie Gibbs, as she had presented herself to Craig Lofgren, didn't exist.

It took Ann another twenty-four hours, but she found out why. Julie *had* been born in Waterloo, in a manner of speaking—a Julie Ackerman had married a man named Cameron Gibbs there five years before she met Craig. A divorce, Ann further discovered, was on the books in Chicago.

Cameron Gibbs wasn't hard to find. A building contractor, he still lived in Winnetka.

"Heard from Julie?" he repeated, once Ann had identified herself. "Hell, no! Why would I?"

She explained, and he said, "Poor bastard. That is one strange woman, I've got to tell you."

"Strange in what way?" Ann rested her elbows on her desk, then muttered a curse when coffee sloshed from her mug.

"She was this sweet young thing when I met her. Fascinated when I talked about my day. Wanted nothing more than to be a wife and homemaker. Man, I felt like the luckiest guy in the world the day she agreed to marry me! Lucky. What a joke. We moved to Chicago, see. She's meeting me at the door every night, I can smell dinner cooking. I've got it good. Then, practically overnight, she changed. Started taking art classes, forgot to do the grocery shopping, had all new friends. She ditched me, just like that.''

"People do change.''

"Huh?'' He sounded as if she'd interrupted a well-worn refrain. "Yeah, sure they do. Only, this wasn't like that.'' She sensed him struggling for a way to explain. "I encouraged her to take classes. I wouldn't have cared if she'd gone to work, or found a career. I've remarried and my wife is a real estate broker. Let me tell you, the phone always rings at the worst time. But with Julie, it was more like…like someone took over her body. She looked the same, but she wasn't. I'd stare into her eyes and my skin would crawl. You can believe me or not. She was weird.''

Ann thanked him and asked whether Julie had to his knowledge ever used another name. He told her no, then agreed to look at a photo Ann would fax to confirm they were talking about the same woman. When she called again, he agreed, "That's her.''

He promised to call in the unlikely event he heard from Julie.

Ann hung up and stared into space. Would Julie have gone back to a maiden name? That didn't seem her style, but it did have the advantage that she'd be able to get a copy of her birth certificate, thus starting over again most easily.

"Learn anything?" Diaz appeared in her line of vision. He grabbed a chair and sat in his favorite position straddling it, with his arms crossed on the back.

"Huh?" She focused her eyes. "Oh. Yeah, actually, I did." Ann told him what she'd learned.

"Poor bastard, is right. Lofgren has to have been through hell since she disappeared. And now it's looking like she just walked out." He swore and shook his head.

Ann said what she'd been thinking for a long time. "If Dad had really looked for her…"

"He might have found her." Juan Diaz's dark eyes met Ann's. "He screwed up."

She summoned a wry smile. "I thought he was invincible."

"We all make mistakes."

"Mistakes?" She tried the word on for size. "He didn't make a simple mistake. He didn't conduct a real investigation, because he took a dislike to the husband." She shook her head. "Everybody admired him because he wouldn't let this one go. He was determined to nail Craig Lofgren in the name of the pitiful, defenseless women everywhere whose husbands wouldn't let them go."

Diaz was silent.

"He always had a thing about arrogant, rich SOBs," Ann realized. "That was what he always said. What he meant was, men who made him feel inferior. He didn't care about Julie. He cared about bringing down her husband."

The knowledge was bittersweet. It left her feeling as if her vision was distorted. Not fuzzy, but extra sharp, as if she was trying on someone else's glasses with a prescription that was too strong for her. It also made her wonder who she was. Maybe nobody. She'd spent a lifetime trying to measure up to her father, the god. He was her mirror, which now lay in shards on the floor. She couldn't see herself anymore, only the world around her with this strangely altered perception.

Diaz smiled at her, his hard face becoming more gentle. "You did good." He gave a nod, slapped a hand on her desk and stood.

She gaped as he walked away.

EXHAUSTED, Craig should have been in bed. He hadn't slept well in days. In some ways, this past year and a half he'd valued the anonymity of the hotel rooms and restaurants in foreign cities. This time, he just wanted to be home. He needed to be there, if Ann Caldwell learned anything new.

He'd come to believe that he would spend the rest of his life in limbo. Never knowing what had happened to the mother of his children, never resolving the mystery. Never being able to walk into his neighborhood grocery store again without being aware that people stared, and that they judged.

Tonight, he'd gotten home in time to say good-night to Brett. His father, yawning, had gone to bed in the guest room. Craig had stood in Abby's doorway for a long time, watching her in peaceful sleep and wondering how she'd handle the news that her mother had left her.

And Brett. What would the realization do to him? Or had he already come to terms with it?

Craig had his suspicions that Abby had mourned a mother snatched away by fate, while Brett had raged at a mother who'd abandoned him. Part of him had wanted to think he'd imagined her goodbye, because he'd rather believe she hadn't chosen to go. But he'd known, deep inside.

As Craig looked in on Brett, who was now sound asleep, anger clawed at him. He could have slammed his fist through a wall. How could Julie have done this to them?

Restless despite his tiredness, Craig went downstairs. He glanced in the refrigerator and decided he wasn't hungry. Almost reluctantly, he picked up the phone. He'd better check his voice mail. The mechanized voice told him that he had five new messages.

Beep. "Mr. Lofgren, this is Officer Caldwell. I wanted to keep you apprised of the investigation." In a dry manner no different than that of an airline employee informing him of a schedule change down the line, she continued, "I've discovered that your wife was married previously. Her maiden name was Ackerman. Gibbs was the married name. I've spoken to the ex-husband who agreed with your assessment that she was 'weird.' She changed almost overnight on him, he says. I'm hoping the maiden name gives us something further to go on."

Beep. A perky voice said something he didn't hear as he grappled with the information that Julie had left out such a huge chunk of her past when they talked.

Maybe, to her, it really hadn't happened. Or it had happened to someone else.

Shaking his head, he replayed the message he'd missed.

Beep. "This is Jessie at Safeway. The film you left to be developed is now ready for pickup."

Beep. "Hey, Brett. Mal. Call me."

Beep. "Lofgren, this is Ross Buchanan." Buchanan was an old friend of Craig's from the Navy who now flew for Continental. Occasionally, they were in the same city at the same time. "I'm at SeaTac. Have a layover. You in town? I thought we could have dinner." The message had been left yesterday afternoon.

Beep. "Mr. Lofgren, this is Officer Ann Caldwell again. The delivery driver just phoned to say he thinks the license plate on that Volkswagen van was from Oregon. However, your wife has not applied for an Oregon driver's license under any of her known names. Please think about whether Mrs. Lofgren seemed particularly interested in any area, asking questions, checking out books from the library." She left her phone number—as if he didn't have it—in case anything occurred to him.

The telephone company's disembodied voice informed him that he had no more new messages.

Craig hit End and set down the phone.

Julie had been married to someone else and divorced. He'd always wondered about her childhood, but it had never occurred to him she had an ex-husband in her past. Why *wouldn't* she mention him? What was the secret?

But he knew his first instinct was right. This Gibbs fellow just didn't exist to the woman she'd become. She'd kept his name as her own because…who knew? Because she didn't go back?

She apparently *hadn't* kept the name Lofgren. In his numbness, Craig thought that should sting. His name had been left with her purse on the kitchen counter. But the knowledge didn't hurt the way it should have, because on her terms the decision was logical. She was walking out on two children without going through the motions of getting a divorce. She'd probably realized someone might come looking for her.

If she could calculate like that, did she qualify as mentally ill? He had no idea what the experts would say. He didn't know if people with multiple personalities could live in each one for months or years before becoming somebody else entirely. Maybe her problem was something entirely different

He bent his head and made himself take slow, deep breaths. She was crazy. Her running away had nothing to do with him.

God, he hoped her form of mental illness wasn't hereditary.

He finally turned out the lights and went up to bed, where he lay on his back trying to decide whether he wanted to confront Julie if Caldwell located her.

In the early months, he'd fantasized about finding her, reducing her to sodden tears of guilt and regret before he turned on his heel and walked away. He'd pictured her begging for his forgiveness, for the chance to come back. He had wanted to be cruel, to make her *hurt,* the way he and the kids had hurt.

Now... Now he didn't know. He felt almost dead inside. He could send divorce papers, get her signature without ever having to see her again. He doubted any judge would grant her visitation rights after the way she'd taken off.

But he knew she wouldn't want them. Maybe Julie Lofgren had loved her kids. Julie Ackerman/Gibbs/Whoever might scarcely remember them.

Slowly he peeled away the numbness as if it were a thick rind. Beneath were so many emotions he struggled to isolate one at a time. Hurt was there, sure. So were anger and bitterness and grief and bewilderment.

But the strongest, by far, was simple relief and even gratitude. Relief that he hadn't spent a year and a half hating her, only to find out she'd been murdered by a passing serial killer, that she'd never meant to leave him and the kids at all. Relief that he and the kids would soon know. Relief that he might soon be free to sell this house and start over.

And maybe, most of all, relief that he might soon be free to kiss Robin and ask whether she'd be willing to start over, too.

Last weekend in the hot tub had she offered to make love with him? Or to promise till death do us part? He wished he was sure.

Craig rolled over, punched the pillow and willed himself to be sleepy. Half an hour later, he continued to feel wired despite his tiredness, as if he'd had a dozen cups of coffee today.

"Crap," he muttered, and turned on the bedside lamp. Could he concentrate on a book?

His mind took a sideways jump. What was it the cop had asked him to do? Think about whether Julie had been doing any research on a particular area.

If she had he hadn't noticed. He'd felt her restlessness, her increasing desperation, but never guessed the outcome. He hadn't caught even a hint of how she was channeling her hunger to change her life.

She hadn't been much of a reader, but she liked magazines.

"It doesn't matter if I get interrupted," she would say, with an impatient shrug. "They have snippets. I can dip in."

She had a basket. Unless the kids had rooted through it because they needed to cut out pictures for a school project, it sat untouched. Julie had thrown in magazines and catalogs—she liked to browse those, too. He'd moved the basket at least once a week to vacuum the family room. It had been as familiar and therefore invisible as the end tables and floor lamps.

Wearing a T-shirt and pajama bottoms, he made his way downstairs, bare feet quiet. He didn't even turn on the hall light. In the family room he flicked on one lamp and lifted the basket onto the coffee table in front of him.

On top were a bunch of catalogs that he vaguely remembered tossing in here himself: *Coldwater Creek, J. Jill, Exposures* and a dozen others that had arrived in the weeks after Julie first disappeared. At some point he'd started recycling her catalogs and magazines. He couldn't even remember consciously making the decision. Saying to himself, *She isn't coming back.* But at first, he'd believed on some level that she was. So these catalogs and a couple of magazines, unread, sat on top. He set them aside.

More catalogs, none with corners turned down, as she'd done when she thought she might want something. She might have glanced through these; he couldn't tell.

A *Good Housekeeping* magazine. *Victoria's Secret.* She'd bought their bras, he knew. After a moment, he set that catalog aside. What if she still bought bras from them? Was that the kind of habit a person would carry with her into a new life? He guessed the police could get some kind of warrant to find out.

Below it was a *Sunset* magazine and below that one on Northwest travel. She'd subscribed to *Sunset,* but not the travel magazine. Each had a corner turned down.

His hand was shaking when he flipped open the first magazine to a feature on central Oregon. It lauded the crisp, dry weather, the beauty of ranching country and tiny lakes nestled at the feet of Mt. Bachelor and the Sisters. Photos showed skiers and downtown Bend with boutiques and restaurants and a rancher checking fences on horseback, white-topped mountains in the distance behind him across dry range land.

The second magazine fell open, as if naturally, to another spread on central Oregon. Colorful quilts hung from eaves and storefronts on a quaint, western street. Sisters, he read in the caption.

Heart thudding in his ears, he set the magazine

aside and dug deeper, but below were more catalogs
and a few magazines with recipes marked. Nothing
surprising.

He wouldn't have thought anything of these two,
if he'd noticed them before. He might have guessed
that Julie had intended to suggest a family vacation
to Oregon.

Now he looked at the magazines as if they were
banks of deep gray cloud hiding bolts of lightning and
vicious whips of wind.

Almost hating to touch them, he nonetheless picked
up the *Victoria's Secret* catalog and the magazines
and carried them up to his room, where he set them
on the bureau. Craig climbed into bed, turned out the
light and lay sleepless, waiting for morning.

THE MINUTE she'd hung up from talking to Lofgren,
Ann started making calls. Two hours later, she hit pay
dirt.

"We arrested a couple on June twenty-first," the
Deschutes County deputy told her. "Julie Ackerman
was the woman. They were selling marijuana, but we
only got her on possession. He was chivalrous enough
to take the blame."

"He?"

"Thomas Seebohm." The deputy spelled the name.

"Do you have an address?"

After hearing her story, he gave her that, too. "It's
a commune. Probably thirty people there. They grow
flowers and sell them. The group runs a restaurant in
town specializing in organic vegetarian food. I hear
it's pretty popular with the ski crowd." His tone sug-

gested that he didn't set foot in any place that didn't serve prime rib, rare. "The property was a resort, way back when, and it has a main lodge and a dozen cabins on a creek. This Seebohm's brother is their guru, or whatever you want to call him. Courage Seebohm, he calls himself." His tone had become dry. "He encourages them to choose names that speak from their heart."

"A commune."

"Bunch of hippies is what it is."

"I don't suppose you'd know whether Julie Ackerman is still there?"

"I could check, if you want," he offered.

"No. No, thanks. I don't want to scare her off. I may need to come down and confirm that she's our Julie Lofgren. More than that..." She hesitated. "I think her husband deserves a chance to present his divorce papers in person."

"Just so he doesn't get ugly," the deputy warned.

"He's not that kind of man," she said, and wished she'd seen that from the beginning.

A minute later, she dialed Craig Lofgren's phone number. When he answered, she asked, "How do you feel about taking a little trip?"

WHEN THE PHONE RANG that evening just after Malcolm had gone to bed, Robin knew who was calling. But it was more than that; her heart took a funny bump, and something between anxiety and anticipation fluttered in her stomach.

She saved the chapter she was writing on the computer and picked up the receiver. "Hello?"

"Robin? Craig again."

"Hi. What's up?" Very nice, she congratulated herself. Casual but friendly.

"Caldwell thinks she's found Julie."

The flutter turned into beating wings. "Where?"

"In a hippie commune in Oregon. She got arrested a few months back for possession of marijuana." He was silent for a moment. "God."

"Oh, Craig." Tears stung her eyes, and she couldn't have said why. "I don't know whether to tell you that the news is wonderful or say I'm sorry."

"Yeah. I don't know what to feel about it, either." He made a rough sound probably intended to be a laugh. "That's not true. I decided relief was predominant. But there's a lot more, too."

"Have you, um, told the kids?"

"No. No. I'm dreading that. In fact..."

When he hesitated, she prompted, "In fact?" Anxiety tickled again.

"I'm going down there tomorrow, Robin. The kids think I'm working. I want to be sure it's her, hear her story, before I tell them."

"Yes, of course." She imagined how awful that would be, to prepare them only to find this was the wrong woman. "Are you going to be okay, seeing her?"

He made that same, raw sound. "I don't know. I have moments when I want to kill her for what she's done to the kids and to me. But Officer Caldwell is going, too. I guess she'll keep me from getting violent."

"You wouldn't anyway," Robin said with confidence.

"Probably not." His wryness was painful to hear. "I'm a civilized man."

"It's almost over," she said.

"For better or worse." He was quiet for a moment. "Poor choice of words."

"It could have *been* worse."

"Yeah. Yeah, I do know that. What if they'd found her body in a shallow grave half a mile from the house? I've been so damn angry…" He broke off. "I just wanted you to know."

"I'm glad. I mean that," she said with sudden fierceness. "For your sake."

"Thank you."

The silence that followed grew uncomfortable.

To fill it, she started to say, "Let me know—"

At the same time, he began, "Robin—"

They both stopped.

Sounding awkward, Craig said, "I, uh, I hope you don't mind if I call when I get home."

"You'd better!"

His voice lightened. "Okay. I'll see you when I get home."

She bit her lip. "I'll be thinking about you."

"I'll hold on to that. Good night, Robin."

"Good night," she whispered, and hung up. She would be holding on to the knowledge that he had wanted to talk to her.

THE POLICE CAR jolted over the rutted road between ponderosa pines and a pair of split rail fences. Dust followed in a rust-red plume. Craig clutched the arm rest and gritted his teeth as the car dropped into a pothole and lurched out. The county deputy who was driving muttered a profanity.

"Here we are," he said a minute later.

The dirt road emptied into a clearing in front of a lodge built of logs. Through the trees, Craig could see scattered cabins. Half a dozen dusty vehicles were parked in a haphazard row. His gaze went straight to the Volkswagen van in the middle. A thin layer of red dirt lay over a faded blue paint job decorated with flowers and rainbows.

A pair of men turned from where they stood by a pile of sawn logs they were apparently splitting. One held an ax; both wore long hair tied back.

The police car stopped. For a moment the two police officers and Craig sat in silence as the cloud of dirt settled and the two men stared.

Ann Caldwell was the first to move. "What are we waiting for?"

After a brief consultation, the man with the ax stayed by the wood pile, watching; the other approached as the three strangers got out of the police car. The air had a bite this close to the mountains in November. Craig shoved his hands in the pockets of his polartec jacket.

"Welcome!" The man nodded and smiled. His dark hair was gray-streaked, the stubble on his gaunt jaw glinting silver. "How can I help you?"

"We're here to see Julie Ackerman," Officer Caldwell said brusquely. "Which of these places is hers?"

"We own them in common," he corrected her, his

expression kind. "Our sister stays in a cabin by the creek. She may be in the kitchen right now, however. Can you tell me what this is about? She's a gentle woman. I don't want to see her in trouble."

"Your 'sister' didn't bother to say her goodbyes before she joined you." Caldwell stared him down. "Sometimes you can't walk away without ghosts following you."

After a moment, he nodded. "Come with me."

He led the way up the rough plank steps onto the wide covered porch, then into the lodge. Inside was what appeared to be a large common room used for dining, with benches and long tables to accommodate as many as forty or fifty people. The room was empty, but voices came from an open doorway.

"Please, wait here," their guide said. "I'll bring Sister Ackerman."

Craig and Ann Caldwell glanced at each other. Finally Craig nodded. They were taking a chance that Julie would flee out a back door, but he disliked the idea of confronting her in front of a bunch of other women.

The graying man disappeared. When he came back a minute later, Craig tensed.

Behind him was a woman in a broomstick skirt and T-shirt, her long blond hair in matted dreadlocks. Her face was bare of makeup, her feet shod in battered work boots. He knew her, and yet he didn't.

He made a strangled sound.

Sister Ackerman looked at him with a peaceful, mild smile, and said, "Hello, Craig."

CHAPTER SIXTEEN

"DADDY!" ABBY FLEW into Craig's arms when she came in the door after school.

Outside, he heard the bus lumbering away.

"Cool! You're back." Brett swung his book bag off his shoulder. "I have stuff for you to sign. We're going on a field trip next week."

"I'm glad to be home." Craig planted a smacking kiss on his daughter's cheek, swung her in a circle and set her down. "I want to talk to you two."

"Where's Grandad?" Abby asked.

"He went home already. He said something about a hot date."

Brett made a face. "Yuck. He told us about her. She's into genealogy. Like, all she does is search the Internet for long lost ancestors. What do you suppose they talk about? How her great-great-great-uncle died?"

Craig laughed. Damn, it felt good. "I'm betting they find something more contemporary than that. She also teaches yoga classes to senior citizens, you know. I imagine she has many facets."

He had to explain "facets" to Abby, who listened seriously.

"Grandad has lots of facets, too," she informed

him. "He taught me to play poker. He always wins, but he's teaching me to bluff. I just look like this—" she demonstrated a stone face "—even when my cards are bad."

"Bluffing, huh? Well, you're definitely getting the hang of it." Craig ruffled her hair.

Brett had been watching. "What kind of talk are we going to have? Is this like a new rules talk, or…" Seeing his father's expression, he stopped. "Or…" His voice cracked.

Craig put a hand on his shoulder. "It's about your mom."

His son flinched. Abby stared up with widening eyes.

"About Mommy?"

"Let's sit down."

He settled them on the couch in the family room and sat on the coffee table facing them, his knees bumping theirs. Abby inched over so she was just touching her brother, who didn't object for once.

"The police have found your mother. She's fine. That's where I went yesterday—to see her."

They both stared. Neither said anything for far too long. Then, in a small voice, Abby asked, "Is Mommy coming home?"

Craig shook his head. "I'm sorry, sweetie. I wish I could tell you that she is, or at least that you'd get to see her sometimes, but…" He took a deep breath. "She's changed."

Abby burrowed against Brett, who put his arm around her.

His chin high, he said, "She changed before she went. Didn't she?"

Craig nodded. "She didn't mean to cause the trouble she did. She didn't know my flight had been canceled. It never occurred to her that the police would think she might be dead, or that they'd be suspicious of me. If it hadn't been for the fog at SeaTac..."

"You wouldn't have come home." Brett sounded...older. Too old. "Then nobody would have been here. We'd have been really scared."

"She didn't think of that, either." There was one hell of a lot Julie hadn't considered, in her desperate rush to escape a life she hadn't been able to bear. "You'd have called Grandad, or one of your friends' mothers."

Brett sat silent, his expression hard. He knew the truth: their mother had abandoned them without a second thought, without caring how frightened they would have been when they got home to an empty house and her purse and car keys lying on the kitchen counter.

"Doesn't she..." Abby swallowed. "Doesn't she *want* to see us?"

With one hand, Craig cradled his daughter's face, his heart aching at the sight of her distress. "Your mom has problems, sweetheart. She knew she couldn't be the mother you need. That's why she left. She thought we'd be better off without her."

His pretty, vibrant daughter seemed to shrink. She nodded as if she understood, but he knew she didn't. She couldn't. Mothers didn't do this. They sacrificed to give their children what they needed. They didn't abdicate.

He talked until he was hoarse, mixing truth and white lies. Abby, he thought, bought into some of the lies, perhaps because she needed to. Brett, stiff and pale, didn't.

"I hope the day comes when she realizes you'd have loved her even if she couldn't be a perfect mother. But, selfishly, I'm glad she didn't want to take you to Oregon, where she's living, which would mean I could have you here only during vacations." Once he'd seen where she was taking them, he'd have found a way to get them back anyway, but he didn't say that. "I love you guys, and I like us being a family together."

Abby flung herself forward onto his lap. She sobbed silently, her shoulders shaking, tears wetting his shirtfront. Craig laid his cheek against her head, squeezed his eyes shut and felt his own tears leaking out.

When her weeping slowed, he opened his eyes to see Brett watching them both with that stony look.

"I hate her."

"She's the one suffering a terrible loss," Craig said. "I think she knows that."

He'd come home less bitter, because he had seen her serene facade crack when they sat at one of the long tables facing each other, the two police officers waiting a distance away. At one point Julie had said, in a broken voice, "I just couldn't do it anymore. I tried. I did try." Head bent, she asked, "Do you have any pictures?"

From his wallet he took their latest school pictures and handed them to her. He saw a fine tremor in her hand as she took them. She looked at the pictures for a long time. A breath shuddered through her, then she thrust them back at him, crying, "I wish you hadn't come!"

"Why? So you wouldn't have to think about them?" he had asked. "They think about you every day. Abby has quit asking where Mommy is, but she hasn't quit wondering."

"I'm not her mommy. That person I was, it was a lie."

Anger he had buried deep clawed free. "Which one was a lie? The potter? The career woman? Mommy? Or were all of them lies?"

"I didn't know they were! But then…then I'd see that I was pretending. Here, I can be myself."

Until she saw one day that this Julie, too, was an illusion. He wouldn't want to be her, reaching inside and finding nothing, constantly donning new costumes to disguise the emptiness. For the first time, he felt pity along with the anger and bitterness.

Brett, too young and wounded to see anything but his own loss, said with shattering intensity, "I still hate her."

Abby, limp and exhausted, lay against Craig. With his free arm, Craig reached out and drew his son into a bear hug.

"I know," he murmured, when he felt the first sob rip the boy. "I know."

WHEN THE KIDS, seeming drained, asked to watch TV, Craig took the opportunity to call his father. After telling him about their reactions, he asked if his father could come over.

"You don't have to tell me that Brett's a responsible kid. They'd be okay for an hour or two on their own. But…"

"Not now," his dad concluded.

"If you're busy, this can wait."

"You've waited long enough, son. Robin will be good for all of you."

"I've never even taken her on a date. You're taking a big leap there, Dad."

"You spent a weekend together, didn't you?" he scoffed. "Who needs a date?"

Craig had intended to wait until after dinner, but the minute Hank Lofgren arrived, he said, "I can feed them. Go on. Get out of here."

Craig went. He sure wasn't hungry.

He hoped Malcolm would be doing homework in his bedroom and he and Robin could talk privately. Maybe he should have waited until tomorrow. Phoned her. But he wanted to see her, not listen once again for nuances that might be imagined.

Her car was in the driveway, and she came to the door as soon as he rang the bell. Just the sight of her stole his breath. He couldn't imagine why, married or not, he hadn't fallen in love with her the first time he saw her. How had he ever thought her too skinny, nothing to look at compared to Julie? In plush brown corduroy pants and a sweater striped in rust and orange and deep green, her hair swinging loose, she was the most beautiful woman he had ever seen. Inside *and* out.

"I hope you don't mind my coming unannounced…."

Her soft brown eyes searched his face. "Did you find her?"

"Yes. It was her, Robin."

"Oh, Craig," she breathed. "I'm sorry, and glad, and…"

"Yeah. Me, too." He reached out and squeezed her arms, wanting to kiss her and see what happened, but aware they were standing on the doorstep, visible to the world. And Malcolm might walk into the living room. Letting her go, he asked, "Can I come in?"

She bobbed her head and backed away. "Of course you can! Oh, gosh. I worried all last night when I didn't hear from you. Did you just get home today? Surely you've told Brett and Abby? I want to hear the whole story in order. I can't help babbling. You found Julie." She sounded amazed. "After all this time!"

Following her into her house, Craig said, "She was married once before. Did I tell you that? If I'd known, we'd have found her sooner. All she'd done was go back to her maiden name."

Robin led the way into the living room. "You did tell me. That's so odd. What if she'd had other children?"

"The thought has occurred to me. She might still have more." He remembered the longing and torment in her eyes when she looked at Abby's and Brett's school pictures. "But somehow I doubt if she does."

"Do you want coffee, or...?"

"No. Thanks. Nothing for me." *Just you.* "Where's Malcolm?"

"He's at a classmate's working on a school project. I have to pick him up later." Robin sat at one end of the couch and patted the cushion beside her. "Sit," she ordered. "Talk."

So he did, telling her about the entire bizarre journey, flying to Bend, Oregon, with the police officer who admitted she'd taken over the case to finish what her father had started.

"We didn't talk much on the way down. More on the way home." He looked down at his hands. "She loosened up a little. Maybe I did, too. She says I symbolized the kind of man her father resented. She thinks he genuinely believed I'd killed Julie, but in a roundabout way she also admitted that his investigation wasn't as thorough as it should have been because he took a dislike to me. He thought I was smug, laughing at him behind his back." Craig shook his head. "Laughing! I was in shock. Stunned that Julie would have left without even scribbling a note of explanation. When I finally understood that the police thought I'd murdered her and gotten rid of her body, I was..." He made a sound. "I probably don't have to tell you what I felt. It was like wandering into another dimension. 'This can't be happening,' I kept telling myself. 'She'll call tomorrow. The cops will discover she bought a bus ticket.' *Something.*"

Robin's hand crept out and took his. He turned his hand in hers and squeezed, probably too hard, but she didn't protest. He needed to hold on to her.

Somehow he found he was talking, describing the commune on the banks of an offshoot of the Deschutes River. The red dirt that rose in tiny puffs under each step, the lodge and cabins and view of volcanic Mt. Bachelor, the woods that felt sparse compared to western Washington's deep green forest.

He told her about Julie's calm greeting and his crazy notion that she wasn't the same woman at all, that she was an imposter who had been told about him.

Fingers laced with Robin's, he said, "She acted as though I was someone she'd known a long time ago. A casual friend from college, maybe, not seen in twenty years. But she didn't try to deny that she was my wife, and she actually seemed surprised that there had been any fuss because of her departure."

"It didn't occur to her that there would be doubt about what had happened to her?" Robin asked with open incredulity.

"I knew she was unhappy—she said so. As if from that I should have assumed that she'd disappear one day." He let out a ragged breath. "She did take a thousand dollars, she was sorry and hoped I didn't mind. She believed I was in the air on the way to Paris, so there really was reason for her to be surprised that the police would ever have suspected me of having anything to do with her disappearance."

Robin's expression wasn't forgiving. "She could have left a note."

He grimaced. "She says she tried a couple of times to write one, but she didn't know how to describe what she felt, and saying goodbye was hard. So she just didn't.''

"Oh, Craig,'' Robin murmured.

"She signed the divorce papers and relinquished custody of the kids. That was the one time when I could see that she remembered, really remembered, who she'd been, and that it hurt. I offered to have Abby and Brett write to her in the future, send school pictures once a year, but she asked me not to.''

"What did you tell the kids?''

The warmth of her hand in his, her palm meeting his, felt like a lifeline. As if she was recharging him with her strength and compassion.

That, too, he described: the mix of truth and lies he had offered the children in an attempt to soften the reality of their mother's desertion without giving them false hope that they would ever see her again.

"Abby is crushed but grieving, in a way that seems healthy to me. Brett says he hates his mother. The sad thing is, I believe him.''

Robin took her hand back. She nodded, worried lines furrowing her forehead. "Hurt and anger make a volatile brew. That's what we've been seeing all along in him.''

"He's been doing so much better.''

"The counseling…''

"I don't think that has much to do with it. I think you and Malcolm have made the difference. But this has to have hit him hard. Is he going to regress?'' Craig asked.

"I don't know,'' she admitted. "He was really quiet today in school. Just…withdrawn. I wondered if he'd guessed where you'd gone and was worrying. It seems like resolution has to be a good thing, even if it's not the one he wanted. Anyway, once word gets out, the attitude of the other kids will change, which may help."

"Will it?" Craig made a sound in his throat. "Belated sympathy and regret aren't going to be very meaningful. I sure don't give a damn either way, and I won't blame him if he doesn't."

Robin straightened and squared her shoulders. She looked into his eyes and said, "When do you intend to move?"

"Soon. I'll put in a request to the airline immediately and get the house up for sale. With luck, we do it over Christmas, when the kids'll be out of school anyway."

She was quiet for a moment. "Oh. That *is* soon. Are you sure a move right away is the best thing for them?"

Watching her, he said, "Can you honestly tell me you think it isn't?"

Emotions he couldn't read skittered across her face. Finally she shook her head. "You know I can't. Maybe a fresh start *is* what they need. Brett especially. Leaving her friend Summer is going to be hard for Abby."

"I know it is, but she's always had a gift for making friends. And maybe I'm wrong—" he had a flash of incredible weariness "—but she doesn't seem as traumatized. She's lost some confidence that the world is always predictable and joyful and safe. But she's never felt the anger Brett does, and that worries me more.''

Robin bit her lip and nodded. Her eyes were bright; too bright. But she smiled as if she wasn't about to cry. ''At least your dad won't be able to complain that he's not ready to put his house up for sale.''

Craig gave a rough laugh. ''True.''

She scooted forward to stand. ''You know, I think I'll grab a soda. Can't I get you something?''

''Robin.'' He wrapped a hand around her arm and stopped her. Thank God her son wasn't in his bedroom down the hall.

She went very still, seated on the edge of the couch cushion, not looking at him.

''I'm hoping like hell I'm not way off base here.'' Damn, this was hard. His heart was slamming in his chest and he was scared like he couldn't ever remember being in his life. He let go of her arm. ''I've never even taken you out to dinner. Never kissed you good night.''

A tremor ran through her.

''You said once that if I asked for almost anything, you'd give it.''

She gave a thin laugh. ''I think I begged you to forget I'd ever said that. If you're trying to explain why our friendship can't be more, please don't, Craig.''

''That's not it.'' Not even close.

She turned wide, shimmering eyes toward him. ''Then what is it you want to say?''

He swallowed, his throat dry. ''I'm trying to figure

out a way to ask if moving might be something you'd consider.''

''Moving?'' The echo, the question, was a mere breath.

He was doing this badly. ''I don't expect an instant answer. I shouldn't even be asking you. I should invite you to dinner, romance you, wait a few weeks before I suggest you disrupt your life and your son's.''

''Disrupt?'' She stared.

''You've got a job you love, Malcolm has friends. Moving is hard for kids. He doesn't need to start over. And you sure don't.'' Craig felt sick. Why on earth would she marry him? She'd be giving up so much more than she gained.

She blinked. ''Are you suggesting that Malcolm and I move, too?''

He tried to smile at her. ''In my incredibly clumsy way, I'm asking you to marry me.''

For a moment, she simply didn't react. Then, in a voice that didn't sound like hers, she said, ''Are you thinking that the kids need a mother? I've become fond of Brett, but…''

He reached out, pulled her into his arms and kissed her. He should have done this ten minutes ago, instead of talking in circles.

For a moment she was stiff. Then, with a tiny sob, she melted against him and wrapped her arms around his neck. Craig kissed her with all the hunger he'd suppressed for months now, with the desperation of a man who had never expected to be able to act on need that had become part of him. It flared now, the ache sharpening.

Her lips were luscious, soft. The inside of her mouth tasted of mint and coffee and Robin. He wanted to take this slowly; not to scare her with what was, after all, a first kiss. But desire and sheer urgency poured through him, robbing him of restraint and even reason. She was in his arms at last, she was kissing him back. Robin made small, throaty sounds, whimpered when he wrenched his mouth from hers long enough to rain kisses down her throat.

"I love you," he said raggedly, and captured her mouth again.

The next time he surfaced they were lying on the couch, his weight pressing her into the cushions. Her sweater was twisted and up around her breasts, exposing her pale belly and the bottom edges of a purple bra. He stroked her smooth skin and said, voice thick, "I don't want a mother for my kids. I want *you*."

Tears filled her eyes, and her mouth trembled. She whispered his name.

Fear stopped his heart. She didn't feel the same. She'd kissed him as if tomorrow didn't exist because…oh, hell, because she wanted him.

But she didn't love him.

"Don't say it." He covered her mouth with his. His kiss was deep, frantic, hopeless. The salty taste of her tears made him groan and lift his head. "Oh, God, I'm sorry."

Unbelievably, she was smiling through the tears, sniffing, then laughing. "I love you. Is that what I can't say?"

He lifted a shaking hand and wiped tears from her upper lip. "If you love me, why are you crying?"

"Because I'm happy." She wriggled her arm free from beneath him and stroked his cheek. "Because I was so scared that you were going to leave, and I'd never see you again."

"You had to have known how I felt." He'd cracked often enough, despite his noblest intentions.

"Sometimes I did think—" Her cheeks pink, she broke off. "And then I'd decide you were just being friendly. Or that you were, well, maybe a little attracted to me just because I'm the only woman who was being nice to you."

He feathered a kiss across her mouth. "You," he murmured, "are the only woman who ever looked past the newspaper headlines. The only one with the compassion and guts to intercede to help a kid headed for trouble. Is that why I want to kiss you?" He did so, sucking gently on her lower lip, watching her lashes flutter down, her head tilt back, hearing her sigh of pleasure. "Is that why I want to be inside you so desperately I couldn't even let myself kiss you?" He kissed her neck, inhaling her scent. "Hell, no," he finished, voice deep and even harsh. "Is that why I love you so much, I dread the days when I won't see you? Yeah. Partly. It's who you are, Robin McKinnon."

"I'm...I'm no saint. I reached out to Brett because I felt guilty for losing touch with him, not because I put on my cloak to save every child in distress."

"Maybe." He smiled at her, letting her see everything he'd hidden. "But I'm betting you put on your cloak and try."

"I…"

"Don't argue." He nipped her earlobe. "We can put off moving until summer if that will be easier for you."

She shook her head, her eyes shimmering again. "But I'd see your face when we go somewhere and people stare. That closed look. Your eyes getting flinty and your mouth—" she touched his lips with her fingertips "—hard. You're so remote I can feel you willing yourself elsewhere. And that won't change, will it? People will keep staring. And they might try to say they're sorry, and you're such a nice man you'll tell them it's okay, only it's not." She sounded fierce. "It's not."

A barrier he'd erected to protect himself crumbled in that instant, boulders dissolving into piles of sand and grit. Until now, he hadn't known how far inside he'd burrowed, how thick his wall had become just so he could make it through each day.

Closing his eyes, Craig rested his forehead against hers. "Yeah," he said, "it is. Thanks to you, now it is."

She kissed him, her face wet with tears again, her lips soft, her arms tight. He sank into the kiss, into her, as if he'd found heaven on earth. And in that moment, he knew: the gates of purgatory had sprung open and he'd walked through them.

When at last he lifted his mouth from hers and they looked at each other again, she said with absolute certainty, "I'll give my notice tomorrow. They can use a sub if they haven't found a replacement by the end of Christmas break. We move as a family.''

Humbled, he said, ''You don't want to talk to Malcolm first?''

''He needs a real father, and a brother and a sister. He may not know it, but he does.'' She smiled, her face radiant with happiness and that amazing certainty. ''He'd miss Brett, you know.''

''Brett worships you.'' His lips teased hers. ''The kids don't know I'm asking you to marry me. I can hardly wait to tell them.''

She moaned, her neck arching for his mouth, her breasts pressing against his chest. ''As in—'' she sounded breathless ''—you want to go tell them right now?''

His rejoinder was succinct and would have insulted his children deeply. But it seemed to please her, because she laughed, a throaty, sensuous sound. ''Oh, good,'' she whispered, just before he pulled her sweater over her head.

He looked down at this extraordinary woman, creamy skin and rich brown eyes and shimmering hair spilling over the couch, breasts swelling above deep violet satin, and he knew: freedom was the least of his rewards.

This woman, who would be his wife, was the greatest prize.

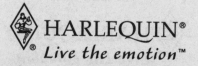

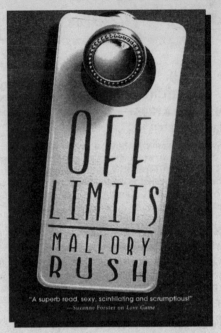
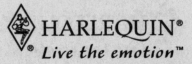

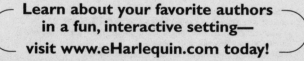

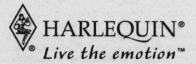

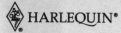

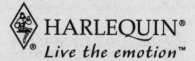

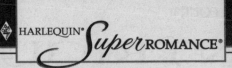

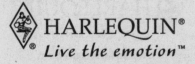